PUBLICITY STUNT

BERNADETTE MARIE

Copyright © 2024 by Bernadette Marie, PUBLICITY STUNT

All rights reserved.

This is a fictional work. The names, characters, incidents, and locations are solely the concepts and products of the author's imagination, or are used to create a fictitious story and should not be construed as real. No part of this book may be reproduced in any form or by any electronic or mechanical means, including information storage and retrieval systems, without written permission from the author, except for the use of brief quotations in a book review.

Published by 5 PRINCE PUBLISHING & BOOKS, LLC

PO Box 865, Arvada, CO 80001

www.5PrinceBooks.com

ISBN digital: 978-1-63112-369-6

ISBN print: 978-1-63112-377-1

Cover Credit: Marianne Nowicki

04232024.2 04262024.3

To Stan,
It's all about the likes, the loves, and the #HappilyEverAfters!

ACKNOWLEDGMENTS

Creating amazing stories is never a solo project. I'd like to thank my husband of thirty-one years, our five kids, my mother, and my sister for always having my back, supporting me, and loving me always. Trust me, writing is an emotional and time-consuming career. To have people who love you while you're manic, head down, hungry, and creating imaginary people is important.

Thank you to Cate Byers who has been working with me for nearly a decade to make my stories shine. She is the mastermind behind keeping my stories straight and looking good—well, reading well.

Thank you to Marianne Nowicki for designing my amazing covers that entice readers to pick up my stories. Thank you to Laurie West and Christian Black who bring my characters to life. Thank you to Jessica Mehring who gives my books one final eye and makes it shine.

And of course, thank you to my loyal and amazing readers. I love writing for you, and I will continue to do so.

ALSO BY BERNADETTE MARIE

THE KELLER FAMILY SERIES

The Executive's Decision

A Second Chance

Opposite Attraction

Center Stage

Lost and Found

Love Songs

Home Run

The Acceptance

The Merger

The Escape Clause

A Romance for Christmas

THE WALKER FAMILY SERIES

Walker Pride

Stargazing

Walker Bride

Wanderlust

Walker Revenge

Victory

Walker Spirit

Beginnings

Walker Defense

Masterpiece

At Last

THE ROM COM MOVIE CLUB

The Rom Com Movie Club - Book One

The Rom Com Movie Club - Book Two

The Rom Com Movie Club - Book Three

FUNERALS AND WEDDINGS SERIES

Something Lost

Something Discovered

Something Found

Something Forbidden

Something New

THE DEVEREAUX FAMILY SERIES

Kennedy Devereaux

Chase Devereaux

Max Devereaux

Paige Devereaux

STANDALONE TITLES

The Happily Ever After Bookstore

Liz's Road Trip

Publicity Stunt

THE MATCHMAKER SERIES

Matchmakers

Encore

Finding Hope

THE THREE MRS. MONROES TRILOGY

Amelia

Penelope

Vivian

THE ASPEN CREEK SERIES

First Kiss

Unexpected Admirer

On Thin Ice

Indomitable Spirit

THE DENVER BRIDE SERIES

Cart Before the Horse

Never Saw it Coming

Candy Kisses

ROMANTIC SUSPENSE

Chasing Shadows

PARANORMAL ROMANCES

The Tea Shop

The Last Goodbye

HOLIDAY FAVORITES

Corporate Christmas

Tropical Christmas

Date for Hire

Mistletoe Memories

VALENTINE FAVORITES

Secret Admirer Pact

PUBLICITY STUNT

CHAPTER ONE

CHRISTINA

What the press doesn't know could fill a library. "It was the shattering heard 'round the country. Christina Malloy threw a coffee mug at her co-star Graham Crowley. Though no one was hurt, these are the kinds of stories we hear coming from the set of the Love Is in the Air network stars."

My stomach growls as I sit uncomfortably in the back of the limo.

My assistant Penny sharply turns her head to look at me. She heard it. I'm sure everyone outside of the car heard it, too.

Her eyes are wide and there is a look of panic that washes over her face. I'm not sure if she's worried that it'll make that kind of noise in the theater, or if she's worried that I'm so hungry, I might pass out.

"Don't mind my body," I say flatly. "It's just underfed, overstressed, and I can't freaking breathe in this dress," I complain as I move ever so slightly to try to adjust myself.

My mother, who is sitting on the bench across from me,

checks her lipstick in her compact mirror before closing it and tucking it away in her clutch. I know she hasn't eaten all day long either, but she doesn't seem to be fazed by it like I am.

"You look magnificent, darling," she says with that practiced tone, and not even one glance in my direction. With a gentle nudge to my father, she draws his attention to me. "Doesn't she look magnificent, sweetheart?"

My father scans a look over me as if he's only now realized I'm in the same car with them. "Yeah. You look great, sweetheart. Real great."

I lift a brow. "Thanks," I say in a tone as flat as the compliment I'm thanking him for.

Being the only daughter of one of Hollywood's biggest producers and the founder of a chain of exclusive spas, I'm used to the short bursts of attention I get from my parents. Sometimes I'm surprised I was ever born. They only give one another short bursts of attention, too.

My mother fancies herself a doting parent, but let's be honest, she falls short—extremely short. I mean, when your only daughter has the lead in Annie at the age of ten, and not just some school production, but a professional production, you don't take that as the opportune time to go to Europe and tour all the spas for research for a pet project. But that's what my mother did. She spent six weeks in Europe building her business while I sang my heart out, wishing for the sun to come out tomorrow.

My father, on the other hand, doesn't even try to dote on me. Oh, I can have anything I want. After all, I am his baby girl, even at thirty. And by anything, I mean as a teenager, my credit card was always paid off and never questioned. My first car was a Lexus. And yes, I have a condo in Beverly Hills that is paid for, and I've lived there since I was eighteen. It was a graduation gift.

But, if I want his attention, then I must be in one of his movies—in which I've so far only been an extra.

He won't invest in the "silly" movies I star in. He doesn't see the appeal of romantic comedies, even though they are box office gold with the right duos. His money, and time, go into productions where the world gets blown up, every-single-time. Where F-words are much of the script, and where there is on-screen sex to fill the space. His premieres are the kinds where you see action heroes on the red carpet looking sexy as hell next to a waif of a model who might pass out at any time. And always, my father in his tux, his sunglasses on, and my mother and I at his side for show.

"You're presenting with Graham Crowley?" my mother asks as she adjusts her breasts in her dress.

"Thanks for the reminder," I say, hoping that my voice resonates the displeasure I feel about that.

I can see my assistant's eyes glass over when I talk about Graham. She's a fan. I am not. I've worked with the man for years and am probably one of the few women who finds him flawed and annoying.

Once movies began streaming, and they began using ensemble casts, I found my home filming romance movies for the Love Is in the Air network.

I'll admit, when they announced that Graham Crowley was joining the cast of my first movie, I was smitten, too.

He has those sexy, boy-next-door looks. The kind that say, "You remember me. I used to deliver the paper, but now I want to rock your daughter's world."

But then I met him, and I kissed him—contractually, of course. Talk about a lack of sparks.

It could be that he finds it humorous to eat bags of Doritos before our kissing scenes. And he hurries from the set to his trailer and hides out there. He's always distracted, as if he's working on some devious plot against me.

And let's talk about the fact that I'm usually in the same state I am now—starving. So maybe it's not the stunt he's pulling with the Doritos, but the fact that he can eat a freaking bag of nacho chips and still have sex appeal. Seriously though, what kind of professional leaves cheese dust on their co-star?

Part of being a first-class actress is not letting on that the romantic scenes between me and Graham are anything but romantic. I work my ass off to not react to the smell of him or the taste. It's led to more than one heated exchange.

We can't stand one another. That's not an exaggeration either.

He murmurs words under his breath as he walks away to his trailer, and I have been known to throw objects at his head.

We do our jobs, and by the ratings and the numbers of fans that show up to our fan events, we know we're convincing.

So, we collect our paychecks, and smile in public. When we're at fan events, cons, or just happen to be out in public at the same place, we'll smile at each other, hold conversation, and I'll even hold his hand—as he tends to grab mine. Now that I think about that, I wonder if it's an insecurity he has. Is he afraid that I'm the string his shiny star hangs from? That he can't risk me getting too far from him?

Knowing I'm going to be presenting an award with the man, while I'm sewn into a dress and my stomach is growling, makes me even more irritable. I'll bet he's eaten full meals today and his stomach won't growl.

My father tucks his phone into the inside pocket of his tuxedo jacket. "Okay, we're the next car up," he says.

My mother taps her fingers to her cheeks to give them some color as my father removes his reading glasses and hands them to my mother to put into her clutch. It's probably the most married-couple thing they do.

He then takes out his sunglasses and puts those on. It's dark outside, but what would Hollywood be if you could see everyone's eyes?

Penny hands me my clutch. "Your phone is inside, as well as powder and lipstick."

"Thank you," I say, watching the lights to the theater come into view.

The streets are lined with people corralled behind barricades and being monitored by security guards.

The car slows and comes to a stop.

I can see Graham already talking to the press. In less than a minute, he'll come toward me smiling as if he's been waiting for me all day. That's the plan that I was told, and I don't like it. I don't need him as arm candy. I can manage the press on my own. I hate it, but I can do it.

Penny gives me a reassuring smile as the door to the car is opened.

In well-practiced protocol, my father exits the car and there are hushed applause and a few camera flashes. Producers aren't instantly recognized or appreciated like the actors that people see on TV or in the movies.

While my father buttons his jacket, my mother reaches for the hand offered by one of the ushers and steps out of the car. My father is too busy taking in the scene and shaking Graham Crowley's hand to help his own wife out of the car.

There are a few more cheers for my mother. She's not an actress, but she's the face of her chain of exclusive spas, so people see her all the time on TV or on billboards and in ads. She's elegant, graceful, filled with Botox, and as sewn into her dress as I am.

Graham heads toward the car. Now my growling stomach clenches.

I move to the door and take the hand that is offered to me.

"Thank you," I say as I step out, my hand clasped in Graham's.

He flashes that smile that makes the ratings go up, but makes my stomach churn.

Dark locks are brushed back and look to be as secured with lacquer as my curls. He's cleanly shaven, and his signature woodsy scent hits me hard as I step in next to him.

"Nice to see you, sweetheart," he says, annunciating the t's sharply.

"Oh, you too, darling," I say through gritted teeth.

He interlaces our fingers and begins to wave as the crowd's cheers grow louder. This little stunt is pissing me off. Him walking me on the carpet just gives him double the time in front of the press. This is my entrance. With him holding my hand, he's taking *my* cheers, and now he's in all *my* photos.

I squeeze his hand hard while wearing a brilliant smile. My nails dig into his flesh.

"Ouch, darling," he leans in toward my ear as if he's saying something intimate. "Perhaps you can ease up?"

Through my gritted teeth, smile still brilliantly in place, I say, "Maybe you could give me some space."

"The press expects us together."

"To present," I say as we walk toward the first of many reporters, stopping intermittently to pose for pictures.

"Oh, honey, haven't you seen the rag mags or the talk shows? We're a hot item."

When he says that, I stop walking and turn to him.

The extra flashes from cameras don't even register when I yank my hand from his.

"What?" I nearly shout.

Graham looks around, his smile still in place. "Oh, don't do it, Malloy," he says, calling me by my last name. "Don't make a scene."

"Why do they think we're a couple?" I'm whispering loudly.

He leans in close again. "It's what fans want."

"I'm not in on this."

People begin to call our names, a chant, if you will. I look around and realize that this little conversation is being recorded on every cell phone within a mile radius.

I put the smile back in place on my lips and let Graham take my hand again. "We need to have a talk about this," I say.

Graham maneuvers his hand out of mine and wraps his arm around my waist to pull me in closer while flashes from cameras blind us. His fingers are pressed to the exposed flesh at my waist, as the designers saw it fit to make sure I was somewhat exposed.

"No doubt, princess. But for now, let's be in love. We can hate each other again when this is over."

I'm already there.

CHAPTER TWO

GRAHAM

And the caption read, "Keep your friends close, and your enemies closer."

Christina's perfume is expensive and clogging my nose. I find it interesting that her parents haven't once looked back at her. They're so self-consumed, I'm not sure they remembered she was in the car.

Somehow, she's wedged her elbow into my ribs as I stand with her closely tucked up against me.

Her skin is cold beneath my fingertips, and I'm not surprised. The woman is actually some kind of ice queen.

I can hear her stomach growl, which happens a lot. She probably hasn't eaten in three days either.

Fans in the crowd call out our names, and we both give them smoldering smiles as I keep her pulled in tightly to my side.

I would have thought that her people would have told her about the story that surfaced about us being in a relationship—a nonexistent romantic relationship. How the hell they came up with that story, I have no idea. Anyone who has ever been on set with us knows that we are tolerant of one another at the most.

I mean, did everyone miss the story about her throwing the coffee mug at my head?

It's a credit to our talents that the streets are lined with fans chanting our names. We've now starred in four movies together where we were love interests, and two where we were siblings.

That's the glory of ensemble casts and viewers' suspended reality.

The fact that we crank out movies with silly romantic tropes on a streaming service still blows my mind. But looking at the people who have come to see us, and the ratings that the movies get, it's the cushiest job the whole world. I'm guaranteed steady work. The shooting schedules are short, so I have a lot of time off to pursue other hobbies, like my writing.

Romance channel viewers are much like those who get into their comic book movies and shows. The fandom is huge. I can honestly say, I never thought I'd be doing the fan con circuits, but I do—we do.

People line up and wait to have their pictures taken with me and Christina—and I don't mean separately. They are there to see us together. I don't know what would ever happen if either of us made time to see other people. Would it demystify the on-screen fantasy?

But the fans make this cushy job what it is. It's their need for more content that keeps us employed and the money rolling in.

If the fans want to see Christina and me in public with my arm around her, well then, I'll offer them that. I need them to believe the hype and tune in the next time one of our movies plays. Hell, the residuals alone should keep me comfortable for a long time.

Of course, the moment we are clear of the cameras, we will step away from one another. Oh, we might heat it up on a TV screen, but there are no sparks here—not really.

Okay, I'm only human. The woman hates me, but let's be honest, she's gorgeous and feminine and I notice.

An entertainment channel has a reporter stationed to pull us in and talk to us. I can see Christina's parents have gone on and are entering the building. Had I not moved in, as I'd been instructed to do, would they have just left her to tend to this mob on her own? I mean, I've seen her do it, but really?

"Graham Crowley and Christina Malloy," the woman says with a hint of surprise swirled into her excitement. As if she didn't know we'd be stopping by. "You two are picture perfect," she continues, scanning a look over both of us.

Christina's body has gone rigid, and she leans into me. That's a bit surprising, except that we've done enough of these stupid things that I know she hates to be grilled with a microphone in her face.

"Thank you," Christina says, and her voice rises in pitch.

The reporter asks her who she's wearing and Christina rattles off some name of a designer I've never heard of.

The microphone is now aimed in my direction. I might lose it if this gal asks who I'm wearing. I'm in a freaking tuxedo.

"You know, Graham Crowley," she sighs as she says my whole name, "hearts are breaking."

"Are they?" I ask. Where Christina's voice rose in pitch, mine is flat.

My agent and publicist, as well as the execs at the studio want us to play up this rumor that we're seeing one another. Honestly, I thought they would have mentioned it to Christina, and she would have fought them off. Maybe that's why they didn't tell her, and just threw her to the wolves. It's a little funny, I suppose, but not cool.

"So, the two of you?" the reporter asks. "How long has this been a thing?"

Christina's smile is plastered on her face, and she turns to look at me. There is a plea in her eyes to get her out of this.

"You know. You spend all this time with someone—" I begin.

"It's bound to happen, right?" the reporter interrupts and finishes my thought. "We've had polls on our website of celebs that people want to see coupling up. You two have always had the lead."

What a waste of resources.

I eye my agent, who waves me toward her. My hand slips from Christina's back, but she grabs for my hand as if I'm her lifeline now.

"You two look cute together," Sandra, my agent, says as we make our way to her.

"Oh, do we now?" My voice is lacking in any humor as I lean in toward her, fully aware that all eyes are still on us. "No one gave her the heads up," I whisper and nod my head in Christina's direction.

"No?" Sandra asks and Christina shakes her head. "That's unfortunate," she says as if it doesn't matter. "Anyway, you look perfect together. You're presenting the fourth award. We'll come and get you before."

We know the drill, but the teams of people we keep around us know it's their job to get us where we need to be, so we'll hear this same thing all night long.

Christina's fingers twine with mine. She doesn't want to be here. I don't want to be here. She doesn't want to be touching me, and frankly, I feel the same. But we seem to be one another's support for the evening. Does that make us a couple?

We follow Sandra into the theater and are escorted to seats next to Christina's parents. Everything is mechanical. There is some socializing, but that's mostly saved for after-parties. This part of the evening is all for getting people in place for the cameras. For the next three hours, they're going to be focused in on how Christina and I sit next to one another. Will we touch? Whisper? Hold hands?

After the rehearsal yesterday, I'm surprised there are any

rumors. We didn't speak to one another as we were walked through protocol. The few minutes we sat, we were both on our phones. I guess proximity is enough to fuel rumors.

In fact, I'm not sure we said anything to one another the entire day.

There's never a need to. The princess at my side never has anything nice to say. Well, when your stomach growls as much as hers does, maybe she's nasty because she's always hungry.

To be honest, I'd rather give the stupid award and then get the hell out. But these silly movies on the Love Is in the Air, all romance, all the time channel, has my name out there. Sandra has sent me three scripts for feature films, and I've had talks about starring in an action film. An action film!

Christina's father is the king of the action movies, and I know that Sandra has been passing my name to him. I could be the next Bruce Willis or Vin Diesel. The thought makes me smile wider.

"What are you thinking?" Christina whispers through gritted teeth and a plastered smile.

"Exit strategy," I say, and she turns a horrified glance my way.

"You're not sneaking out, are you? You can't leave me—"

"Not an exit strategy for tonight. Don't panic."

"Okay, thank you," she says, as if my sticking around will give her comfort. Maybe she finds solace in us both being miserable.

I don't ever know what this woman thinks. But I do know for a fact she'll blow a gasket the next time we have a kissing scene and I eat Doritos before it. It only fuels my fire to do it more often.

Actually, she won't have to worry about the Doritos. I have plans to down a bag of Funyuns before our next romantic scene. I had my roommate buy a case of them from Costco just for eating before the kissing scenes.

With Christina's hand still in mine, I grin at my plan. Sometimes my joy comes from just irritating the woman.

CHAPTER THREE

CHRISTINA

And the self-help manual said, "Take a deep breath, if you can."

There is nothing that I can do to make myself more comfortable. I'm grateful that these kinds of award shows aren't all the time. You're herded like cattle in dresses you can't breathe in. There are hundreds of faces, more famous than mine, yet the camera is equally on me and Graham.

My parents are poised, and not even acknowledging me. Graham has his legs crossed and is brushing lint from his tux.

I can feel a panic attack coming on, and there is nothing I can do about it. Nothing. I just need to remind myself to breathe or try to. Seriously, this dress is too tight.

Graham leans in close to me. "What's wrong? You're jittery."

I turn my mouth to his ear. "I don't want to be here."

"You and the other thousand people who are here tonight. You're not alone."

I press my lips together, hoping to keep the worried crease that forms between my brows from appearing.

"Are you sure you don't have an exit strategy for tonight?" I whisper.

Graham raises a brow. "You want to escape?"

"More than you could possibly know."

He doesn't move his head, but his eyes dart around the room. "I can make one."

"Would you?"

Something lights in his eyes. "For both of us?"

My shoulders drop slightly. It would be just like him to leave me stranded here, alone, with my parents, who don't even seem to remember that I'm sitting next to them.

"Yes, for both of us," I say, still sharply focused on making it look like a friendly conversation, and not the urgent words of a woman ready to run.

"If you and I leave together, and don't return, that rumor mill will explode," he whispers. "What people are already saying will escalate."

I consider that. "Unbeknownst to me, it apparently already has," I say, to which Graham simply nods.

"I'll get us out of here, and we go our separate ways."

"Even better," I agree.

"We have to present," he reminds me.

"Obligated, I know." It's not like I'm asking to leave right now.

He nods again, and this time he takes my hand, laces our fingers together and rests them on his thigh. "There are millions of women who would like to be in your shoes right now," he teases.

"They haven't kissed you to know your breath stinks," I say, and he chuckles.

"Yeah, well, when I really kiss a woman, you know, for real, her body doesn't go all rigid. A real kiss from me would make your panties melt off."

I try to tug my hand free, but Graham grips it tighter.

"Tonight, you're my girl," he says, shooting me a smile. "You're an actress. You can pretend to love me."

"Then you'd better send in the submission of me doing so to the committee, because it'll be Oscar-worthy," I say, and again he chuckles as the orchestra begins to play and the chaos around us begins to settle.

∼

We are the fourth presenters, and we are nearly an hour into this production. Between the commercial breaks and the monologues, my butt has gone numb, and when they come for us, Graham nearly has to pull me from my chair because I can't feel anything in my legs. The tightness of this dress has caused my circulation to stop flowing.

The people holding our seats sit down as we are led backstage. Graham is a good three feet in front of me, and I'm trying to catch up.

Backstage we're told what to do, which we've already rehearsed, but again, I know it's their job to make it go right.

Graham is handed the envelope with the winners, and I am offered his arm.

When the commercial break is over, the emcee, a daytime actress who has been nominated for one of these silly awards six times and never won, takes the stage to talk about our category. We're presenting for the best actress in a short series, or something like that. With all the ways people can consume entertainment now, there is a category for everything.

Music plays, and Graham and I walk out on the stage.

There is an eruption of cheers from the upper balconies where fans are allowed to watch the show.

I give a little wave, and the volume of the cheers increase. Okay, I can't help but smile at that.

I exchange a glance with Graham, who has that movie star smile glowing.

I love knowing that people enjoy the work we do. They love the characters, and Graham and I have a unique chemistry—when acting. I love being one of three leading ladies for an entire channel of movies. Someday, I'll have another leading man. My stories will get fresher, and more in-depth. And maybe those people who are cheering my name will be equally happy when I fall in love with a real man, and not this puppet on a string, whose arm I'm holding.

We reach the podium, and someone shouts out, "Graham, I want to have your baby!"

There is some laughter from the crowd in the balcony, but those in attendance in the industry are mostly not amused.

Graham clears his throat, and his cheeks have pinked. Did he get embarrassed by that? Interesting.

When everything settles in the theater, Graham begins to speak.

"In the category of Best Leading Actress in a Limited or Short Series, the nominees are…"

"Olivia Chase for *Christmas at Carson Pier*," I say, and there is a round of applause as the big screens show the woman, sitting among the crowd, smiling wide.

"Pauline O'Donnell for *Love Is All Around - A Tale of Bravery*," Graham reads the second name, and I watch the monitor to see the face of the woman who is one of the spokespeople for my mother's chain of spas.

"Gwendolyn Addams for *Go Get 'em, Tiger*," I say.

"Jacqueline Thomas for *Once Upon a Valentine's Day*," Graham quickly adds because there is someone making motions with their hands that we're taking too long. As if an hour was the right amount of time to get to the fourth award, but now we must hurry.

"And Laura Gray for *Letters from a Prison*," I add, my voice now shaking because the director of this shindig is staring at me as if this lapse in time is my fault.

"And the winner is . . ." Graham says as he hands me the envelope to open.

I pull the ribbon that lifts the seal and look down at the name.

"Olivia Chase for *Christmas at Carson Pier,*" I say, but Graham says it too, louder and enough to drown out my voice. *What an asshat!*

Olivia Chase stands up in the crowd, only a few seats from where Graham and I had been sitting. She hugs the people around her and then begins her walk toward us.

Her black skin shines with specks of gold glitter that match her dress. A long braid is draped over her bare and well-defined shoulder.

Graham moves toward her to give her a hand as she climbs the stairs, and she leans into him, kissing his cheek and lingering to whisper something at which his eyes flicker.

As she moves to the podium, I step back, but not before she scans a long look down the front of me, and then winks at Graham.

Graham moves in next to me, and now I can smell Olivia Chase's perfume on him, and her lipstick is on his cheek. Talk about leaving a mark.

We stand there, smiling wide, as Olivia gives her speech. When she's done, she turns to Graham and wraps herself around his arm as he escorts her from the stage with me following. Well, this is awkward. Surely someone who is promoting this stupid thought of us dating will pick up on this little *thing* between them and make it some kind of newsworthy event. It happens all the time.

He can be the asshole, and I'll be the innocent bystander girlfriend who was blindsided.

As we clear the stage, Olivia whispers in Graham's ear again, and he smiles. She's then whisked away for photos.

"A bit intimate there," I say as I move in next to him.

"Worried, *sweetheart*?" he says, enunciating his t's as he did before.

"Why would I even care?"

"Why would you?"

Graham starts toward the back of the stage, and I follow. The last thing he's going to do is ditch me now. He promised me an out, and I'm going to take it.

CHAPTER FOUR

GRAHAM

And the gossip magazine said, "And where did they go in the night?"

I had promised I'd get us out of the rest of the night. Sandra helped make that happen, and a call to Christina's assistant, Penny, made it so that we quietly walked out the back door of the theater without any incident.

Now, in the back of Penny's Kia, I undo my bow tie and unbutton the first few buttons on my shirt. I can't get out of this tux fast enough.

"Maybe this isn't the best idea. They're going to know we're gone," Christina says, turning around in the passenger seat and looking through the back window as if she assumes someone will be following us.

"Of course they're going to know. There are a couple of seat fillers who probably are supposed to fill other seats. Oh, and if, just by chance, your parents bother to look to where you'd been sitting, they might remember they rode with you to the theater."

"Don't be an asshole," she bites back, but it doesn't resonate in her eyes.

I'd have assumed she was oblivious to the situation, but obviously she was not. Her parents couldn't have cared less that they were there with her. I wonder sometimes if her parents even know what she does for a living. In the years that I've known Christina, I've seen her power couple parents parade her around like a trophy, but otherwise, they don't seem to remember that she even exists. Yet, her father shook my hand and called me by name.

"But, instead of us being assholes, we'll be some loving couple who just couldn't wait to get some time alone," I say, still playing up this stupid trope of our lives that someone has decided we're living.

"Anyone who knows us will know that's not true."

"Yeah, well, it's the millions of people who don't know us that think it's true."

"I don't like that," she says.

"You don't get much say in the matter. You were raised in this. You know that the press runs what people think."

Christina turns around with a huff but aims her glare at Penny. "Did you know about all of this? That someone released something that says we're dating?" she shoots the question to Penny, who grips the steering wheel tighter.

"Well, um, yes. Well, I mean—"

Christina holds up her hand to stop her. "I don't care tonight. Tomorrow, I'm making a call to my agent. I didn't agree to any of this, and I don't want to be part of it."

I laugh in the backseat, and she turns her narrowed eyes on me. "What?" she shouts.

"You're such a diva. I don't think you get a say as to what people say about you in the press. We signed up for that when we started in this line of work. Besides, what does it matter if this is what people think?" I ask.

"It matters."

"Why?"

Christina purses her lips. "Do you love me?" she asks.

"Oh, hell no," I reply with an emphasis on hell and no. "I have a hard time stomaching you altogether, but I think you know that."

"The feeling is mutual, you know."

"I know, and it only makes this that much sweeter," I grin at her, and I'm sure if it weren't dark in the car, I'd see her cheeks turn red with anger.

"You know that if you're attached to me, then you can't see anyone else." Her voice teases as if she's found a loophole in this scheme that is going to wreck me.

"Says who?"

"Says those fans you think so much of. If they want you with me, they won't want you with anyone else."

I consider that for a moment, and she's right. Not that I date a lot or do anything else that goes with dating. The truth is, I'm a homebody. I'd rather have one woman in my life than a string of them. Where is the true satisfaction in that? Well, at least that's how I was raised. And even with people thinking I sleep around; it's how I live my life that counts. I know the real me. No one else does.

"I guess I'll just have to keep my affairs in order and keep them quiet," I shoot back.

She huffs again and turns around.

"Where am I supposed to take you both?" Penny asks. Her posture is tense as she nearly strangles the steering wheel.

"You're not supposed to take *us both* anywhere," Christina says. "He needs to get out of the car and go his own way."

I let out another burst of laughter. "What, are you going to have her drop me off on the street corner?"

"Maybe," Christina says.

I rattle off my address to Penny. "Get me close and I can walk."

"But you're in a tuxedo," Penny says, her eyes darting to me in the rearview mirror.

"It won't be the first time, even tonight, that you see someone walking the streets in LA in a tuxedo," I say.

"She'll take you home," Christina grunts. "And then she'll take me home, because we need to discuss how much of this she knew."

Penny's brows draw in and she worries her bottom lip.

I wonder if Penny is really worried about what Christina might say. Things I've learned over the years from working with the woman, she has no bite. If she digs her teeth into you, you won't feel it.

See, Christina Malloy isn't as hard as her mother or father. Now those two, they can make you quake in your boots. Christina, she just doesn't have it in her to be ferocious. Though it doesn't appear that Penny knows that.

Oh, I've seen Christina try to lay down the law, and things change because she comes from Hollywood elite, but really, it's not her that makes things happen. It's the dropping of her parents' names.

But what do I care if she thinks she's tough? We're on equal ground when it comes to our jobs. The network likes us. They keep writing stories for us and we keep getting paid. Long live the serial romance, and God bless the lovers of unrealistic romance movies that are produced by the dozens.

Penny pulls up in front of my house and stops the car.

"I guess this is my stop," I joke from the backseat. "Has anyone texted you to ask where you are?" I ask Christina.

She looks down at her phone. "No."

"Didn't think so. Well, thanks for the ride," I say to Penny, and she returns a smile. "Later, lover," I tease Christina as I open the door.

"Go to hell," she replies.

Things are normal between us. No matter how many pictures show up on TV tomorrow or in gossip columns, Christina Malloy will still loathe me, and I will still try to get under her skin.

CHAPTER FIVE

CHRISTINA

And the agent said, "In sickness and in health, until the agreement runs out."

The ringtone that I have set for my mother rings from my purse. I pull out my phone and connect the call.

Without me even saying hello, my mother says, "Darling, do you *need* me there? Really? It's just Sal. When have you ever needed me to talk to your agent?"

I grip the phone tighter in my hand. "I just thought some moral support would be nice," I say as I walk down the hallway toward my agent's office.

"You know I support you in anything. I don't have time to come over there, though."

Of course she doesn't. Not only that, but she also has no idea what I need her support on.

"Fine," I say sharply.

"You'll be at the grand opening on Thursday, right?" she asks, and it twists me up inside.

Oh, she can't meet me at my agent's office for a meeting about how my career is being handled, but I'm expected to be at her grand opening? The worst part is, she's not asking me to be there because I'm her daughter. It's free publicity for her if I, Christina Malloy, star of the Love Is in the Air network, am there.

"It's really not a—"

"Christina Abigail Malloy, you promised me," her voice drops into a pout, and I can imagine her face matches.

I set my jaw and stop outside the door to my agent's office. "I'll be there," I say.

"Have to go, honey."

And with that, the call is dropped. It's been two days since I snuck out of the awards show with Graham Crowley, and my parents haven't said a word. Two days and they hadn't even wondered why I didn't get back into the car with them at the end of it all, or even return to my seat.

The press noticed. Pictures of Graham and I were on the entertainment blogs and TV reports. His hand on my waist. Conversations we were having, in which we were talking through forced smiles, looked intimate. No one seemed to notice Olivia Chase's cheek-to-cheek whispers, or how she wrapped herself around him.

My parents are oblivious to it all.

The only thing my mother cares about is me showing up for the opening of the new spa in Beverly Hills. It'll be an exclusive new concept in a new posh hotel. And I'll have the eyes of the million fans that dote on the movies that the Love Is in the Air network puts out, and she's literally banking on that.

The door to my agent's office opens and Penny is standing there.

"We thought the door might be locked since you were just standing out here in the hallway," she says.

I breeze by her, my Gucci purse in the crook of my arm.

My heels click on the marble floor, and I pull my large, dark sunglasses from my face.

I know the drill. I walk straight to the boardroom where my agent Sal, his assistant Barbara, and three publicists sit around a table.

Sal stands and moves to me. He's wearing sunglasses inside, which is a trait that makes me crazy. My father does that as if the room is always too bright. As if their own glow might blind them. It's ego, and it's ugly.

But this man has me a solid contract to make six more movies, and from there the franchise will just keep going, and I'll be at the helm of it all.

"Sweet Christina," he says as he kisses both of my cheeks. His breath is already laden with alcohol and cigars. It's only eleven in the morning.

"Sal," I say without the same enthusiasm.

It's Penny who pulls a chair out for me, and I sit on the edge of it, crossing my legs, hoping that the skirt that I chose doesn't ride up and distract my agent. I'm not about using my body to get my point across. I'm about using my mind to tell this sleazy man who controls my career that a mistake has been made and I want no part of it.

"You look great, darling. How was the award ceremony?" he asks.

"Boring. Predictable. Annoying."

He gives one curt nod. The others just watch our interaction as if they are sworn to silence unless spoken to directly.

"Can I get you anything?" he asks.

"I just want to discuss something with you."

"You want to discuss Graham Crowley."

I inhale and look toward Penny, who has her eyes diverted to the iPad in front of her as if she'll need to take notes on this.

I look back at Sal. "Yes."

He looks toward the door behind me. "Right on time," he says as the door opens, and he stands.

Walking into the room are Graham and his agent.

Sal shakes Graham's hand and then Sandra's as well.

Penny moves down a seat, leaving a chair between us, which Graham is all but pushed into by Sandra.

"Feels like the principal's office, doesn't it?" Graham whispers as he takes his seat.

"Or an ambush," I say, bouncing my foot under the table.

Sal heard that, and he lowers himself into his chair.

"So, let's just lay this out," he begins. "I'm guessing that you called me to discuss the relationship between the two of you?"

I rest my forearms on the table and my bracelets thud against the wood. "There is no relationship between us," I say slowly so that the point isn't missed.

"Right. Well, tabloids say otherwise," he counters, easing back in his chair.

"And why is that? Why do the tabloids think this at all?"

Sal pulls a cigar from his pocket and clenches it between his teeth, but doesn't light it. Instead, he looks toward Graham's agent.

Sandra steeples her fingers to her chin. "Listen, it's all in the interest of what's hot right now, and that's the two of you. That romance channel is blowing up. Their streaming service with your movies is a fan favorite. There are watch parties. There are social media parties. There are fan clubs. You name it. The two of you are money in the bank."

"We know that. We're the ones that attend their fan parties and romance cons. We smile for their pictures. We sign their swag. That doesn't mean I have to fall in love with this asshat," I say, and Graham feigns insult. "Oh, you don't feel any differently about me?" I snap.

"You're right. I'm not fond of you at all."

"The whole package?" I sit back in my chair and swivel it

toward him so that our knees almost touch. I cross my arms and watch him, waiting for him to examine me as most men do.

Without giving me the satisfaction of a scan, he leans in toward me. "Did you want a list of things, your highness?"

I hold out my hand toward Graham. "Do you see what I put up with?" I ask Sal, who is grinning so widely that his cheeks push up his sunglasses slightly.

"Listen, doll, it's publicity. The story is out there, and we think you should roll with it. The network is even offering some incentive."

Now it's Graham that leans in. "What incentive?"

"You're contracted for six more movies. Four of those, you're love interests."

I groan, and Sal holds up a finger.

"They're willing to give a bonus, a big bonus, to sign on to do six more after that. They want to do a fan cruise, and, doll, I have a hot lead on a big-screen rom-com written just for you."

It's bait. *It's bait.* The sirens are going off in my head, but I can't help it. I have to ask.

"Who is writing it?"

"Penelope Mondragon," he says, and there is a collective gasp that goes through the room.

Penelope Mondragon is the greatest thing next to Nora Ephron; may she rest in peace. Working with Penelope Mondragon would be solidifying my place in rom-com history with Meg Ryan, Sandra Bullock, and Reese Witherspoon, just to name a few.

My mouth is actually watering.

"There are two people involved here," Graham says, as if to remind them all that he needs some bait too.

His agent presses her hands flat on the tabletop. "Charles Malloy is asking for you," she says.

Graham exchanges a look with me, and I can assure you my

look is one of pure mortification at the dropping of my father's name at the table.

"Well, what do you know?" he says, the corner of his mouth lifting in a cocky grin. "No doubt he sees my action hero potential."

I can feel my neck and cheeks heat. A bead of sweat is rolling down the back of my neck. I swear, if my father is behind this . . .

"Listen," Sal says leaning back in his chair, examining the cigar he hasn't lit. "A love affair between Christina Malloy and Graham Crowley is gold. I don't give two shits that you can't stand one another. I haven't talked to my wife in three years," he says as if it's the same thing. "Your fandom wants it. They're willing to pay for it. This is gold."

I clasp my hands together on top of the table and think about what to say.

"What if I'm involved with someone else?" I ask.

I can see Sal's brow lift. "You?"

"Yes, me," I say, more than a little insulted.

"Tell me about this," Sal eases in over the table, his cigar now balanced between two pudgy fingers. "You're seeing someone?"

I uncross my legs and cross them again. A look at Graham's smirk tells me that no one believes I could be involved with anyone else. This team that's supposed to support me doesn't believe in me at all.

Graham leans in, too. "They just want a public presence?" he asks, getting me out of answering the question that had been posed to me.

"What more is there?" Sal asks.

"I mean, we don't have to get married or anything, right?" Graham asks.

Grateful that he asked that, I turn my attention back to Sal.

He's grinning, and I swear the tint on his sunglasses is even darker than before. "Just some photo ops, some outings, that kind of thing. No weddings. No babies," he says, and I actually choke.

Penny hands Graham a glass of water to pass to me. I take it and sip.

"You'll have to play it up on the set, because that's where these people get their info," Sal says, and it's Graham that chokes out a laugh.

"Anyone who has been on set with us knows it's tense."

Sal agrees with a nod. "Yeah, well, now it needs to be full of sweet love."

"I mean, I don't have to sign a contract to be nice to her, do I?" Graham asks.

"No."

"If it doesn't work, it doesn't work?"

"If it doesn't work, I can't promise the other things will fall in your lap," Sal says with his brows raised.

Graham pulls his bottom lip through his teeth. I know what he's thinking. If he pisses me off, I could run to Daddy.

But I'm thinking about Penelope Mondragon. Being in one of her movies is like a dream come true. It'll be the catalyst for the career I really want.

"Can we discuss this?" Graham asks. "Alone?"

The publicists are the first to stand, followed by Penny and Barbara. Sal pats my hand and rises from his seat. Graham's agent stands and touches his shoulder as she walks out of the room.

A moment later, we're alone in the boardroom. I'm guessing this is just the start of me having to be alone with this guy.

CHAPTER SIX

GRAHAM

And the caption read, "A love affair that reads like a romance novel."

With everyone else out of the room, I sit back in my chair and think about what's been laid on the table. I've done more for less money. I already work with this woman, and I know how to tolerate her fancy shoes, her coffee made just so, and her incessant question asking.

I can live with the Chanel No. 5 scent, which I find appalling, and well, I can mess with her, because if she's in on this, she can't react. Oh, this could be just the thing I've been searching for.

I'm humored now, and when I chuckle, she turns those dark eyes on me.

"What's so funny?" she asks.

"This whole thing. I can't believe we're being asked to fake date. What are we, in some romance novel?"

"I don't hear anyone asking anything. I think we're being bribed and forced into this."

"We don't have to do it," I remind her, but I really want that part in her father's film. I can't help but think that if Charles Malloy thinks that I'm dating his daughter, it'll carry some clout.

"If we don't, you know what will happen?" She leans in toward me. "They'll bury our careers. We're not in control here," she whispers.

She's right. We're puppets, but if we do this, the payout will be worth it.

"So, what does it hurt?" I ask. "We're familiar with one another."

"Right, so much so that the fact that you chew your ice makes me want to throw something across the room at you," she says, and I think about the time she did that.

"Yeah, well Chanel stopped at number five for the name—it's not a suggestion for the number of ounces you should put on in a day," I counter, and she gasps as if I'd just slapped her.

"You chew with your mouth open," she says, crossing her arms in front of her.

"Honey, it'd be nice to see you eat. I assume that's why you're so bitchy."

Again, she gasps. I'm sure she'd like to slap me, but we're trying to work this out, not air our grievances.

I hold up a hand. "We either get on board with this, or we don't, and we decide we're screwed."

She studies me as if she's considering her options. "Fine. How do we do this?"

"We need to be seen together. We need to have PDA and smile when the other one talks. Starbucks runs, walks through the freaking mall, or on the street. I guess we study Affleck and Lopez, see what they're doing, and copy that."

She groans with a shake of her head, but honestly, they have it figured out. An Instagram post here or there and a TikTok dance won't hurt.

"I know that it all sounds horrible," I say, "But Penelope Mondragon," I remind her.

Her eyes widen. She wants it. She wants it so bad, she can taste it.

"I'm not speaking to my father about the movie on your behalf," she says.

"I wouldn't ask you to. It sounds like it's already something. But to be honest, if he's in on this thinking that you and I are together, maybe it'll help."

She worries her lip. "I'm not sure it will. But I want in too."

"On the relationship?" I ask, raising a brow.

She shakes her head. "I want to be in my dad's film, too."

"You're getting Penelope Mondragon," I shoot back, because now she's encroaching on my givens, and she has her own.

"Yes, but my father doesn't see me as an actress. He doesn't think I have real talent."

"I'm supposed to convince him of that?" I ask.

"Not exactly, but if he wants you, and he thinks I'm with you, I can ask to be involved. He'll do it then. Otherwise, I'm nothing."

There is a sadness in her eyes when she talks about her father and his opinion of her. I may not care for her personally, but this woman has massive talent. It's not showcased in these little streaming movies. A Penelope Mondragon movie is where she belongs.

I consider what she's asking for. I don't see what it'll hurt. The man will never let her in his film, no matter what say I have in it. Hell, he didn't even know she left the awards ceremony. Christina is on her own in this town, even if she is the child of Hollywood royalty.

I just want the part, and I'm willing to sell out my reputation to get it.

"Fine," I say, agreeing to her being in the film, as if I have any say.

"Fine," she says.

"Just remember not to fall in love with me." I wink at her.

Christina rolls her eyes. "As if that could ever happen."

"It could."

"It won't."

There is a tapping at the door and Penny pokes her head into the room. "They want to know if you've come to a decision. They want to make some kind of press release."

I look at Christina and she looks ill. This could very well backfire and blow up in our faces. But if it doesn't—well, I just have to consider what great things will come my way.

"We're all in. You can tell them," I say.

Penny nods and closes the door.

"I feel sick," she says.

"You look sick."

"See what you do to me?"

"You'll have to get over that, you know."

"What?" she asks as if she's confused by it.

"The snide comments. Especially in public. From now on, we need to be a high-profile couple in love. There can't be any slip-ups. The press is going to be looking for that."

"I hate this," she says, gathering her purse and pulling her phone out.

"Yeah, well, honey, it doesn't appeal to me either. However, my name on a marquee as the star of one of your dad's films, now that appeals to me."

She scrolls through items on her phone and then drops it back into her purse with a huff.

Turning in her seat, she looks at me. "There's nothing in writing. How do I know you won't stab me in the back?"

"How do I know you won't do the same?"

"I promise," she says, resigned.

"I can't see where that carries weight. You hate me enough, you just might do something to see me crash and burn."

Her eyes narrow. "I don't *hate* you."

"You sure aren't a fan."

"I appreciate your talents."

Well, that's something. "Let's shake on it."

"That's going to stop us from screwing one another over?"

"I'm a man of my word. You should know that."

Christina thinks it over as she studies her manicured fingers. Finally, she holds out her dainty hand and a diamond bracelet dangles from her wrist. "I'm a woman of mine."

I shake her hand and then hold it there. "I'm going to have to kiss you."

She eases back. "We're alone. You don't have to kiss me."

I laugh. "Not now, but I'm going to have to do it in public. You're going to have to react like you do when we're filming, only there won't be angles to just get the one reaction. You're going to have to act as if you enjoy it."

"Then you'll have to enjoy kissing me," she counters.

Admittedly, it's one of the things I do enjoy about working with her. Though, I assume it's because when I'm kissing her, she's quiet.

"Then we're in agreement. We're a couple," I say, needing verbal conformation.

"We're a couple," she chokes out the words, and to be honest, I'm not sure she's not going to be sick.

I let out a long and steady breath.

"Well, let's go out into the world and give our fans what they want."

"So that we can get what we want," she adds, as if saying it aloud validates what we're selling out for.

"Exactly."

CHAPTER SEVEN

CHRISTINA

And the woman who gossips in Sal's office says, "I bet you ten bucks she gets him fired before this is over."

∼

I'd feel better if there was a contract. Something written on paper that says, *If I pretend to be in love with Graham Crowley, I absolutely get a Penelope Mondragon film.* But this is a handshake deal, made with a man I can't stand, among others who are out to reap the benefits of me selling myself out.

I've never been "attached" to a man before. I've dated, but no one cared.

Yes, I was born into a Hollywood family. Yes, I'm depicted as the California princess. But no one has ever looked my way—until now.

I don't want to credit Graham for that either. I got my own parts and I'm holding my own. Sure, timing helps. I was one of the first actresses in the films that the Love Is in the Air network contracted for multiple films.

My father didn't do that.

My mother didn't do it either.

And my coupling on screen with Graham Crowley didn't do that either.

But now I've sold my soul to the devil for a bigger chance. Hollywood is full of people living with this same regret. At least I don't have to take my clothes off to have made this deal.

Graham takes my hand in his as we exit the building and head toward my car.

My first instinct is to pull back, but it's as if I have a little demon on my shoulder whispering in my ear the reminder of what I've done. The man gets to touch me and kiss me in public. If I want the rewards that are to come, then I need to let him do just that—touch and kiss me in public.

"What do you say to lunch?" he asks.

I turn my head to look up at him as we stop at my car. "You're asking me to lunch?"

"I am. We can split the bill," he says with a grin.

"Why would I want to go to lunch with you?"

"Because you're my girlfriend," he reminds me. "Actually, I was thinking that we could just go to Whole Foods, grab some take-and-go thing, and head back to one of our places. Perhaps mine, since I came with Sandra, so I don't have a ride."

I nod slowly and slip on my sunglasses.

"Fine, but when we get to your place, I'm not touching you."

He lifts a brow. "Why would you say that?"

"I mean that this ends when we're in private. I don't have to be nice to you."

"So, it's fair game that goes both ways?" he asks.

"I guess so."

"Fine. Give me your keys."

I grip my purse to my chest. "I'm not giving you my keys."

"Yes, you are. One of the first signs that we're together and that you trust me is you letting me drive your car."

I narrow my eyes at him, not that he can see that through the darkness of my glasses. "Only I drive my car."

"Well, now, so does your boyfriend. C'mon, I'll open the passenger door for you, honey."

"We'd better get our payoff soon," I growl as I walk around the car and Graham laughs. I'm just not sure how long I can do this.

Deciding not to go all out yet, we stop at a boutique grocery store, rather than a chain. Graham takes a selfie of us looking at the shelves, and I smile sweetly. He sends it to me and tells me to gram it when we get back to the car.

We still have a few stunned onlookers, but at least there isn't a mob. Graham takes a selfie with someone while I am turned around looking in the deli case, and the woman who checks us out is a bit star struck, but admittedly, we make it through a public venue, holding hands, smiling sweetly, and back to the car.

Graham puts our bag in the back seat, and I climb into the car.

I take a moment to just catch my breath. This man is no stranger. I'm familiar with him at my side, with his hand in mine, and his voice in my ear. But this is a whole new level of chaos that has my body buzzing. I just hope I don't regret my decision.

As Graham climbs into the car, I take out my phone and bring up Instagram. There's a heaviness in my chest as I bring up the picture of us shopping. I will never admit this aloud, but we are cute together.

I pop in the picture and add some fluff to it by saying that we're going to have a lovely lunch, just the two of us. It posts and I feel ill.

As Graham situates himself behind the steering wheel of my car, I let out a breath and cross my arms.

"Hungry?" Graham says, his lips twisting up in a smirk.

"Don't go accusing me of being bitchy because I'm hungry. I'm already exhausted, and all we did was walk through a market."

"Exhausted? Maybe you need more sleep," he says as he starts the car.

I turn, pull off my sunglasses, and level a look at him. "It's not about how much sleep I get. I'm exhausted trying to smile while you're in my presence."

"It's going to be happening a lot. So, get used to it."

"Only in public," I counter.

He turns in his seat to face me. He's still smiling. "If you think that laying into me when we're in the car is safe, you're wrong. I will guarantee that if we sit here more than two minutes, there will be pictures of our little lovers' spat all over the internet."

I grit my teeth and slide my sunglasses back on. I hate that he's right, and I'm not going to tell him he is.

He puts the car in drive and starts driving.

We don't speak as he drives through town, and I realize he's headed to my place, not his. I didn't realize he even knew where I lived until he pulls up in front of the security gate.

"I thought we were going to your place," I say.

Graham shakes his head. "Yours was closer. Code please," he says and my mouth gapes open. Does he really think I'm going to share that with him?

"No way."

"I can just sit here, or you can reach over me and type it in. I'll close my eyes."

I swallow. I hate this. I hate this. I hate this!

I unbuckle my seatbelt and start over the center console, and him, and through the open window. I feel his hands on my back.

"Don't touch me," I growl as I try to reach the buttons on the control pad for the gate, my breasts squishing up against the door.

"If I sit here with my hands in the air, it looks weird."

"This whole thing is weird," I say as I try to ease myself back into my seat and fix my skirt.

Graham pulls through the gate.

"Which door?" he finally asks, and I point to the correct one and push the button to raise the garage door.

The door to the garage goes up and he pulls the car in.

"Security gate and private garage. Nice place," he says.

"Don't tease me."

"Who's teasing? I mean it. Nice place."

I eye him coolly. He hasn't even seen my place to tell me it's nice.

"And your little bungalow in Burbank isn't nice?"

"Not like this. No security. Garage door doesn't work well. I need to get it fixed. I have a roommate and a dog."

"You have a dog?" I find it odd that I don't know that.

"Yep. Black lab named Loki."

"Loki?"

He pulls his sunglasses from his face and hangs them from the front of his shirt. "Yeah, Loki. Thor's brother?" he says in the form of a question, as if that's supposed to make me know what he's talking about. "Seriously? You were born and raised here, and you don't know Thor and Loki?"

"I don't know Loki, but I've heard of Thor."

"Heard of Thor." He shakes his head. "Shit, what kind of isolated island do you live on?"

"Are you seriously going to sit in my car, in my garage, and hassle me over this?"

"Yes," he says with confidence. "No one in Hollywood doesn't know Loki. Marvel Universe. The god of mischief."

I purse my lips. "I only know of Thor, but I know Iron Man."

He laughs. "It's a start. We have to remedy this."

"I don't think we do."

Graham opens the car door and steps out. "Oh, yes, we do. I'm staying here until you've seen at least two Marvel movies with Thor and Loki."

"I really—"

"Oh, my sweetest love," he grins, "you have no choice. Let's go."

CHAPTER EIGHT

GRAHAM

And the entertainment reporter says, "We can't get enough of Christina and Graham, but how long can it last?"

~

I understand the lack of Thor knowledge once I step into Christina's condo.

My bungalow sits on a quarter acre and has four bedrooms. It's no mansion, but I'm happy there. But this...

Marble floors, open space, extravagant furniture, mirrors, collectibles, and a professional-grade kitchen that appears to never have been cooked in.

I set our bag from the market on the island and take in the view from the large bank of windows.

"How long have you lived here?" I ask.

Christina sets her purse on the counter, putting her sunglasses in the case before dropping them inside. "A while," she says, but then chews her bottom lip.

I can't help but notice how her eyes go dark when I ask

personal questions. Or how her lips grow pinker when she gnaws on them.

"I can find out," I say, leaning my hip against the counter.

"You don't really have to learn about me. It's not like we're really dating."

"Well, we've been working together for years, so it's not like we're strangers either," I say, but in fact, we really are strangers. We've never gotten to know one another. That's equally on me.

"Don't you think you're pushing it?" she asks, crossing her arms in front of her. "I mean, you're in my home. You drove my car."

"And I guarantee you that someone noticed."

Her nose wrinkles up. "It still doesn't mean I need to share intimate details of my life."

"I only asked you how long you've lived here."

She continues to chew on her lip, and I'm worried she's going to make it bleed.

"Don't judge me, okay?" she asks sincerely as she moves around the island and stands across from me.

"No judgement zone, except about the Loki thing."

She rolls her eyes. "I've lived here since I was eighteen."

I purse my lips so that I won't react. An eighteen-year-old alone in this place? Was she banished here?

"You're judging." She folds her arms in front of her again and shifts her weight from side to side.

"I'm sorry. I don't mean to. I respect your upbringing."

"Oh, no you don't," she accuses. "You think I'm a spoiled brat."

Well, who wouldn't think that? But then I think about how her parents treated her at the awards ceremony. An extravagant condo given to an eighteen-year-old seems appropriate. And, she didn't say they gave it to her, but, yeah, I'm assuming—I'm making judgement.

She moves past me, and I reach for her arm. "Hey, it's a nice place."

Christina studies me. "It's not like I don't work, you know."

"I know. I'm there with you, remember?"

She nods, and somewhere we come to a truce.

I drop my hand and she moves to the refrigerator. "I have sparkling water, flavored water, Sprite Zero, and sugar free apple juice."

I purse my lips. "No Coke?"

"I don't drink sugar drinks."

"That's too bad. I guess I'll need to bring some over."

"I don't see that you need to do that," she says, pulling a flavored water from the refrigerator.

"I'll take one of those," I say, and she nods as she hands me one. "Thank you."

"We can eat in here, or out on the balcony," she offers.

"Where is your TV?"

Her brows draw inward. "In my bedroom."

I purse my lips again to keep from laughing. "Your house is this big, and your TV is in your bedroom?"

She tucks her hair behind her ear and lifts her eyes to meet mine. They're still dark and defensive as they settle on me.

"It's really the only room I spend time in. This is a big place for one person."

Interesting. She's lonely.

I could ride this until she's in tears, but standing in her kitchen, I feel protective of her. I'm seeing a different side to this Hollywood princess. Maybe these were questions I should have asked her when they first paired us up.

Nah, she wouldn't have let me.

"So, I'm going to guess you're not going to invite me to watch a Marvel movie?" I study her as her eyes go wide at my suggestion.

"Not in your lifetime," she confirms.

"You know, why don't I get an Uber, take my lunch, and head out."

She opens her bottle and takes a sip.

"That's probably a great idea."

I nod and pull out my phone. She gives me the actual address of her place and I input it.

Christina moves to the other side of the island and sits on one of the stools.

On any other day, I would have done anything to get out of her presence as quickly as possible, but today, I guess I feel as if we are forging a friendship of sorts. Why? I don't know, but I've been enjoying myself, even if it was for show.

But that's not what Christina and I do. We don't enjoy one another's company. We don't hang out or share details of our lives with one another. The fact that I knew where she lived seemed to surprise her enough.

I look at my phone and realize that my Uber driver is only three minutes away. I move to the bag from the market. I take out her lunch items and keep mine in the bag.

"When do you think we should see each other again?" I ask.

"We start production in four weeks."

I wrinkle my nose. "I think we're going to need to see each other a few more times before then."

She twists a tendril of hair around her finger. "I have to be at a grand opening for my mother's new spa on Thursday," she says.

"Another one?"

Christina nods. "This will be the sixty-fourth one to open. But this one is a new concept spa."

"I don't understand that at all."

She laughs. "I can't say that I do either."

"I could pick you up and take you there."

Lifting her bottle to her lips, she takes a sip and studies me. Her eyes have softened, and her shoulders have dropped. She's easing around me, even if ever so slightly.

"I suppose that would be okay. There'll be a lot of press there."

"All the better."

She wipes her fingers over her lips. "I hate this," she says, but it's more sad than angry.

"It's not forever," I say, taking her feelings a bit personally. But what I don't understand is why it matters to me.

This woman sitting across from me isn't my friend. She's someone I'm forced to work with, and now, in order to get all the things I want, I'm forced to spend time with.

But seeing her in her own home, I feel something. Let's call it compassion. I know her mother doesn't drop by with leftovers because she's worried that her daughter doesn't eat.

I see my mother at least three times a week when she drops by, or I take her to lunch.

My father invites me to go golfing or hiking a few times a month. I wonder when Christina last had one-on-one time with her father—or if she's ever had that.

Even though we've worked together for a while, I don't know if she has siblings, though I assume she doesn't. I have my brother. At least when we are irritated with our parents, we have each other. Who does Christina have?

I look at my phone. "My driver is here."

"I'll text you about the grand opening, and we can make plans."

I nod. "Okay."

I pick up the bag with my lunch and head to the front door. As I walk through her house, I look around again. There isn't one personal effect out. No shoes. No miscellaneous articles of clothing. Not one single photo.

Maybe this Hollywood princess isn't the hot mess of perfume I think she is. Maybe she could just use some attention.

CHAPTER NINE

CHRISTINA

And the chef on TV said, "If you don't make something of it, it will spoil and be tossed out and forgotten."

With the salad I'd picked up for lunch in my hand, I lock my bedroom door and settle on my bed to eat just past seven o'clock. I never ate earlier, so I decide to make this my dinner.

Penny emailed me my schedule for the week. They'll send the script to the next Love Is in the Air production next week, and we'll do our read-through the following week.

I didn't like him asking personal questions today. Sure, we agreed that "we're dating," but it doesn't mean we have to spend alone time together. I was glad that he decided to Uber home. It felt as if he were looking around and judging me while he was here. It was nerve-wracking enough for him to know where I lived without me telling him.

Glasses on, and my hair pulled up atop my head, I aim the remote toward the TV and scroll through the channels.

I stop when I get to the Love Is in the Air channel. I can't help but look to see what's on.

It's *Grand Central Christmas*. This was my first movie with Graham. I wince when I watch the scene where we're having our first intimate conversation on a bench at the station.

I'll never forget that day.

We'd been working together for more than a week when we filmed that scene. It was just enough time for me to decide that he was an asshole.

He'd called me out for what he said was excessive use of my perfume, and I'd come back at him for his language on the set. That only gave me a glorious rendition of the F-word used in its many, many forms.

It wasn't long after that that he decided to start making our kissing scenes something of a challenge.

Our long-standing irritation with one another only grew more intense from there. He comes to set with his lines half memorized, whereas I have the entire script memorized, which includes everyone else's lines too.

He shows up right on time, except for the first day of shooting when he's there hours early. I don't understand that thought process. Why only on the first day?

I'm always early. You can't just walk on set and assume that everyone is just waiting for you. Sure, we might have the luxury of being the stars, but it's the crew that makes the magic happen.

I hit the menu button on the remote. I can't watch Graham and I act like we love each other a moment longer.

As I scroll through the channels, I see two of my father's movies, and I zip right past those. I try not to watch commercials, not wanting to see my mother talk about her true love—her spas.

But I grin when I see *Thor: Ragnarok* is on. What are the odds?

Stopping on the channel, I set the remote next to me, pick up my fork, and start in on my salad.

I surely won't understand anything in this movie. Seriously,

I've seen *Iron Man*, but I still don't know who Loki is. But only a moment later, I'm educated.

There, in all his glory, is Tom Hiddleston in an ornate costume. So, this is Loki?

I settle in against my headboard and watch. There's humor, action, and I appreciate the handsome leading men.

I wonder if Graham's dog is untrustworthy to receive a name like Loki.

Before I know it, I have sat through the entire movie, and I enjoyed every moment of it. I pick up my phone and scroll my contacts to Graham's number, fully intent on telling him that I watched the movie and now know all about Loki, but I stop before I even start.

I don't need to text him. I don't need to talk to him when it doesn't matter. What we're doing is for show only, and there's no one here to see me talk about an Avenger movie with Graham.

Setting my phone down, I turn the channel again and stop on the Food Network. This is how I'll spend my time until I fall asleep—just as I do every night.

∼

When should I pick you up? The text appears on my phone Thursday morning, and I squint to read it.

Sitting up in bed, I wipe the sleep from my eyes and try to comprehend what the text is about.

A few deep breaths and I look at the time. It's nearly nine o'clock. I haven't slept in that late in a very long time. Picking up the remote on my nightstand, I aim it toward the windows, and open the room-darkening drapes.

I wince as the light fills the room, and then I look back down at my phone.

Christina? Another text appears.

The last time Graham texted me was two years ago, according to the text thread that comes up.

The text he had sent me was scathing. *The damn line is, "You're extraordinary, Mr. Greene. If I weren't betrothed to another, I'd marry you." It's not that damn hard!*

I blow out a breath. Why had I not deleted this thread and blocked this asshole's number? They'd nearly rewritten that entire script, and since I'd memorized the first one, I stumbled a bit, and he couldn't help but call me out on it.

He texts again, *Just call me Sherlock. I looked it up, the grand opening. The event starts at 1pm. I'm going to pick you up at 11 and take you to lunch first. See you soon, sweetheart.*

I swallow hard. I don't want to have to face my mother today, and I seriously don't want to face her with Graham Crowley. I fall back into the pillows.

Penelope Mondragon. Her name rushes into my head, and I remember why I'll tolerate Graham Crowley in my life. I want that movie so bad, I can taste it.

I'll be ready, I text back and then toss my phone to the end of the bed and pull my comforter up over my head. This is an interesting kind of hell that I've fallen into.

∼

At eleven o'clock, my phone buzzes, and I pick it up from the counter.

I'm here. How do I get in?

I grin down at the text. I could leave him outside and never answer.

I'll buzz you in, I text back, deciding that I'd better just put up with this.

Standing, I walk toward the window and watch him drive into the lot and park after I buzz him through the gate. Moving to the front door, I pull it open and wait for him to walk up the steps.

"Good morning, beautiful," he says with a grin. His eyes are shielded by a dark pair of sunglasses. But when he pulls them off, those dark eyes shimmer as he looks up at me.

The strangest pulse goes through my body—like electricity.

I swallow hard and try to regain some composure.

"You don't have to keep up the pleasantries when it's just us," I remind him as I turn back into my house and walk to the kitchen to gather my purse.

"I realize you find the sight of me appalling, but we're both so greedy about getting what's promised to us, perhaps you should just get over it," he says as he follows me to the kitchen.

"Greedy?"

"Yes," he says firmly. "And I said we're both greedy, so don't go getting on your high horse, princess."

"Don't call me that."

"Then don't act like that." He crosses his arms in front of him. "Listen, we need a truce. It's not like we don't know how to act civil to one another. That's sorta what got us into this in the first place."

"No, people lying got us into this."

"And we agreed to it so that we can get what we want," he says, moving toward the island and pressing his hands flat on it. "I'm not a bad guy."

"You're opinionated. You're egotistical. You sabotage our scenes."

He holds up a finger. "I eat Doritos before I kiss you," he says with some humor.

"Sabotage. Do you know how hard it is to make that seem real?"

"Then I guess it just makes you a better actress. Maybe you should thank me."

I let out a low growl and pick up my purse, slinging it over my shoulder.

"This isn't going to work. People are going to see right through this," I say as I walk past him.

Graham reaches for my hand and stops me. I turn and look up at him.

There's something in his expression that carries seriousness, and perhaps some regret.

"I want that movie," he says. "I know it's greedy, but I want it. I deserve it."

"Fine."

His fingers linger against my skin. "You deserve something more too."

I lick my lips. I want that movie more than I've ever wanted anything else.

Graham steps in closer to me and my breath catches as I look up at him. "We can do this," he says softly, his fingers grazing my arm gently.

I blink hard as he continues to close the gap between us.

"We can do this," I say, my voice a bit airy.

Graham leans in. Instinct has me closing my eyes.

I've kissed this man hundreds of times, but this—this is different.

The air grows heavy as he leans into me. I can't breathe.

It's then I feel his tongue slide over my cheek before he steps back. My eyes fly open, and Graham slips his sunglasses back on his face as he laughs that maniacal laugh.

"Don't tell me you don't want me, doll," he says, still laughing as he walks toward the front door.

I might just kill him before this scam is over.

CHAPTER TEN

GRAHAM

And the Instagram post read, "In Hollywood, famous actresses eat lettuce and famous actors can eat anything they want."

~

Christina is fuming as she makes it to my car and pulls open the door. I can't hear what names she's using for me, but there is a string of them being muttered under her breath.

Seriously, this could be a lot of fun.

She settles into the passenger seat and puts on her seatbelt.

I don't say anything to her. I start the car and drive out of the parking lot.

I've made reservations at a restaurant in the hotel in which her mother's new spa is going in. I've asked for a corner table, but not a private area. We're supposed to be seen, but I don't think either of us is ready to be seen in the middle of the dining room.

When I pull up in front of the hotel, Christina turns to me. Her large, dark glasses shield her glare, but I know it's there.

"We don't have to be here for another hour and a half."

I unbuckle my seat belt as the valet walks toward my car. "I thought we'd eat here and then we won't have to hurry over."

There is irritation in her sigh as the valet opens her door and holds his hand out to help her from the car.

I watch her climb out with practiced elegance. I can appreciate that she's flawless on the outside.

Once the valet closes the passenger door, he starts toward my side. I step out and hand him my key and a twenty. He thanks me, and before we even walk to the front door, my car is driving away.

I'll never not think about *Ferris Bueller's Day Off* when it comes to a valet.

I catch up to Christina and rest my hand at the low curve of her back as we enter the front of the new posh hotel.

"You don't have to touch me," she growls as she takes off her sunglasses.

"Then that wouldn't be realistic, would it?" I ask.

Her shoulders push back, and I can see that defensive stance go into place. I'm used to it. I can make her standoffish just by saying hello most times.

We walk through the lobby toward the restaurant, and there are eyes on us. A few phones have been less than discreetly lifted to take pictures.

Christina steps up to the counter, and I step to her side to give the hostess my information. She tries to not appear star struck, but it's there. By the way Christina's face has gone hard, she's not much in the mood for showboating today. To be honest, I'm not sure if that's my fault or her mother's.

The hostess walks us to a corner table, just as I'd requested. I pull out Christina's chair, but she doesn't thank me. She sits and begins to tuck away her sunglasses.

I take my seat and look around the room.

There isn't much of a lunch crowd yet, which is good for one of our first public appearances.

Christina picks up her menu and studies it. I study her.

Her dark hair is pulled back into a sleek ponytail. Large diamond studs adorn her ears. Her fingernails are a different color than they were the other day. I wonder if she did that herself or if she had a salon day yesterday, since I didn't see her or talk to her.

She has on the same diamond bracelet she wore to the award ceremony, and a single silver band on her right middle finger.

There is something about her that screams simple elegance, but I know she's probably spent hours looking this *simple.*

Christina sets her menu down and picks up the water that was poured for us. She sips and then replaces the glass. Easing back in her seat, she crosses her legs and rests her hands on her knees.

She's taking in the room.

"See anyone you know?" I ask as I read over the menu again.

"Bob Hanson is having lunch with his assistant," she says nonchalantly, as if she's a spy and feeding me information. "Gretta Jones and Martha Bloom are having martinis. Bob Mills is at the bar, alone, except for some fan girl who just approached with an actual autograph book."

I can't help but grin at that. Is her tone disgust or jealousy?

"Bob Hanson is having an affair with his assistant," I say as I put down my menu and steal a quick glance in Bob's direction.

"How do you know that?"

"Everyone knows that," I say.

"Maybe the media just made that up. Maybe they don't like one another at all."

I shake my head. "First of all, Bob Hanson makes the deals; he doesn't take them. And second, what would his assistant gain in a fake relationship?"

Her lips twist, and she picks up her glass of water again. "We're greedy."

"We established that the other day," I remind her. "We're in a different place compared to them."

She nods.

We both want to further our career, and it's being handed to us for the price of our personal reputations. I know that this is going to be a short-lived thing, this story between us. Soon, she'll have her Penelope Mondragon rom-com and I'll have my Charles Malloy action movie. In another year or so, no one will remember the cheesy romance movies we made together, or that we were ever associated with one another. But for now, it'll have to work for both of us.

No surprise that when the server comes to take our order, Christina orders some overpriced salad that probably doesn't have enough calories in it to sustain her until I get her home in a few hours. A glass of sparkling water is added, with a twist of lime.

I'm working with my trainer later, so I'm going to eat. I order some gourmet burger with sweet potato fries and a beer.

"You're driving," she points out when the server leaves the table.

"I am. It's one beer before noon, and I'm not leaving this building for at least another two hours. I think we're okay."

She nods and looks down at her napkin, trying to avoid looking at me or having any unnecessary conversation.

I scroll through my phone until our lunch arrives, then I tuck my phone into my pocket.

"You're welcome to any of my fries if you'd like," I say.

Christina looks at my plate. "I'm good, thanks."

"Maybe when we're done with your mom's event, I can drive you through an In-N-Out and get you something to really eat."

"I said I'm good."

"I think you're going to pass out one of these days. Is that all you ever eat, or is that all you ever eat around me?"

She stabs her first round of greens with her fork. "It's not the same for men in this town. One ounce. One wrinkle. One bad Botox injection and a woman's career is over."

I snort out a laugh as I take a big bite of my burger. "You think it's different for men?"

"Um, yes."

"I don't see it anymore. I mean, look at the women in this industry who are in their seventies and eighties still making a name for themselves. I think times are changing."

"Okay, but those actresses are established. They did their time starving themselves, and in a time when they weren't protected by the venomous predators out there."

I chew thoughtfully. "So, you're going to starve yourself on the merit that if you're too big you won't be looked at, yet you feel bad for the veterans who didn't have a choice but to be looked at? You don't make any freaking sense."

"I want to work."

"Then be good at your job," I counter.

"I am good at my job."

"Good enough that the masses think you love me."

She narrows her gaze at me. "I loathe you."

"Ah, it's a bright and sunny day in Hollywood, my love," I say as I take another big bite of my delicious hamburger.

CHAPTER ELEVEN

CHRISTINA

And the entertainment reporter says, "It must be serious if she has him making appearances at her mother's grand openings."

~

I hate that my body is reacting to my lunch and my stomach is growling as Graham and I walk toward the new spa my mother is opening.

I know he can hear it, and to his credit, he hasn't said anything.

It's not until we are on the outskirts of the crowd that has amassed around the balloon arch and the podium that he finally reaches for my hand and interlaces our fingers.

This is it. Not that my parents have paid any attention to the media, but my mother will see me holding hands with Graham now.

I hike my purse up on my shoulder and put on my biggest smile as we walk through the crowd.

Penny sees us and moves to me. "Your mother is in the office and wants to see you before she makes her appearance."

My thought is that she should already be working the crowd. But this is normal for her. She must know what she's doing.

I give Penny a nod and turn back to Graham. "I have to go see my mother. I'll be right back," I say.

He nods, but as I try to pull away from him, he pulls me back by our joined hands. I look up and him and he leans his head down and moves toward me, pressing a gentle kiss on my lips.

Smiling, he eases back, but I'm worried that my expression is terrified.

"I'll be right here," he says gently and softly, as if it were meant just for me to hear, and not for those who are watching us.

I give him a nod and follow Penny into the office where my mother is having her makeup done.

"Sweetheart, you made it," she says, keeping her head still as the woman applies lipstick.

"Of course I did," I say, wondering if I had an option. "I just had lunch in the restaurant."

"I heard you were in there with Graham Crowley."

I swallow hard knowing how quickly news travels. "I was. He's here with me."

"Since when do you see him socially? I thought you didn't like him."

I look around the room at the few people I don't know. There is a look people have when they're trying to do their job and act as if they aren't listening for personal information. I've been around it my entire life. So, you watch what you say and when you say it.

"Things seem to have worked out differently for us," I say, and then decide to change the subject. "There's quite a crowd out there."

"Honey, this concept spa is going to be big," she says, turning in the chair as the woman doing her makeup begins to put away her brushes.

"I look forward to having the new services," I say.

"You can book before you leave."

No special treatment for me, I think selfishly. I know they have couples' services. Maybe I could book for Graham and me.

I suck in a breath the moment I realize that I've lumped us together. I don't want to spend time with him like that. What in the hell was I thinking?

"What do you think?" My mother stands before me and does a little spin in an elegant green suit.

"You look stunning," I say.

She reaches for my hands. "Make sure you have some champagne," she says before her publicist ushers her out the door.

I stand in the room now with the women who had done my mother's hair and makeup, and Penny, who is watching me. I've all but been dismissed by my mother so she can go be in the spotlight.

Penny moves to me. "Can I get you anything?" she asks.

"I'm good. Really, you don't have to stay for all of this," I say.

Penny's eyes go wide, and her mouth opens and closes as if I've taken her by surprise.

"Are you sure?" she asks.

"I'm sure. Enjoy your day."

Her mouth twitches as if she wants to smile. She thanks me and hurries out the door.

I think about what just transpired. Do I not allow her time away from my social agenda? I consider it for a moment. No, I don't. I'll need to be more aware of that. Penny should have her own life, too.

Checking myself in the mirror, I retrieve a tube of lipstick from my purse. I fix my lip color and drop the tube back into my purse. Before I leave the room, I smile at those who are quietly watching me.

The moment I step out of the office and into the crowd, I look for Graham. He's standing to the side talking to Penny, but I notice the cameras and phones aimed at him taking pictures.

I move to him, and Penny says goodbye and heads out.

"Are you okay?" he asks.

"Yeah. I'm fine," I say, smiling up at him, and then I slip my hand into his. Honestly, I never thought Graham Crowley would be my comfort.

∽

"You're awfully quiet," Graham says as we drive away from the hotel. "Are you sure everything is okay?"

"I'm sure." I turn in my seat and look at him. "I guess the press got what they were looking for today, huh?"

He grins. "We're still not the hottest couple out there," he says.

"Enough to make life a bit interesting, I guess."

He lets out a low hum. "Interesting. That it is. Do you think your mother even realized we were there together?"

"She mentioned it when I went to see her before she spoke."

"And?"

"And she asked what that was about. She thought I didn't like you."

A grin curls up the side of his mouth. "You don't like me. So, what did you tell her? Did you tell her it's just a publicity scam?"

I brush my hands over my skirt. "No. She doesn't need to know that. I just told her things worked out differently for us, and she let it go at that."

"Interesting. I'm surprised I haven't heard from my mother about it yet. I mean, we're nearly four days into this," he says with a laugh.

"Don't you speak to your mother?"

"All the time. That's why it's interesting. But she doesn't watch gossip shows. She just doesn't care about it."

"You're in the industry. Doesn't she keep up on it for that reason?"

"My brother is a marine. She cares about the danger he might be in, but she's not into following politics. I'm in the entertainment industry. If I were being stalked, she might care. Me being seen with a woman I work with, that's not newsworthy to her."

I'd like to say my family was the same, but he knows that's a lie. My mother is obsessed with seeing herself in the press, and though my father doesn't say anything about it, he's equally obsessed. It's not always easy either. Though big producers don't always get the same amount of applause when they step out into public, their dirty laundry is shouted equally loud.

Uncomfortable with the intimate conversation, I change it. "What plans do you have for the rest of the day?"

"I'm working out with my trainer."

"Oh," I say. Of course he has things going on. I'm probably one of the only people in this town that's lonely if I'm not working.

"Would you like to work out with us?" he asks.

"No," I say quickly, and he lets out a little chuckle.

"You're considering that In-N-Out offer, aren't you?" he asks, a bit too amused.

I purse my lips, but the smile breaks through anyway. "Yes."

"How about we get it and take a drive down the coast?"

"But you have plans."

"Plans can always be changed."

Now I smile at the consideration he's giving me. "Thank you," I say. I guess I'm desperate for companionship. I mean, I'm agreeing to more time with Graham Crowley.

Graham laughs. "Thank you? Are you kidding? I'm excited to watch you eat. It'll be like an event."

"If you're just going to tease me—"

"I am. But I like teasing you because your cheeks get all red when I get under your skin."

"Well, it's not nice."

"I'm sorry," he says sincerely, and he reaches for my hand. "This isn't easy on either of us."

I look down at our joined hands and wonder why he did that. But I don't pull my hand back. For some reason there is comfort with our palms pressed together and our fingers entwined.

"What's not easy? The being nice?"

He gives that some thought. "Yeah, I guess that's what I mean."

"Just because I agreed to food doesn't mean I like you."

"I get that. Just because I want to feed you doesn't mean I like you either."

"Good. I'm more comfortable loathing you."

He grins, and I can't help but smile too. Surely the meaning of loathing one another doesn't mean the same thing as we hold hands.

"Double-double, animal style?" he asks and my mouth waters at the mention of the menu item at the hamburger chain.

"Make sure to get animal style on the fries too," I say, and he actually laughs.

My decision is made. I'll hate him tomorrow.

CHAPTER TWELVE

GRAHAM

And the text read, "Dude, are you seriously dating that chick? Don't forget my house has cameras."

Armed with bags of burgers and fries, I head toward the coast. I've called in a favor with a friend who lives right off the beach. He's out of town, and we can walk out onto the beach, away from tourists, right from his back door.

I haven't cleared that with Christina, but it still fits into our plans. It'll be a good place for her to calm down. She's been a bit tense since we left the hotel. And who could blame her?

I've now been around her and her mother twice, and I can see the energy that takes on Christina's part. Her mother wanted her there for the event, but once her mother was the center of attention, she didn't even acknowledge her daughter—or us, for that matter.

Christina kept moving us to the edge of the crowd, and she held onto me as if I were her lifeline. Photos were taken of us, and we talked to a few industry people while we were there. All along, we played up our little relationship, so it looked like we couldn't get enough of one another.

It didn't go unnoticed that her father hadn't bothered to show up. I wonder if he's invested in her mother's spa business or not. Are they married in name and appearance only? Is it any different from what Christina and I are doing? The thought weighs heavy in my chest.

"How long have you lived here?" she asks me.

I've put the top down on the car and the sleek ponytail she'd been wearing now has loose strands flying around her face.

"You mean in the area?" I ask.

"California. I know you're not from here."

That surprises me. I can't imagine that she'd have bothered to know anything about me.

"I've lived here since I was fourteen," I say.

"Where did you live before?"

"Ohio."

She turns her head and studies me. "Ohio? What made you move from Ohio to California?"

"I got a part in a TV show."

I watch as she bites down on her lip. This is the part that seems to be news to her.

"When you were fourteen?" she asks.

"Yep. *The House on the Corner*," I say. "I was the next-door neighbor for three seasons."

Now she shifts with the bags of food on her lap and looks directly at me. "Chip?"

I laugh. "Yeah, that was me."

"God, I had the biggest crush on you," she laughs, and it's genuine and sweet. "On Chip, I mean."

"And you didn't know that was me?"

Christina shrugs. "My nanny and I used to watch that on Monday nights after dinner."

"You and your nanny? How old are you?"

"I'm not that much younger than you."

I push my hand into her shoulder as a jab from across the car. "How old are you?"

"I'll be thirty in May," she says sheepishly.

"Five years," I say. "So, you were nine when I took the role of Chip."

"See, I wouldn't have correlated that it was you. I liked Chip, not Graham."

I grin at her. "Yeah, but you had a crush on me. That's something."

"It's not valid now. I don't have a crush on you anymore."

I shrug. "It's just nice to know you once pined for me."

She laughs again, and I realize I like the sound of it. In fact, unless it was scripted, I can't say I've ever heard her laugh before.

I drive down one of the streets lined by houses that back to the ocean. I slow and pull into the driveway of one of them.

"What are you doing?" Christina asks with urgency laced into her voice.

"Parking. Actually, I'm going to park in the garage," I say as I put the car in park and open the car door.

She reaches for my arm. "You don't live here. Why are we here, at this house?" Her voice shakes as if this is a trigger for her.

"This is the house of a buddy who is out of town. He said I could park here, and we can sit on the back patio overlooking the beach."

She worries her bottom lip as she does when she's uncomfortable.

"I'm not going to try anything on you or abandon you in some strange house. We're here to feed you and enjoy the beach." My voice is straining because she's making me crazy with this hot and cold attitude of hers.

"Fine. But we eat and you take me home."

I nod, because suddenly getting her home won't come fast enough.

. . .

Christina follows me through the house. Is she just taking it in, or is she freaked out that we're here? I can't tell. All I know is that this was a mistake. We do fine in public. We know how to do that. But any time alone, we fumble until it becomes uncomfortable.

"Whose house is this?" she asks as we walk through the state-of-the-art kitchen toward the sliding glass doors that lead to the patio.

"Craig Mason's," I say.

Christina stops and looks around. "Dodgers?"

I chuckle. I'm surprised she knows that. "Yes."

"Okay. I think I'm impressed."

I raise a brow and pull open the vertical blinds that cover the sliding glass doors. "Why are you impressed?"

"You have famous friends."

I eye her coolly. "I know a lot of people," I say.

She bites down on her lip and thinks about that. "I just don't see you out hobnobbing. I mean, it's not in the entertainment news and all."

"Meaning you don't see me courtside at the Lakers games or in a suite at a Dodgers game?"

"Exactly."

"I'm not famous enough for anyone to care," I say, and I hear the bit of jealousy that hangs in my voice. "Just this little affair we're having seems to be newsworthy. But trust me, you're not the only person in my life, honey," I say as I open the sliding door.

I don't wait for her. I walk out onto the patio and take in a deep breath. The serene view calms me, and at this moment, that's what I need.

The reason Christina and I don't get along is because she's hard to be around. She's hot. She's cold. She's a princess. She's fragile. I can't keep up.

Sure, I'm not all that serious when we're working. I want to enjoy my job. What the hell makes people want us together, I don't know. But the network keeps casting us together. It's going to happen when you're working with an ensemble cast. I've done a few movies with other actresses for the channel, but they don't have the same ratings as when I'm paired with Christina.

We are network gold, and I'll never understand it.

Ratings go up when our movies play. Advertising spaces cost more during our movies. We get our own panels and meet-and-greets at fan events, when everyone else is forced to do them as a group.

I move to the railing and grip it. Taking in another breath, I hear her come through the door and set the bag of food on the small table.

"This is nice," she says appreciatively.

"It's a great place to just come and collect yourself," I say.

"Do you do that a lot?"

Oh, she has no idea how soothing this place can be after a day of working with her. "Yes," I say before turning toward her.

Christina brushes off the small chair at the table and sits down. I sit down across from her and open the bag of food.

"Promise me you'll eat this," I say as I pull out a wrapped burger and hand it to her.

"I'll eat it."

I set the fries between us and watch as she immediately takes one and eats it. She hums, and I wonder if she thinks that's all she's going to eat. Honestly, if she doesn't eat that burger, I might force it down her throat.

"I forgot how good this is," she says.

"That was one fry."

"Yeah, but it was really good."

I watch as she unwraps her burger completely and finally takes a bite. Her eyes close, and she chews thoughtfully. I wonder if she can even finish that burger. If she chews each bite so thoroughly, we might be here all day.

What happens after she finishes it? Will she be happy and satisfied? Or is she one of those people who is going to run to the bathroom and throw it up?

That thought horrifies me.

"Thank you," she says.

I lift my sunglasses to the top of my head and study her. "Why?"

"For treating me like a human."

"Because I bought you a hamburger?"

She nods. "It actually means a lot."

CHAPTER THIRTEEN

CHRISTINA

And the neighbors said, "Look who is walking on the beach."

∼

Because Graham doesn't say anything, I finish the burger and most of the fries. I'm stuffed, but it was so good.

He's right. I don't eat. You can't afford to eat in this town, or your career is over. Sure, there are some actresses that are making it as plus-sized, and I admire them. I really do. I wish we could all just be normal. But it's not how I was raised.

I remember seeing my father watch women walk down the street. He was screening them, even if they weren't actresses.

"Look at the arms on that one," he'd say. "She could skip a meal or two," he'd say about another.

There were times when he'd criticize my mother at the dinner table, and well, that kind of stuff trickles down.

I'd watch her go without eating, taking diet pills, getting sick after meals. As a child, you just assume that's the norm and those are the expectations.

Penny and Sal even try to work my schedules around my period. There's just no need for extra bloat when you're on camera.

I scan a look over Graham, who has helped himself to his friend's beer. He's sitting in a chair across from me, feet kicked up on another chair, finding ease in the middle of his day.

He's unbuttoned the top few buttons of his shirt and taken off the tie he had on.

He ate at the hotel, and then had another burger with me. Now he's having a beer and there's not a care in the world going on in his head right now.

I want that. I'm envious of that.

"There's not many people on the beach today," I say, and he turns his head to look at me. We've been sitting in silence for a long time while I ate.

"It's Thursday, in March," he says, as if that's enough for people to stay away.

I nod. "Right."

He puts his feet on the ground. "Besides, this part of the beach is quieter, more private."

"That's nice."

"It is. I'll come down here and run this stretch of sand, or just sit by the water when I need some time to think," he says.

I look out over the ocean. I don't utilize its power very often. In fact, if I'm not working, I'm usually just wandering around my condo—alone.

"Do we have time for a walk on the beach?" I ask, and he sets down the beer.

"Are you feeling up to it? You did just eat a full meal."

I purse my lips and take a breath to lash out, but he holds up his hand.

"Sorry. That was uncalled for." He drops his shoulders. "Yes, we have plenty of time for a walk on the beach."

We tend to react to one another rather than interact. Maybe this is a good time to think about that really hard.

I'm finding some enjoyable qualities about this maniac, but I wouldn't dare tell him that. Maybe it's just familiarity. I know him. Or I think I know him.

And to be honest, I feel safe around him.

We pick up our lunch trash, and he sets it by the back door so that we can take it with us when we leave. Then we head down the steps and out to the beach.

There are a few people walking about, some laying on the sand, others in the water. We walk close, but we don't touch.

"What was your first role?" Graham asks me.

I lift my dress a little so that the hem doesn't drag in the sand. "*Itsy Bitsy Bites*," I say.

He purses his lips. "That's baby food, isn't it?"

"Toddler," I correct.

"So, you were pretty little?"

"Yep. Other than that, it was bit parts here and there. But I was Annie when I was ten."

"No shit?"

His admiration of that makes me smile. "My parts were nothing like you playing Chip. I mean, if you didn't know where to look for me, you didn't see me."

He nods. "What was your first show?"

"I had a walk-on part in *Cosmic MD*."

He laughs at that. "I've never heard of it."

"You'll never find it either. It was the pilot, and it never made it. Honestly, I didn't do much until I landed the Love Is in the Air network. It's been everything to me."

Now he reaches for my hand and laces our fingers together, just as he had in the car. It's comfortable, and I don't feel the need to pull from him. Though we're in private, he really doesn't need to touch me.

"You're really good at what you do, you know?" he says.

That causes me to stop, and it tugs on his hand, forcing him to turn toward me.

"Are you serious right now?"

He steps to me. "I'm serious."

I study him from behind my sunglasses. "I suddenly don't know when you're messing with me."

"Honey, I can say nice things."

Now I want to lash out at the use of *honey*, but I don't.

"Do you really think I'm good at what I do? I mean, all the characters I play are basically the same."

He shrugs. "Mine too. I guess that's why I want an action role. I can do more than drive an old pickup truck and pretend to be some Christmas tree farmer or dress in a pretentious suit and pretend to be some CEO."

That makes me laugh, and I cover my mouth with my other hand. "It's so predictable, isn't it?"

He smiles. "That's why it's popular. People say they want new entertainment, but they don't. They want comfort. That's what we give them. They want the happily ever afters they don't have at home. They want the meet cutes and the first kisses. It's all relevant."

I pucker my lips. "But you want to shoot people?"

"I can't help it. I'm a guy. I'd like to play a sports hero, too, someday, but I'll take what I can get. Right now, I have a gig that includes a girlfriend."

My jaw goes slack. He said that as if it didn't mortify him as much as it did a few days ago.

This relationship, though fake, has some realism. We're the only two people going through it, and we're doing that together. But in the end, we both get something we want, and it doesn't have to involve the other person.

"Are you bothered by being associated with me?" I ask.

Graham studies me again and then takes my other hand in his as well. The hem of my dress drops and skims the sand.

"If I were, I wouldn't make movies with you. I'd have asked to be released."

My mouth has gone dry, so I lick my lips. "We don't get along."

"It'll take some work on both our parts."

Okay, I'll admit I find some joy butting heads with him all the time. Maybe I could find some joy being his friend, too.

"You're right," I say. "I'll work on it."

"Me too."

We stand there for another moment, neither of us moving. Our hands are still grasped in one another's, and our gazes are set.

"Maybe we should head back home," I say. "I mean, you should take me home. You have plans."

He nods slowly, but we don't turn back to the house.

"I want to do something first," he says.

"What?"

He takes off his sunglasses and hooks them on the front of his shirt. Then, he takes my sunglasses and pushes them to the top of my head.

I wince from the brightness of the sun.

He cups my face with both of his hands.

I swallow hard. I've seen him do this before. I've been part of it. This is how he kisses. This is his move in.

We've tried this a million different ways, and this is his signature move, the one they can get in one take—from his perspective.

I'm prepared for him to lick me, or head butt me, or hell, just to walk away. So, I keep my eyes open and watch him.

The corner of his mouth turns up. "I'm actually going to kiss you this time," he says.

"Why?"

"I want to know what it's like when it's not scripted."

"I'm a bit leery," I whisper.

"You should be, but I'm being honest."

I worry my lip and he watches me. "No one is watching," I say, as if that's the only reason someone would want to kiss me.

"I know. I just feel like it's the right thing to do." He eases even closer to me, closing the gap between us.

This forces me to wrap my arms around him just to keep my balance.

"I could count it down if you'd like." His breath is warm against my mouth. And though we just ate onions on our hamburgers, there is no hint of Doritos. He's kissing me without the purpose of sabotage.

"Maybe that's a good idea," I agree.

"Okay." His thumbs brush my cheeks. "One. Two."

We both say, "Three," at the same time and move in.

His mouth is on mine, and it's hot and open. This isn't a well-practiced kiss, this is one of feeling.

Our kisses are always hard and firm. But I open to him and one of his hands moves to the nape of my neck. The other slides down to my waist, pulling me in closer.

His tongue moves against mine and my head swims. I've never felt this before when we've kissed. We don't kiss like this. My body isn't rigid like it usually is, and it goes pliant under his touch.

I gather the back of his shirt, and I can feel his hand at my lower back. He's gripping my dress in his fingers.

The sun is hot. The ocean loud. My skin is damp from sweat and probably from the increased activity my heart is feeling as it thuds in my chest.

When neither of us can breathe, we ease apart. Needing a moment, we rest our foreheads to one another's.

"Okay, well . . ." he says on a ragged breath, but doesn't go on.

"Yeah, well . . ." I agree.

I watch his throat work as he swallows. "We should get you home. I need to get to my trainer."

Without another word, we put on our sunglasses and walk back toward the house.

I wonder if he feels the same way I do. We've just crossed a line we can't uncross.

This farce just became very real.

CHAPTER FOURTEEN

GRAHAM

And the guy on the radio said, "Enjoy the drive, because it's going to be a long one."

~

If someone had asked me what my plans were for the day, I would have grumbled something about having a commitment to a grand opening. I might have dissed Christina in some way, annoyed that I'd have to spend the day with her and pretend to love her. But never would I have thought that I'd be driving away from her house pent up over having kissed her on purpose.

We didn't talk all the way from Santa Monica to her house in Beverly Hills. Our arms and hands brushed from time to time when one of us would move, but we didn't touch otherwise.

When I dropped her off, we sat in awkward silence for a moment before she stepped out, thanking me again for feeding her.

I'd take her to eat three meals a day if I thought it would change the attitude she harbors toward me.

But I'd kissed her on the beach, and that was huge. I didn't do it to appease a crowd. I didn't do it for publicity. I didn't do it just to shut her up. I did it because I wanted to.

The only problem is that now, I want to do it again.

I jump when my phone rings. I look down and see that it's my roommate, Milo.

"Hey, what's up?" I answer the call on my hands-free. The wind blows through the car, but there are enough traffic lights in this town, I won't be going too fast to hear him anyway.

"Loki ate something and got sick," he says. "I don't know what it was."

"Shit. Like food? Did he catch a bird or a rodent?"

"I just told you. I don't know. All I know is that I came home from lunch to let him out, since you said you had plans. There's vomit in the kitchen, the living room, and on his dog bed. He's laying out on the floor moaning."

I wince. Now I wish I could just bypass all these stoplights and get to him.

"I'm on my way," I say, turning at the next light, hoping that it'll shave off a few minutes on my drive.

The house smells, and I have to hold the back of my hand to my nose so that I don't gag.

"I told you it was bad," Milo says, walking out of the kitchen with an apron on, rubber gloves over his hands, and a mop.

I walk toward Loki. He turns those dark eyes up to me as if pleading to make him feel better.

I kneel and run my hand over the top of his head. "What happened, boy?"

He cries in response.

"Let me get some blankets and towels, then I'll get you in the car."

Yeah, he doesn't feel good. I said I'd put him in the car, and he didn't run out the back door to hide behind the house.

"I can't go with you," Milo says. "I have to get back to work."
"It's okay. I'm sorry you had to walk into all of this."
Milo shakes his head. "I hope he's okay."
"Me too," I say, running my hand over Loki's head again.

An hour later, I'm sitting with Loki at the vet's office. Luckily it appears he didn't eat anything toxic. He's got gastroenteritis, and some IV fluids will help. When I get him home, there will be meds to give him, and the poor guy gets a bland diet for a few days.

The vet's assistant knows who I am. She hasn't said anything, but she can't take her eyes off me. And when I catch her eye, her cheeks flush and she grins as if she has a secret.

I'm more worried about my dog than I am about appeasing a fan right now.

While Loki is resting, I walk down the hall to the bathroom, only to notice that the Love Is in the Air channel is on the TV in the waiting room.

I blow out a breath as I see an image of Christina and me on the screen. *Seaside Beach House*, I think is that movie. I laugh, because I'm not sure anymore. They all run together at this point.

I do know that we weren't love interests in that movie. We were siblings, so the banter was more authentic when they weren't getting along.

The thought makes me chuckle. I lift my phone and take a picture of the screen.

The afternoon entertainment at the vet's office, I send the text with the picture to Christina.

When I return to the room where Loki is, Christina sends a text. *Not one of our better performances.*

I laugh. *I was thinking that feuding siblings was right up our alley.*

Why are you at the vet? I thought you were going to the gym, is her next text.

I look at the dog next to me who is sleeping while the IV does its job.

I send her the picture of the chocolate lab laying on the bed. *Loki isn't feeling well. The afternoon took a turn.*

My phone rings in my hand and I answer it quickly when Loki's eye pops open and then closes again.

"Is he okay?" Christina asks immediately. "What happened?"

"He's fine," I say, lifting my hand to him and running it over his side. "Just a stomach bug."

She sighs. "Good. He's beautiful," she says.

"He is. He looks better when he's up and running around."

"I'm sure. Maybe we can take him to the beach one of these days, when he's feeling better."

I sit back in my chair and cross my legs. "I think that would be nice. He'd enjoy that. What are you doing?" I ask, as if it's normal for me to wonder about her.

"I just finished doing some yoga. I'm feeling a little bloated from lunch."

It's horrible that this town is obsessed with working out after you eat. I'll bet Christina had that yoga session planned to combat the salad she picked through at the hotel and had to do extra for the hamburger and fries.

"How long do you have to sit at the vet clinic?" she asks.

"I don't know. They're giving him an IV and some meds. It's better to be here. Milo was cleaning up the mess at the house. If I sit here long enough, maybe it'll have aired out."

I can hear her laugh, and again, it's a sweet sound. "Poor baby," she says, and I know she means Loki and not me or Milo. "Who is Milo?"

"My roommate."

"Oh," she says, and it lingers there for a moment. "They sent the script over," she changes the subject.

"Did they? I'll bet mine is waiting for me then. Have you read through it?"

"Not completely. I know they did a few rewrites, and there are a few steamier scenes than we're used to."

I let out a low hum. "Interesting. I wonder when those rewrites happened."

"Do you think this rumor about us made them rewrite?"

"It was a thought."

"Maybe we can read through it together."

I run my thumb over my bottom lip and think about the kiss we shared earlier, and how pleasant this conversation is.

"I may have to stay home the next few days just to make sure Loki is okay."

"Of course. If you want to, I could come to you. But only if you—"

"I think that would be great. Let me call you tomorrow and we can make plans."

"Okay. Let me know if you need any help with Loki. I don't have any plans until we start filming."

And that statement tells me just how lonely this woman really is. It also makes me realize that she could quickly attach herself to me if I let her. Do I want that?

CHAPTER FIFTEEN

CHRISTINA

And the caption read, "The view from the beach is worth its weight in gold."

The city is slower to come to life on Saturday morning. I sit on my patio and enjoy my morning coffee. I have lunch plans with my mother today, but she doesn't lunch until one o'clock. I have plenty of time to do some yoga, give myself a facial, and maybe rethink my outfit.

I haven't heard from Graham since Thursday, when he was at the vet's office. I don't know if Loki is okay or if something else happened. I just know that I offered to do a read through of the script we received, and then I've heard nothing.

There's no reason to read into it. Graham and I aren't really a couple.

I sink into my chair, wrapping my robe around my legs.

But we kissed.

I bat the tears that sting my eyes. God, why am I such an

emotional twit? Yes, we kissed. I have kissed that man more than any man I've ever dated, which isn't many.

This is all fake. I know it's all fake. So why am I so freaking emotional about it?

Picking up my phone I scroll through my emails, and I stop at one from Penny.

This was just posted the subject reads.

I open the email and there is a picture of Graham and I kissing on the beach the other day when I thought no one was looking.

Well, shit.

He played me.

He knew someone was looking.

The tears that had been stinging my eyes fall now, and I don't even bother to wipe them away.

I fell for it. I thought he kissed me because he wanted to. But the whole point of us pretending to be dating is so that people see it. They want their Love Is in the Air movie couple to be real, and Graham and I agreed to it so that we could be handed opportunities that mean so much more than cookie-cutter scripted movies. I signed on for this.

Well, I just need to keep my priorities straight. It's all about Penelope Mondragon—not about Graham ghosting me.

I do not have feelings for Graham Crowley, no matter how amazing that kiss was.

I don't care that he can be kind and gentle, because now I know that's all part of this act.

I can respect his acting talent.

My phone rings in my hand and I jump. It's my mother.

I swallow hard, hoping that my voice won't crack when I speak.

"Hello, Mother," I say, and it sounds light enough.

"Christina, what is this picture that I see on social media?"

I wince, but then shake my head at the silliness of her

question. My mother has now been around Graham and me twice where we held hands or were close. She's even asked me about seeing him and commented about me not liking him.

This she notices and decides to mention?

"What picture?" I stand, pick up my coffee mug, and walk back into my condo.

"What picture? My agent just sent me a picture of you and Graham Crowley kissing on the beach in Santa Monica. What are you doing?"

I dump out what's left of my coffee into the sink and rinse the mug before putting it into the dishwasher. The top rack is now full, so I decide to run it. I consider for a moment that all I have in there are coffee mugs and one plate. Someday, I need to learn to cook and eat at home. As it is, I have a refrigerator full of pre-made, portioned meals that I choose from when I feel like eating.

"You've seen me and Graham together, Mom. Why is this a surprise?"

I hear her gasp at the question. "I thought you didn't like him."

I don't, but I can't even tell my mother that. It's a bit eye opening to realize that even if I tell my mother the truth, then this fantasy I'm living is over. My mother can't keep gossip out of her mouth. She'd say something to someone, and the next thing I know the headlines would read *Christina Malloy, daughter of producer Charles Malloy, is lying to everyone.*

That might happen no matter what.

Well, shit.

"Mom," I say calmly as I lean my hip against the counter. "Things change. Graham and I have worked together for years. We've figured it out." The words taste vile on my tongue and my stomach growls as if it, too, objects.

"You brought him to the grand opening."

Did she just figure that out? Seriously, he got more press for being there than she did.

"Yes."

"Oh, Christina. This isn't good for your reputation," she scolds.

"I beg your pardon?"

"He's a playboy. A flirt."

"I dare you to find a man, or a woman for that matter, in this town that isn't one," I counter, suddenly very defensive over this man that I don't like. And, if I'm being honest, he might be a flirt, but I don't think he's some playboy.

"Christina, your reputation is sweet. Do you really want to have pictures of yourself kissing a man on the beach? Please tell me you didn't take him home with you."

"Mother!" The word echoes through my kitchen.

"Well, this is bad, Christina."

"No, it's not. Graham Crowley is a nice guy," I say, nearly choking on my words. "We're seeing each other and working together. Besides, Dad must not think he's too bad a guy. He wants him for one of his movies."

There's silence for a moment. "He hasn't mentioned it."

I'm sure my parents haven't had a conversation about their jobs in years. Talk about a power couple that shows up to be photographed. I don't think my mother realizes that's them.

"It's what I've heard," I say. "I should get going so I can be ready for lunch, Mom."

She hums into the phone as if she's deep in thought. "Don't forget, The Palm," she says as if I don't have a full itinerary in my email about the lunch.

"I won't forget."

"I'm sending a car for you."

"I can drive," I say.

"Why don't you invite Graham to join us?"

That takes me by surprise.

Great. How do I even approach that?

Before I can explain that he probably can't make it, she says goodbye, and the call is dropped.

I blow out a breath of frustration and click on Graham's contact info.

I know this is very short notice, and you're probably very busy, but are you free for lunch at one?

The text goes unread.

I start the dishwasher, wipe down my counters, tie up my trash, and carry the bag down to my garage.

Still no answer.

Well, she can't say I didn't ask.

It isn't until I've finished my yoga workout, sat in my sauna, and applied a facial that he finally texts back.

Sorry I didn't respond quicker. I was walking Loki and forgot my phone at home.

I read the text, and instead of being disgusted by his name popping up on my screen, I smile.

No problem. I don't mention the lunch again. It's right there if he wants to accept or not.

So, why lunch?

See? Neither of us find the need to see one another outside of public events. I shouldn't have even asked.

My mother and I are going to lunch. She saw the picture of us kissing on the beach in Santa Monica and had some questions. And she invited you to lunch.

My phone rings, and it's Graham. I'd rather just text. I suppose I could just not answer, but it's not like he doesn't know I'm holding my phone in my hand.

"What do you mean the picture of us on the beach?" he asks.

I laugh. Not only do I laugh, I snort because it's so funny.

"I mean the picture of us kissing on the beach. You orchestrated that. Don't tell me you didn't know someone was watching."

"I didn't," he says quickly. "I kissed you to kiss you."

"Well, I don't believe you. Not when Penny sent me the picture and then my mother saw it, too."

"Fine," he snaps out the word. "Don't believe me."

"I don't."

"I don't think going to lunch is a good idea," he counters.

"I didn't think so either, but I had to invite you."

"I don't think you had to. Just tell her I can't come."

"Oh, I'll tell her." I'm shouting now. This feels more realistic than him kissing me.

"I'll see you at the reading," he snaps out the comment.

"Fine by me," I say and disconnect the call.

Graham Crowley is an asshole, and he just keeps proving it. I can't wait until I get that Penelope Mondragon film tied up and I can drop his ass. I don't even care if he gets his film or not. All I know is I don't want to be associated with him more than I have to be.

CHAPTER SIXTEEN

GRAHAM

And the social media post attached to the photo said, "You never know who is going to show up on my video camera and make out with their co-star."

"Who the hell was that?" Milo asks, sitting on the couch with Loki's head rested on his lap.

"Christina Malloy," I say sharply as I scroll through my phone and find an email from Sandra titled, *Nice Job.*

I open the email and there is the attachment of the photo Christina was talking about.

"Shit," I mutter under my breath and fall into the chair next to me.

Loki lifts his head, jumps off the couch, and comes to rest his head on my lap now.

"Drama?" Milo asks as he picks up the remote and aims it at the TV.

"You could say that."

"Christina Malloy, huh? Why is she calling you?"

I turn my phone around so that he can see the picture.

"What the actual fuck?" he asks, laughing. "When did you start hitting that?"

It's vulgar, but not something that should be making me wince. We talk like that all the time in our house. But the way he says it, it makes me sick.

"I'm not *hitting* it," I say, and I choke a bit as I do.

I can't tell him the truth. One person knowing the truth, beyond the small circle of people orchestrating this, and it ruins everything.

I want that movie. The way to get that movie is to pretend like everything is about me and Christina. But I did not stage that kiss.

We were both vulnerable in that moment. It had been a great day. I kissed her because I wanted to, not because I thought it would get caught on someone's security camera, which seems to be the case. I'm surprised you can even make out that it's me and Christina, but you can.

"How long has this been going on?" Milo asks.

"A week, maybe." I don't know when the rumor mill started.

"I've never heard you say anything nice about her. And that phone call didn't sound all too pleasant either," he says.

I rub my hand over Loki's head. "We're working on better balance," I say, hoping that it makes sense.

"You have a lot of work to do," he laughs, and lets the remote fall to his side when he comes to a Denzel Washington movie.

This is just proof that Christina and I have to watch our step. Not even my roommate believes this, and why would he? I usually come home from a day of filming and make him go to the gym with me just so I can cool down.

Christina Malloy makes me crazy, and now I'm sitting here rubbing the head of my dog, whose name she doesn't even understand, and I'm worked up.

Maybe I should call her back and go to lunch with her and her mother.

Then I quickly rethink that. I've spent time near her mother, and I can't imagine anything more uncomfortable. I guess it's a good thing this relationship is fake, because one thing is for sure, I wouldn't want her parents in my life as in-laws.

I have to consider that I'll be working for her father if everything comes about as planned. But he's just a producer; it's not like I'll have him in my face all the time.

My phone buzzes again, and this time it's my mother.

Were you going to tell me that you were seeing someone?

I blow out a breath, and because I see Milo's eyes shift toward me, I decide to handle this by calling my mother from my bedroom.

I stand and start down the hallway to my room. Loki follows, and I close the door behind us.

Hitting the contact information for my mother, I wait for her to answer the phone.

"Hello, sweetheart," she says, and it never fails to make me smile.

"Hey, Mom."

I don't take for granted that my mother dotes on me, even though I'm thirty-five. It's nice to know I'm appreciated and loved.

"So, tell me about this girl you're seeing," she says, and her tone is sweet and caring.

I sit down on my bed and Loki jumps up next to me.

It's cute how she says *this girl*. There was no jumping to conclusions or questions about what she thought I was doing. My mother is genuinely interested in me, and likewise the people in my life.

"It's Christina Malloy," I say.

"She's your co-star, right?"

"Yep," I say, laying back, but keeping my hand on Loki's back.

"Well, tell me about her."

I smile. She might be digging for the dirt, but I'd much rather go this route than whatever Christina is going to go through while having lunch with her mother.

"Truth is, we haven't really gotten along in the past."

"Uh-huh," my mother says. Yeah, she knows all this.

"Things change. You know, when you work with someone for so long, things just work their way out."

"Why don't you bring her for dinner?"

That has me sitting up. After today, meeting up on set is going to be tense enough. Then again, maybe if I take her to my parents' house for dinner, it'll defuse the situation. Maybe Christina could see how a real family is supposed to act.

"I'll talk to her," I say, hoping to hold off on dinner. "She has a lot going on." I don't even know if that's true. As far as I could make out, Christina has no life beyond her roles for the Love Is in the Air network.

"I'd love to meet her," my mother says. "Brian is coming for a visit," she adds, and now the conversation is changed.

"When?" I ask.

My brother is in the military, so his visits are rare, and a reason for gatherings.

"He'll be here next month. Will you be available to spend time with us?"

I consider my schedule. "We start production in two weeks. So, I'll be filming, but I'll make time."

"Thank you, sweetheart. That means a lot to me."

Loki lifts his head and jumps down from the bed. He needs to go outside, so I take that as my sign to end my call.

"I'll talk to you soon, Mom. I'll see what Christina's schedule is too."

"That'll be wonderful," she says. "I love you."

"I love you, too."

CHAPTER SEVENTEEN

CHRISTINA

And the hostess at the door texts her friend, "Christina Malloy is here alone. I wonder where her eye candy is."

I arrived on time. Of course, I arrived on time. My mother sent a car for me. However, it is one-thirty before she makes her grand entrance.

I stand from my seat as she nears. She's wearing a red dress with a matching red jacket, a pearl choker, and a large pair of black Chanel sunglasses, which she hasn't taken off even though she's inside the restaurant.

Her blonde hair must have extensions clipped in because it's a few inches longer than it was the other day at her grand opening.

"I'll have to make lunch quick," she says, air kissing both of my cheeks so that her red lipstick doesn't leave any marks.

Before she sits, she scans a look over me. I'm in a sundress, which is comfortable, and a cute pair of sandals. My sweater hangs on the back of my chair.

"Don't you have a nice suit or dress you could wear?" she asks as we sit.

"This is nice," I say, looking down at what I have on.

"It's casual."

I thought lunch was casual, so I don't comment.

"And you should wear your hair down more often," she continues her assessment of my look. "You're not twelve."

At least she knows that.

The server comes to the table and my mother rattles off an order for the both of us. I don't mention that I had wanted the salmon. Now I just have a bed of lettuce coming my way.

"I thought Graham Crowley was going to join us," she says, using his full name as she takes her sunglasses off, finally.

"He had other plans."

She crosses her legs and lays her napkin in her lap. "I would think he'd make time for you."

"He's busy," I say, a bit more curtly.

"I don't like seeing you in the tabloids like that."

"I don't think it was in a tabloid."

"Internet," she says, waving a hand in the air. "Same thing."

I agree with that. "Well, we didn't know we were being watched."

"Oh, honey, we're always being watched."

Her nostrils flare, and I know what she's thinking.

My father has been linked to two different women over the years. The thought makes me sick, but I'm not alone in knowing my parents aren't perfect. You're not raised in Hollywood without something like this happening.

In my father's case, it was real.

But leave it to my attention-seeking parents to use the publicity for good. Somehow, they managed through it all and have kept their marriage intact. Though, I don't have any false notion that they are in a *happy* marriage. That's something I've never been around either.

"How serious are you and this guy?" she asks as the server returns with her water and lemon.

I wait until the server walks away.

"We've worked together for years. Now we're feeling out a relationship."

"Feeling it out?"

"I'm not running off and marrying him. Is that better?"

"Oh, Christina, really now." She seems offended.

"He's a nice guy. I'm getting to know him."

My mother sips her drink, holding her glass so that her bracelet dangles daintily and her manicure is featured.

"You're still working, right?"

I pick up my water and take a sip. I don't have my mother's flair to make it look elegant, and to be honest, I'll be lucky not to choke on my water. Did she really just ask me if I was still working? Does this woman pay any attention to the things that I do?

"Yes. We start production in two weeks," I say.

"Something new, or another one of those rom-com things?"

Rom-com things?

"It's a streaming television movie," I correct her, and she nods as the server brings out our salads and sets them down.

"Whatever. You're much too talented to be just making the same movie over and over."

Obviously, she doesn't know the fandom behind these *rom-com things*.

"Sal says there is some interest in me for a Penelope Mondragon movie," I say and that has my mother lifting her eyes from her salad to me.

"That's a big deal."

"I think so."

"Do you think you can handle it?"

For every good feeling I get, it's quickly wiped away.

I stab at my salad and shove a forkful into my mouth. I can see her mortification at me doing so, but at this moment, I just don't care.

I wonder if Graham has a dog just so he always has a friend. Maybe that's what I need. I need a dog. Someone who will be home for me. Someone who will listen to me and not judge me. Someone who doesn't care who I kiss on the beach.

The thought makes me laugh. I raise my napkin to my mouth and finish my bite.

"What's so funny?" my mother asks as she looks at her phone and scrolls with one finger. She's not too worried about what I'm laughing about.

"Do you know who Loki is?"

She turns her head to look at me and lifts a brow. "Loki?"

"Yes. Do you know who he is?"

"Should I? Are you seeing him too? Really, Christina..."

She doesn't even finish her thought before she picks up her phone and begins to text.

I pick up my phone and click on Graham's contact.

What kind of dog is Loki? I ask.

Chocolate lab, he quickly replies. *Why?*

I was just thinking I needed a dog.

A moment later my phone buzzes with a picture of Loki laying in a patch of sun in the yard.

He's beautiful, I add. *And I know who Loki is now, btw.*

My mother pushes her half-eaten salad away and takes another sip of her water. "Darling, I really have to go. The new spa has some VIPs coming in, and I need to be there to greet them. They're worth their weight in gold if they review the spa."

I watch as she stands and leans to air kiss my cheeks again.

"Lunch is taken care of. You can stay and finish. Bye."

I watch her hurry toward the door, where her assistant waits for her.

I'm alone, in a restaurant, and I want to cry.

I'm glad I have fans who want to see me all the time on their

TV, because it appears that no one else wants to spend time with me.

Batting my eyes, I ward off tears that want to fall.

I text the driver my mother had sent and tell him I'm ready to be picked up. He lets me know he'll be in front of the restaurant in three minutes.

I leave an extra twenty on the table for the server, and hope that my mother took care of the bill as she said she had.

Then I head for the front door with my shoulders pushed back and my sweater and purse hanging from my arm.

I can't help but wonder if I called Graham to come over, he would. Right at this moment, I'm feeling extremely lonely, and even his company would be welcome.

CHAPTER EIGHTEEN

GRAHAM

And the entertainment reporter on the morning news says, "Graham Crowley has been seen running on the same beach where just a few weeks ago he was kissing Christina Malloy, but she seems to be MIA."

~

The car pulls up to the studio offices where we're doing the read-through, and I let out a long breath. It's been two weeks since I've seen Christina, but I'm about to come face to face with her, and we're supposed to act as if we're into one another.

I should have reached out to her, but I just didn't have it in me to do so. She exhausts me.

Even after our little blow up, she texted me that day she was having lunch with her mother asking about Loki. I don't get her.

I figured if we just stayed clear from one another, then maybe whatever transpired that day would blow over. But Sandra said that something was mentioned on an entertainment news show about us, and the speculation was that we'd already gone our separate ways.

No news isn't always good news, I guess.

I notice that there is another SUV parked in front of the building. The driver steps out of that SUV and walks toward the back. He opens the door, and the moment I notice the leg that extends from the vehicle, I know that it's Christina. Then I see Penny skirt the back of the SUV and catch up with Christina.

I hurry and open the door, and step out.

"Hey," I call out and both women stop and turn around.

Penny smiles. Her curly hair wildly frames her face. She pushes up her glasses, holding her iPad to her chest.

"Hey, Graham," Penny calls back.

"How are you?"

She exchanges looks with Christina before looking back at me to answer. "Good. Good," she says. "I'll meet you both upstairs."

Christina and I watch as she disappears into the building.

I take in Christina, who is dressed like Holly Golightly. Her hair is pulled back into a sleek bun at the base of her neck. She has on her big sunglasses and a white dress. On her arm is her purse and another bag which I've seen her carry from time to time. I know that it has her script, a small makeup bag, and a water bottle.

"How are you?" I ask her. I can't decide if I can actually feel the indignation resonate off of her.

"I'm good. How are you?"

"I'm good. I'm glad to get back to work."

She nods. "Should we go in?" She turns, but I take her hand.

"Can we have a moment?"

She pulls her bottom lip through her teeth, and it instantly makes me think about the day I kissed her.

"Sure."

I tuck my hands into my front pockets and rock back on my heels. "How have you been?"

"Good. You?"

"Good," I say. "Milo, Loki, and I went camping. It was nice to get out of town."

She nods. "That sounds nice."

"It was." I look down at my feet and then back up at her. Her eyes are still covered with those dark glasses. "I guess we're back on, right? I mean, we've been out of sight for a few weeks."

"You know, if you don't want—" she begins, and I shake my head.

"I'm all in. If you are."

"Did you know about the camera when you kissed me?" she asks, and I wonder if this really was where everything fell apart.

"I swear, I didn't. I kissed you for purely selfish reasons."

"And what were those?"

I smile. "Because I wanted to."

Her lips pucker before she smiles. "Really?"

"Really."

Christina looks up at the building and then back at me. "I guess they're waiting for us. Do we walk in hand in hand?"

"Why not?" I reach for her bag, and she hands it to me. "When we're done, why don't you come home with me and meet Loki?"

"Go home with you?" she asks, and her voice rises.

"Just to see Loki and for dinner. I'll have you home before curfew."

She laughs and holds out her hand. I take it, lacing our fingers together.

We're about to walk into a room filled with people we work with often. They've seen us go at one another yelling obscenities and throwing props because we're angry. Now, we're walking in holding hands, and only Penny, Sandra, and Sal know what's going on.

. . .

That comfort we had somewhat created a few weeks ago is back as we ride the elevator together. We're still holding hands.

"Sandra says that the entertainment news is questioning us already," I say.

"I guess I can understand that. You've been camping and I've basically been hiding in my condo."

I nudge her. "Seriously, what did you do the past two weeks?"

Her eyes go wide. "I mean it. My lunch with my mother was a disaster, and I haven't had anything else on my agenda."

Every time I talk to this woman, I feel as if I should kidnap her and show her what she's missing in life.

There are millions of people who wish they were her. She's the daughter of Hollywood royalty. There's no reason she should sit alone in a sterile condo that's as big as my house, alone.

Maybe I need to be the bigger person here and look past her shortcomings. Christina Malloy needs me—and my dog.

When the elevator doors open, I hold them open with my foot, but I block her exit.

"We're good here?" I ask.

"We're good."

"Then let's try this again, but I can't guarantee it won't end up on the internet."

Christina shakes her head. "You don't have to—"

I press a finger to her lips. "May I?"

Her eyes lock on mine and then scan over my mouth. "Yes," she whispers.

With my foot still holding open the door to the elevator, I reach for her and pull her to me.

I want to say something witty, but instead, I lower my head until our lips brush.

I keep the kiss light, but it must do its job. She sways into me, and there is a moan that escapes her. Before she pulls away, I touch her neck, and she opens her eyes to look up at me.

"Maybe we can explore that more too," I say before I take her hand and we walk toward the boardroom where everyone now waits on us. Suddenly I feel protective of her, and kissing her enhances that feeling.

CHAPTER NINETEEN

CHRISTINA

And the photo that the publicity staff took is posted with the caption, "Back to work. This rom-com might have a lot of extra rom."

~

Sal smiles as we walk into the room, which has gone from loud chatter to a hush.

Penny stands when we enter and pulls out my chair for me. I thank her and take my seat.

Graham rests his hand on Penny's shoulder as if in a sign of solidarity. It's got to be hard to know something that no one else knows. I mean, it's hard enough to be the focus of that secret.

Penny takes her seat and Graham sits down next to me. A moment later, he rests his arm on the back of my seat and looks around the room.

The director, Jean-Claude St. Paul, studies us, and I know for a fact he's not excited to see us in this capacity. Sure, no one wants us to be fighting on set, but sometimes I think when the actors are involved with each other, it's equally hard to keep their attention. I suppose that's something that Graham and I should talk about.

"It's nice to see everyone," Graham says, taking the lead on the meeting. "Are we waiting on anyone else?"

Penny shakes her head, but Sal leans in on his forearms, his sunglasses shading his eyes. "Let's get started."

As it begins at the start of every project, we go around the room and do introductions. This is how we get to know the faces that go with the names. Anyone who is involved in the production is piled into this room that's much too small.

For the most part, the faces are familiar. Members of our ensemble cast sit around the table. Men who have played neighbors, brothers, and additional love interests sit amongst women who have played my best friends, sisters, and bosses. As we make our way around the room, Graham inches in closer to me, his arm still around the back of my chair.

The confused looks from our co-stars don't go unnoticed.

They are often our sounding boards to issues between me and Graham. Or they're caught in the crossfire.

I sip the lemon water that I brought, and before we start our read through, Graham takes a bite of a granola bar and hands the rest to me. He winks and then opens his script.

Under the table, our thighs touch. I've nibbled on the granola bar, and I'm grateful that he gave it to me. I don't eat in public very often, but I was hungry.

As we read through the script, we make notes, and the director asks for some changes.

Since I've been alone for the past few weeks with just the script, I have it memorized. Though, I don't let on. No one needs to know how sad and lonely I really am. I don't even want to admit that to myself.

Graham has his script marked up, and as we make our way to the middle, he turns the script toward me.

Inside, he has a Post-it note.

Our first real love scene, he has written on it.

His hand comes to my thigh under the table, and I'm sure that I flinch. He doesn't seem to take that personally.

Leaning in close to me, Graham whispers in my ear, "This should be interesting."

I swallow hard.

The movies that we do usually don't have anything like this in it. This movie has a shower scene and bed scene—well, a bed scene that isn't just us laying in it. Though it's not extreme in any way, we will still be in bed together—more intimately.

The most we've ever done are kissing scenes. But I guess this is moving forward. This is picking up the pace. This is nerve-wracking.

We read through the scene, and I can feel the heat crawl up my neck.

As soon as we are done with the scene, the director calls for a ten-minute break.

Penny stands. She knows this is her cue to get me a new water, and usually a Tylenol.

Before Graham and I can vacate our seats for the short break, the director comes toward us.

"I'd like a word," he says and walks out of the room.

Graham and I exchange worried looks before he stands and holds out his hand to me to help me from my chair. We follow the director out of the boardroom and down the hall to a private office.

Jean-Claude is pacing when we walk in.

"Shut the door," he says. He has a slight French accent that can often be intimidating, especially when he gets angry.

He stops pacing, folds his arms in front of himself, and then looks at me and Graham standing next to each other.

"This isn't going to be a problem, right?" he asks.

"What's that?" Graham asks.

Jean-Claude motions between us. "Whatever is going on between you two. We've worked together before. You're both professional and you do your work, but you don't talk aside from your lines."

"Now we talk," Graham says as he takes my hand and holds it in his. "Why would this be a problem?"

Moving closer to us, Jean-Claude's tongue moves over his teeth as he studies us. "I have heard how you talk about her," he says, and I feel Graham tense up. He then turns to look at me. "And you. Last time we worked together, you threw a coffee mug at his head."

Graham laughs, but I suddenly feel faint. I did that. God, I did that!

"It won't happen again," I say.

Jean-Claude's eyes move from me to Graham and back again. "This doesn't feel right," he says.

"It should feel better," Graham interjects. "Imagine how this will show up on the screen. Our fans love us together, and this film is different than the rest."

"This film has sex," Jean-Claude states the facts. "It's still just a rom-com for a streaming service." His voice drips with irritation at the project, as if it's beneath him—but here he is.

Jean-Claude throws his hands up as if in defeat and walks out of the office, leaving me and Graham alone.

I shake my head and close my eyes tightly.

Graham takes both of my hands and pulls me to him. "What's wrong?"

I open my eyes and look up at him. "Just another streaming service rom-com? Even he doesn't believe in what we do anymore."

Graham's brows draw together. "You believe in it," he states firmly.

"I used to. Now even you and I are selling ourselves out for bigger and better things."

He looks hurt that I said it that way, but it's the truth. We've made a deal with the devil, and now we're paying.

"I still believe in it," he says. "I believe we'll get those bigger and better things. And I believe that we might even become friends."

I study his face, and I notice that it's softer than I remember.

I consider what he's saying. He has kissed me now—twice—just to kiss me. And he wants me to meet his dog. That's big, right?

Maybe we will be friends.

I think about how lonely I've been, and I wonder if that's what I need. Smiling up at him, I know it's what I need. I need people in my life, and my lack of them has me in this situation. I don't go out. I don't see people. I almost don't know how to act if I'm not being paraded around by my parents. So, when I'm around someone else, the rumors fly.

"I think I'd like to be your friend," I say.

Graham smiles. "Good. I'm tired of only hanging out with Milo," he jokes, and I laugh, lifting my hand to his chest.

"Will I meet him too?" I ask.

"It's possible. But don't judge me based on him. I might be thirty-five, but I live like I'm still in college."

I wrinkle up my nose. "Why? You're a successful actor."

"That's why. I haven't settled down yet, so no need to have the big house and yard. I have just what Loki and I need."

Graham takes my hand, and we walk back to the boardroom, but what he says sticks with me.

He has what he and Loki need, so I wonder where I fit into that. Maybe he doesn't really need another friend, and maybe I'm only fooling myself into thinking this is real, too.

As we enter the room and sit down, the others file in.

I look at Graham as he's in conversation with the actor who will play his best friend. Under the table, he's still holding my hand.

My heart begins to beat faster. We're supposed to be fooling everyone else. But I'm very worried that he's fooling me.

CHAPTER TWENTY

GRAHAM

And the new trailer for the network says, "Where love really happens."

~

Penny canceled the car for Christina, and I ordered Penny an Uber, since they had come together. There are a lot of moving parts to everything in this town.

It would be nice to just make movies. But there are assistants, and agents, and drivers. The list goes on and on.

I sometimes wonder if that's why I try to live so simply with my roommate and my dog. I do what I love, but try to remain grounded.

Shifting a look toward Christina, I realize I'm not grounded at all.

I've fallen into this life of *look at me*. That's what happened, and that's what we're facilitating. Sure, I'll get the big payday at the end, but then I'm just feeding the monster.

Having my entire family move to California when I was fourteen was a big deal. My parents uprooted their lives, and the life of my brother, to move so that I could pursue my dream. I found out firsthand how important it was to have both your mother and father nearby. I watched plenty of friends get caught up in drugs and unwise choices. I count myself as one of the lucky ones. Perhaps I wasn't enough of a child star to have been affected.

That's a lie. It didn't matter how famous you were as a child star. If you didn't have the right support, you just didn't make it.

Of course, the fact that my parents are still married and speaking, that's a credit to their well-established relationship before we moved.

They kept me grounded, and I suppose they still do.

I've had my drunken nights on the Sunset Strip. I've probably ended up in bed with a woman or two that I should have reconsidered and just gone on my merry way, but I didn't.

But looking at Christina as she scrolls through her phone, the city that we've embraced rolling by us outside the window, I think of how different she is.

That condo that she lives in is one of those places people dream of having. They'll work for years just to get to live in one for a few months, until they're unemployed again.

Christina has lived in hers since she was eighteen, and I can't help but wonder if that was her parents' way of just getting her out of their house. Out of sight, out of mind.

Even when they're around her, she's out of sight, out of mind.

I know this thing between us is made up for the cameras, but since that day I kissed her on the beach, I can't stop thinking about her.

Our little argument over lunch with her mother, or whatever it was about, shook things up. Usually, I wouldn't have given it another thought, but for the past two weeks, it really messed with my head.

Even when Milo and I were camping, all I could think about was her.

"What do you like on pizza?" I ask, and Christina slowly lifts her gaze from her phone to me.

"Pizza?"

"You've heard of it, right?"

She turns her phone over in her lap. "I don't eat pizza."

"Why not?"

She lifts a brow as if there is no reason to explain. She just doesn't do it.

I hold up a hand and rethink my question. "It's pizza night at our house. I'd like to extend the invitation for you to have dinner with us."

"Can I order a salad?"

I chew my bottom lip and study her. "No," I say, and she takes off her sunglasses so that she can study me directly.

"No?"

"No."

She huffs out a breath. "I might as well go home."

Before she can scroll again, I take her hand in mine, directing her attention back to me.

"One night. Live a little."

She purses her glossed lips. "Pizza is going to do that for me?"

"And beer," I add.

"Oh, hell no. You're asking me to partake in a carb-filled dinner and add a carb-filled drink? Do you know what that will do to my body?"

"I don't care about your body. I'm thinking about what it'll do to your attitude."

Her mouth drops open. "What?"

"I'm just saying, for one night, let loose a bit. A few slices of pizza and a beer isn't going to destroy you. You certainly could afford to eat a real meal that doesn't consist of just lettuce."

She has an argument brewing. She doesn't know how to not argue with me.

For a moment, I think she's going to tell the driver to take her home. Then she looks out the window, back at her phone, and then at me.

"I don't know how I like my pizza," she admits. "It's been years since I had one."

I'm starting to feel as if she's a project for me to take on. I need to undo all the programming she's had since birth.

"I'll order a cheese one for you, and you can steal whatever toppings you'd like off of mine, then."

The corner of her mouth lifts in a slight smile. I'm going to guess no one has ever conceded anything to her. She's just been told what to do her entire life.

Suddenly, I can't wait until she meets my mother.

Something tells me that Christina Malloy could use a dose of reality—in the sweetest way.

The moment we step out of the SUV, I can hear Loki inside barking.

Christina stops as if she's afraid now.

"He's only excited that I'm home. He's harmless," I say.

She gives me a small nod and follows me up the front walk. I fish my keys from my pocket and notice her looking around the yard. It's well-groomed, and the neighborhood is nice. Even though she's seen my house before, on the night we escaped the award ceremony, I guess it was dark. Something tells me she's a bit surprised that it's a tidy yard.

"I'm going to go in and get Loki settled. It'll only take a few seconds. I'll call out to you."

Christina nods and stands on the front step as I walk inside.

As is the norm, Loki races through the house and straight to me, nearly knocking me over as he jumps up to greet me.

"Hey, pal," I say with equal enthusiasm as I rub his head and his ears. Lowering to one knee, I hold his attention. "I have a friend. I want you to meet her, but you can't jump up on her," I say.

Loki lets out a howl, and I redirect his attention back to me.

"Seriously," I say. "She's in a white dress. You can't mess that up."

He nods as if he really understands me, and I laugh.

With my hand tucked into his collar, I walk him toward the front door.

I push open the screen door, my hand still on the dog. "Come in," I say, and Christina takes a moment to assess me and the dog before she steps into the house.

"Sit," I say to Loki, which he does, but he's jittery. "Loki, this is Christina."

He barks, and she flinches and grips her purse as if it's protecting her.

"Christina, this is Loki," I say because I think she's unsure of what to do. "Shake," I instruct Loki, and he lifts his paw.

Christina looks at me for instruction, and I nod toward his paw. She leans in and takes his paw.

"It's nice to meet you, Loki," she says, but that's when he gets away from me, pulling me forward as he jumps on her, leaving dusty paw prints on her white dress and knocking her off balance.

She teeters on those high heels, and I have to let go of Loki to reach for her, but he lunges again.

My arms come around her and we hit the end of the couch, falling over the arm, and down on one another. Loki takes that as a game and pounces on top of both of us.

"Stop! Stop!" I shout at the dog, who howls in excitement over this new game.

I manage to get off Christina and grab Loki, making him sit as I help Christina off the couch.

Her purse is now on the floor, and her sunglasses had flown off her head and are now on the other end of the couch.

I purse my lips, so I don't laugh.

"I'm so sorry. He's heard a lot about you, so I guess he was excited to meet you," I say, hoping to defuse the situation.

Christina's eyes are wide. She's working to collect herself, and I'm not sure how this is going to end up.

She looks down at her dress and then back up at me.

"I'm so sorry," I say again.

"It's okay," she says, but her voice cracks.

"Let me take him out back, and I'll help you get cleaned up."

"I don't need help," she says.

"Let me take him out. The bathroom is just down the hall. Washcloths are in the drawer on the left," I say as I direct Loki to the back door.

As we pass through the kitchen, I look down at the dog, who looks so proud of himself. "Way to go, bozo," I say with a laugh. "You might want to work on your social skills," I tease as I open the door and watch as Loki takes off to run around.

CHAPTER TWENTY-ONE

CHRISTINA

And the email between agents reads, "They went home together."

I wasn't ready for that.

Stepping into the bathroom, I turn on the light and stand there for a moment.

I don't know what I was expecting when I walked into his house, but it wasn't a dog jumping on me, nor how cute his house is.

This bathroom is beautiful. Seriously, two men live here? Two straight men?

The tile is dark, and the countertop is light marble, but with dark veins so it matches. Even the shower curtain matches.

Obviously this isn't a bathroom that is used daily. This is for guests. I wonder how many guests they get.

I open the drawer where Graham said there were washcloths. I pick one and wet it. I'll have to have the dress cleaned. Had I known I was going to end up at his house, I would have packed a change of clothes.

"Everything okay?" I hear his voice from the other side of the bathroom door.

"Just fine. I'll be out in a moment."

I clean off my dress, wash my hands, and manage to tidy my hair, which got tousled when we fell onto the couch.

When I walk back out into the living room, I take it in.

It's decorated in mid-century modern, and it fits the house. There is an enormous TV on the wall, two couches, and a large chair. Pictures are set up on the end tables, and I can't help but move to look at them.

I pick up one that has Graham and what I assume is his family. I know it's Graham, because he's perhaps just slightly younger than when he was Chip on the TV show he was on. But I remember Chip fondly.

"That's my family," he says from behind me.

"Your mom, dad, and a brother?" I ask, turning to look at him standing there with two bottles of water in his hands.

He nods. "Yeah. That was right before we left Ohio."

"What's your brother's name?"

"Brian. He's three years younger. Marine."

I lift my eyes to him. "Are you polar opposites?"

He shrugs his shoulder. "Not really. We have a lot in common, aside from our parents and upbringing." He chuckles. "Although he is twice my size now, so I don't mess with him."

"I always wanted a sibling."

Graham hands me one of the bottles of water. I take it and set the picture down.

"I like your house," I say.

"We've done a lot of work on it. Want a tour?"

"Sure."

Even in the privacy of his home, he takes my hand and leads me through the living room to the kitchen.

"Wow," I say, looking around at the updated kitchen. "You did all of this?"

"Milo and I did it. My dad helped a lot, too. The house is an investment."

"I thought you said you and Milo live like college kids."

He chuckles. "I did ask you what you wanted on your pizza."

That makes me laugh. He most certainly did.

The rest of the house is updated as well. Milo has the back half of the house, which must have been an addition to the original house. It's like an adult arcade with old, upright video games and a pool table. His bedroom door is closed, but an additional bedroom has been converted to Milo's office. If he were to have a Zoom meeting, no one would know he was only feet from a teenager's dream game room in a bungalow in Burbank, that's for sure.

"Would you like to see my room?" Graham asks.

I know he means nothing by it, so I make sure not to make something of it.

"Yes."

His bedroom is bright, and that surprises me. The bed is made, and it's neat and tidy. He has an ensuite bathroom that has been updated as well.

"This is my office," he opens another door.

I step inside. "What do you do in an office?" I ask, looking around at the shelves of scripts and a few awards.

"I write."

That has me turning toward him. "You write?"

Graham shrugs. "That surprises you?"

"Yes," I say honestly.

"Why?"

I don't really have an answer to that. "I just wouldn't think you'd have time for it," I say, as it's the least negative thing I could say.

"What do you think I do when I hurry off set and to my trailer all the time?"

What do I think? I think he's running away from me. What

else would I think? It never would have crossed my mind that he was creating something.

"What do you write?" I ask.

His lips twist up to the side before he moves toward the desk and picks up a stack of papers that are clipped together with a big binder clip. He hands it to me.

Whisked Away, a thriller by Graham Crowley.

"Really?" My voice lifts, and he smiles as he looks at me.

"You never know when my looks will fade."

That has me laughing as I hand him back his manuscript and he sets it back on his desk.

When he turns back, he scans a look over me.

"I know you're probably comfortable, but would you like something else to wear? I have some sweatpants and T-shirts."

I consider that. "Is Loki going to jump on me again?"

"It's possible. He's very excited to have you here."

"He is, huh?"

"I can't guarantee that Milo won't jump on you, too, when he gets home."

Again, he has me laughing. I didn't expect this side of him. He's easy to be around, and I wonder if that's because I'm in his home. I'm in his space.

No. I was comfortable with him at the house on the beach, and at my mother's open house. I guess I agreed to this because I am comfortable with him. Even if I can't keep myself from fighting with him.

"Maybe I'll take you up on that," I say. "But no posting pictures of me."

"I wouldn't think of it. Anything we do that's not in public is private," he says as if he understands that need for separation of the two.

"Thank you."

"C'mon," he takes my hand and walks me back to his bedroom.

I stand near the door as he moves to his closet and opens it. Inside, everything is organized by color and design. Dress shirts, polos, and T-shirts are all neatly displayed on hangers.

"Your choice. College tee or nonprofit."

I can't help but grin at him when he's like this. "What college?"

He moves a few shirts around and pulls one out. "Berkley?"

I raise my brows. "Impressive."

"Oh, I didn't go there." He shrugs. "When college rolled around, I was doing a movie and that was more important."

I nod. "What movie?"

He wrinkles his nose. "*The Gift of Not Knowing.*"

Now I wrinkle my nose. "I'm not sure that was an Oscar contender."

"We filmed for a month before it got pulled. As I have a nondisclosure signed about it, you'll have to do your own research to find out why."

My smile is even wider now. "I just might do that."

He hands the shirt to me sans the hanger, which he puts on the bottom rod next to the other unused hangers, and shuts the door.

Turning, he walks toward the dresser and opens a drawer. Pulling out a pair of gray sweatpants, he hands them to me.

"You might need to roll the waist and hike up the legs," he says.

"Maybe I should just keep my dress on."

He shrugs. "Your call, but Loki has been outside now. I can't guarantee it'll stay white."

I scan a look over him in his jeans and button down. "Are you going to change?"

"For sure," he says with a wink. "Comfort is everything."

He moves back to the drawer, pulls out another pair of sweatpants, and then another T-shirt from the closet, which he pulls from the hanger and leaves the hanger on the rod.

"I'll change in the bathroom," he says. "You can change in here. Take your time, and feel free to hang up your dress."

"Thank you," I say.

He watches me for another moment before he backs out of the bedroom and closes the door.

I have to admit, this day has become quite a surprise to me.

CHAPTER TWENTY-TWO

GRAHAM

And the entertainment report during the news said, "Love Is in the Air execs confirm that their stars are in fact seeing one another. It goes against the reports we've heard that the duo doesn't exactly like one another and has been known to throw props at each other. This will be interesting to watch unfold."

I've ordered the pizzas and let Loki inside. We've had a talk. No jumping. No barking. No running.

The moment he hears the bedroom door open, he runs down the hall, barks, and I hear Christina shriek when Loki jumps up and licks her face.

"Dammit, Loki," I say, running toward the bedroom.

To my surprise, Christina is crouched down, Loki's head is on her shoulder, and she's petting him.

"Okay, so he didn't eat you," I say.

"He surprised me, but I'm not in heels anymore or a pristine dress. If he messes up your clothes, I don't care."

That makes me chuckle.

I notice that her toenail polish matches her fingernails. I didn't think about her being barefoot if she took off those heels. She doesn't seem to mind, so I won't say anything.

Christina stands, and Loki moves in next to her as if he's her damn dog. I think he's confused.

"What I don't understand is why you gave a sweet dog the name of a villain," she says, her hand rested on Loki's head.

I shrug. "I like Loki more than Thor."

She nods. "Why doesn't that surprise me?" She's grinning, and there's a hint of something sinister to it. I like this playful side of her.

"I ordered the pizzas," I say.

"I didn't realize I took so long to change."

I scan another look over her. She has the T-shirt tucked into the sweatpants, but only in the front. The pants are rolled down at the waist, and she's somehow managed to roll the cuffs of the legs so that they are cropped at her calf, and they look amazing. I can't imagine any other woman on the planet taking that much time to look perfect in a pair of sweatpants and a T-shirt.

"Can I get you something to drink, other than water?" I ask, noticing that she's holding the bottle I gave her earlier.

"I can wait for the beer you promised me when we have pizza."

And that reminds me, I'd better text Milo to get some beer.

I invite her out back to sit on the patio. The weather is mild and sunny. Loki runs through the yard, and we sit at the table under the patio umbrella. Milo promised to get beer and a bottle of wine. He laughed when I told him who I had at the house. Wait till he sees her in a pair of my sweatpants.

"Is that the only book you've written?" she asks me as she watches Loki chase a squirrel out of the yard.

"Yes and no," I say, and that has her turning her attention back to me. "I've got a drawer full of unfinished manuscripts, and a folder on my computer with even more of them. I have a few movie scripts I've started, and a play."

"No kidding?"

I shrug. "It clears my mind sometimes."

Christina nods, twists the cap from her water, and takes a sip. "I do yoga—to clear my head, that is."

"Do you do a lot of yoga?"

She laughs. "I do. I would assume you spend hours writing."

"I do."

"Both are lonely hobbies," she says, and again that nags at me.

I'm not lonely, but I know she is. This town isn't made for lonely; it's made to be on the move all the time. But I can see how when you're not in the spotlight, you could get lost.

I suppose I'm a bit surprised that she and I are in this mess we're in. I don't make appearances to stay relevant, except for the fan conventions.

I'm lucky to have the cushy job I have that makes it so that I don't have to do talk circuits and radio shows and podcasts. She, on the other hand, is paraded around so that her parents stay relevant, but they don't pay her any mind.

Loki tires of chasing the squirrel and comes toward us. But instead of coming at me, he walks right to Christina and lays his head on her lap.

"I've never been around a dog," she says.

"Never?"

"No. I wasn't allowed pets growing up. I did consider it though, when I texted you about what kind of dog Loki was. I thought maybe it would be nice to have a dog around. I mean, my place is so big, and it's just me."

"We're not home with him as much as I'd like us to be."

"Do you share the dog?" she asks.

"He's mine, but really, it takes both of us. Milo's schedule is a bit more normal, if you will."

Christina's hand moves over Loki's head, and I think it's as soothing for her as it is for him.

"What does Milo do?"

"Financial advisor," I say.

She nods thoughtfully at that.

Loki raises his head and looks toward the house. He barks once and Christina looks at me.

"Milo's home," I say. "He'll have the beer and the pizza."

I stand and offer my hand to her. She takes it, and when she stands, we're flush together.

Her eyes lift to meet mine. A beat passes between us. There's no doubt we both consider kissing, but Loki bumps into our legs and we step apart.

We follow the dog back into the house where Milo is setting the boxes of pizzas on the table.

He lifts his head, ready to say something snarky about cheese pizza, no doubt, but his mouth turns up into a wide smile instead.

"Hey," he says, and I take Christina's hand in mine, and she moves in next to me.

"Hey," I say, a little stern so that his smile softens. "This is Christina Malloy."

Milo holds out his hand to her. "Milo Wilson," he says.

Christina shakes his hand. "It's nice to meet you. Thanks for picking up dinner."

"Sure," he says, scanning a look over the two of us in our lounging clothes. "It looks like I'm overdressed. Don't start without me. I'm going to go change."

He passes by us and to his room.

We decide to eat dinner on the back porch. Once the sun goes down, it'll be cold, but for now I want to bask in it.

Milo throws Loki's ball out into the yard with one hand and then eats with the other. I know that Christina is waiting for him to mess up which hand he throws with and which hand he eats with, but Milo has been doing this for years. He's very skilled.

"So, are you slumming today?" Milo asks Christina as she takes a bite of her pizza, which I'm glad to see she's eating. I expected her to pick off tiny pieces and maybe make it through a quarter of a piece. She's on her second slice and I'm cheering her on, internally.

"Why is that? These are his clothes," she says, as if maybe Milo is criticizing her wardrobe.

"I mean just hanging out here. I'm sure your place is nicer."

She exchanges a look with me, but I shake my head. I've never discussed her place with Milo.

"I was invited. Besides, I wanted to meet Loki," she says.

"He's not quite as evil as his namesake," Milo says as Loki brings back the ball.

"I wouldn't think he'd try to kill his own brother," she says, and I grin at her. "I told you I know all about Loki now," she says, confirming what she'd told me about knowing who Loki was.

Knowing she sat through a Thor movie makes me want to kiss her again. I don't know when I've been prouder of someone. She's eating pizza, has Marvel Universe knowledge, and is sitting in the backyard in sweatpants, drinking a beer. I've corrupted her, and I couldn't be more pleased.

CHAPTER TWENTY-THREE

CHRISTINA

And the barista at the coffee shop texts her friend, "Christina Malloy just bought two coffees. I'll die if Graham Crowley is drinking a drink that I made."

I don't remember when I've had such an enjoyable night.

Loki fell asleep with his head on my lap as we watched *Avengers: Infinity War*. I guess that Graham wanted to see if I could keep up.

Milo is funny and kind, and it was nice to just have a conversation with someone who isn't in the industry.

I ate three pieces of pizza and drank a beer. And, admittedly, for the first time in a very long time, I feel good.

Opening my front door, I step into my condo with Graham right behind me. I turn on the lamp, and it only slightly brightens the space.

I think about how much character his house has, and how dull and sterile my place is.

"Thanks for the ride home," I say, setting my purse on the couch, and draping my dress over the back of it.

"My pleasure. I had a nice day."

"So did I. I can't remember the last time I had pizza."

He grins. "I knew you'd cave."

I wrinkle up my nose at that. "I'll get your clothes back to you as soon as I can."

"No hurry. I'll see you plenty."

I step out of my heels. I'm sure I'm a sight in high heels and sweatpants.

Kicking them to the side, I look up at Graham, who is standing there, looking down at me. It's amazing how much shorter I am when I eliminate those extra three inches.

"What is your schedule like this week?" he asks.

"I have fittings tomorrow," I say.

"Mine are on Wednesday."

Awkward silence falls between us for a moment before he steps closer to me. "Can I interest you in dinner tomorrow? I'll bring groceries and we can cook in your fancy kitchen," he offers.

I turn to look toward the dark kitchen and then back up at him. "We could go to your house. Loki will be lonely."

"I can bring him with me, if you don't mind him in your house."

Thinking about having a dog in the house thrills me and makes me nervous all at the same time. But, then too, looking around, there certainly isn't anything Loki can mess up. Hell, it's so impersonal around here, all I need is some cleaner and paper towels to clean up any mess he could possibly make.

I wonder what it would be like if I added some area rugs, and maybe got a TV for the living room. It would probably help if I entertained occasionally, too.

Graham touches my arm. "Are you okay? You're quiet."

I chuckle. "I was just thinking." I draw in a breath. "I would love to have you and Loki over for dinner."

"I'll see you tomorrow then," he says, and we stand there in an awkward silence for a moment before he leans in and kisses me on the cheek. "Have a good night."

It's hard to fall asleep. I have white noise playing. I have the room cool and dark, but my mind wanders.

This thing with me and Graham isn't real, and though we're working toward being friends, I feel something for him. But then I'm just not sure what it is.

My phone buzzes on my nightstand. I pick it up and grin down at his name.

I think Loki misses you, his text says, and it's followed by a photo of Loki's sad eyes looking up into the phone.

I'm grinning at the picture. I sit up in my bed and text back. *I'm not sure he had enough time with me to miss me.*

Sure he did. He's a good judge of character.

I gasp aloud when I read that. Is Graham Crowley saying nice things about me—to me?

Tell him I'll see him tomorrow.

I did. He said he can't wait. A moment passes before his next text comes through. *I can't wait either.*

My heart is racing, and I press my fingers to my lips.

This goes beyond the fake relationship we agreed on. Is this the friendship he said he wanted? God, I am so pathetic I don't even know if this is only friendship or if it's more.

I'll let you know when I'm done at the studio tomorrow, I text.

He sends a smiling emoji. *Loki and I will wait for your text. Have a good night. Loki says sweet dreams.*

I hold my phone to my chest and lie back down. I'm sure to have sweet dreams now.

Penny meets me in the parking lot. Before I've even climbed from my car, she's standing there waiting for me.

It wasn't until recently that I really started to take note of how much Penny does for me. She's always got my back, and I don't think I ever appreciated her enough.

This morning I stopped and got her a cup of coffee.

When I hand it to her, her eyes go wide, and I swear that they mist.

"Thank you," she says and her voice shakes.

"It's my pleasure. Thank you for all you do. I appreciate you always being here for me."

Penny blinks hard. "Um, they're ready for you inside. Can I carry your bag?"

I look at her. She has her own bag over her shoulder, her iPad pressed to her chest, and her coffee in the other hand.

"I'm good," I say, hiking my bag up over my shoulder and shutting my car door.

The alarm engages as we walk toward the building.

"How was your evening?" I ask her, and by her reaction, I realize I never ask her these kinds of questions. That's not how I want to work anymore. I'm not my parents, and I refuse to be so oblivious to others from here on out.

"It was nice. I just watched TV and vegged," she said.

"What do you watch on TV? I'm always looking for something new."

Penny's shoulders soften. "Well, I like anything on the Food Network. I'm a bit of a foodie," she admits.

I laugh. "I tend to watch Food Network a lot, but I'm realizing I'm not a foodie at all."

She smiles as we reach the door, and she pulls it open for me. "What did you do last night?" she asks, but then stiffens as I walk past her and into the building as if she shouldn't have asked such a thing.

"I went to Graham's for dinner. We had pizza and beer with his roommate."

Penny blinks hard as she catches up with me. "You're spending time with him? I mean, I know . . ." She lets her sentence hang there. "Sorry. It's not really my business."

"It's okay. We're spending time together."

"That's good, right?"

"It has been," I say as we walk toward the room where the fittings will take place.

When Penny opens the door for me this time, and I pass through and say thank you, her face brightens.

Maybe this relationship that I'm sorta having with a guy, who I thought I'd have to force myself to be around, is a good thing.

I find myself looking forward to getting home to spend the evening with that guy and his dog.

CHAPTER TWENTY-FOUR

GRAHAM

And the internet quiz says, "Will it last? Yes, or No?"

Loki and I have had a long talk. He's to mind his manners. He's not allowed to pee in her house. And barking must be saved for when he gets home.

Of course he agrees to all my terms, but I'm not sure I trust him after he jumped on her yesterday after we had a talk then, too.

Christina buzzes us through the gate, and I park in the designated space for her condo. I put on Loki's leash and let him out before I gather the bag of groceries that I brought and the bag with his travel items in it.

I knew I couldn't trust him. Loki starts barking the moment he sees her standing in the doorway, watching us climb from the car.

"We had an entire discussion on how he wasn't going to act like this," I say, my hand gripping his leash as he tries to run away from me and to the woman he's been taken with.

She's dressed casually in a pair of yoga pants and a tank top. I'm glad she feels comfortable with me and doesn't need to be dressed up every time I see her. That's something for sure.

Why that makes me nearly giddy, I don't know.

When Loki can't get away from me, and is headed straight to Christina, I let go of his leash.

I laugh as she braces her stance for the incoming dog.

When he reaches her, he lunges. His paws come to her shoulders, and she hugs him as she tries to balance herself.

"You've made a friend," I say as I reach her door.

Christina is now crouched down and playing with Loki, who is still barking his excitement.

"Loki," I say sternly. "Quiet."

Christina laughs as she unclips his leash and he runs around the living room, sliding on the marble floor.

"I'm sorry about him."

She shakes her head as she stands and folds the leash. "He's fine. I'm glad to see him."

She watches him run circles, and I watch her. There's a glow to her that I don't think I've ever seen. Dogs will do that, but I wonder if there's something more.

She hands me the leash, and I tuck it into Loki's bag of items.

I follow her to the kitchen with our bag of groceries and set them on the island.

"I opened a bottle of wine. Would you like some?" she asks.

"I would."

She pours us each a glass as I unpack the bag.

Christina hands me a glass, and with her glass in her hand, she looks over the items on the counter.

"What are we making?"

I look at the items and wonder what she thinks I'm going to make.

"I didn't know if you had a grill, so I decided we'd be better off just making pasta. It's an easy meal."

She worries her bottom lip. Will she even consider eating pasta? But I have convinced her to eat hamburgers, fries, and pizza, so I suppose anything is possible.

"I did bring a salad, too," I add.

The corners of her mouth lift into a smile, and she sips her wine.

"I'm a little closed off when it comes to cooking," she admits.

"I'm a little adventurous when it comes to cooking."

"You don't say?" She lifts her brows.

"My mother loves to cook. She made it look fun."

Christina takes another sip of her wine. "I'm not sure my mother knows where the kitchen is in her house."

After she says it, she tucks her lips between her teeth and watches me for my expression.

I have to admit, I don't have great opinions about her parents, but that doesn't reflect on her.

I lift my wine to my lips and watch her over the rim of my glass.

She's watching me. Even though she's trying not to smile with her mouth, she's smiling with her eyes. Do I do that to her? Is it Loki?

"How were your fittings today?" I ask as I sip my wine.

She shrugs. "Boring. Yvette doesn't have an extensive wardrobe," she says, mentioning her character's name.

"I suppose William will be the same," I say about my character as I take another sip of my wine. "I'm guessing I'll have my share of suits. Another CEO romance story."

She narrows her eyes at me. "You still believe in it, though?"

"I do. But I think it's our charm that makes it work."

Christina laughs hard enough that she covers her mouth with her hand to stifle it.

"That must be it," she says through her fingers.

Watching her enjoy herself makes me want to kiss her again.

Loki won't have any of that, though. He bounds through the

kitchen, plowing himself right into my legs when his paws slide on the marble.

"You're a menace," I say to him as he looks up at us. "Where can I set a water bowl for him?"

She looks around. "I guess anywhere."

I take his bowl out of the bag I brought with a few of his toys and a couple of snacks.

Christina watches me as I fill the bowl with water and set it by the door that leads to her patio.

"Do you take him to visit women often?" she asks, and it's innocent enough.

I give Loki's hind quarters a small pat as I walk back to the island and pick up my wineglass.

"Loki usually only gets to see my mug—and Milo's. I don't take him too many places."

"So, this is a special outing for him?"

I have to tread lightly here. She's searching for something.

"It is," I say, moving toward her.

Christina holds her glass with both of her hands. "I'm not sure I'm worthy of being considered a special outing for him."

"Why not?"

"I'm not special," she says matter-of-factly.

I study her. She believes that.

When I agreed to say we were dating, it was for selfish reasons. It's still for selfish reasons, but the woman needs to know that she's more than just a face on a TV screen, or the image of her parents' marriage.

I can't say that I ever thought she was special either, but it's all different now.

Setting my glass on the island, I reach for hers. Taking her glass from her hands, I set it on the island next to mine.

Her lips part, and she watches me with great interest as I cup her face with my hands.

"You need to know something," I say, and her tongue darts

between her lips as if to moisten them. "This thought that you're not special is crap. Whoever let you believe that was wrong." Though I know exactly who made her believe that.

She blinks hard. "I thought you believed that."

I try not to wince. "Well, I was wrong."

"You think so?"

"I know so. You're so much more," I say, and I watch as her lips turn up into a smile.

"Thank you," she says softly.

"I have to admit, I was only going into this with the expectation that I'd see you in public and do what I had to do to fulfill this agreement." Her eyes dart away from me, but I place a finger under her chin to direct her attention back to me. "But now I can't stop thinking about you."

"Really?"

"Really," I confirm, and press my forehead to hers. "Don't ever think you're not special, because my dog and I, we seem to like you a lot."

She lets out a breath, and her eyes grow damp. "Well, shit." She laughs.

Her lips part again, and this time I ease in and press mine to hers.

Her eyes close instantly because she trusts me now, and her arms lift around my neck.

I turn her so that she's pressed against the counter. My tongue sweeps through her mouth and against hers as her fingers lift into my hair.

It's not the first time I've kissed her, but this kiss is different than any other.

It's hot, quick, and desperate.

I press my hands into her hips and take as much as she'll give me. My fingers grip into her as she presses herself to me, taking everything she needs from this kiss.

No stage kiss will ever be the same between us. And maybe

that's what Sal and Sandra were going for when they decided that we should embrace the rumors.

I can't even care.

All I care about is letting this woman know how important she's become to me in the past few weeks.

Christina eases back, her breath labored. "Are you always going to kiss me like that?"

"I want to," I say.

She searches my eyes as if she's waiting for me to tell her I'm kidding, but I'm not.

Everything has changed.

CHAPTER TWENTY-FIVE

CHRISTINA

And the gossip blog said, "Neither of them is filming, but Christina Malloy attended her father's movie premiere without Graham Crowley. Has she already moved on? Has he?"

~

Reasons I don't date—for real.
 1. I'm too critical of myself.
 2. I don't have time for other people. Correction, I don't make time for other people.

It's been a month of Graham and I "dating," but I haven't seen him since the night he and Loki came for dinner, and he kissed me in my kitchen. Though it's not expected that we see one another, I do miss him, and it's the craziest damn thing.

His fitting was the day after mine, and then he had dinner at his parents' house. I was expected at a showing for one of my father's movies, which was horrific. I don't enjoy people shooting other people's faces off and then gratuitous sex, just to lighten the mood. There's a reason I do happily-ever-after romance movies for a streaming network channel.

I know, I still want a part in his movies, but I'm going to have to be the extra who only serves the characters in a restaurant or something. I can't believe Graham wants a leading part like those in my father's movies.

I should have considered asking him to go to the premiere, only the preview was planned over a month ago, before Graham and I had purposeful conversations and kissed in private.

The thought makes me smile.

There were plenty of questions as to where he was at the preview. I just smiled, posed, and didn't say a word.

We did talk about it on the phone, since we've talked almost every night, and exchanged texts often.

It was extremely nice to hear his voice when I accompanied my mother to Seattle to scout out a new spa location. That was a long few days. But knowing that Graham was on the other end of the phone for each of my remarks, and at the end of the day, it made the trip more pleasant.

Today is the first day on the set, and as much as I love my job, this is the first time I've ever been giddy to get to work. Even stranger is the fact that I'm giddy to get to Graham—that's a first too.

Usually, with the lead up to a new project, I'm filled with anxiety. Knowing I'm working with Graham usually ups that feeling. But not today.

Why does the craft services table always have shit on it that makes you gain ten pounds just by looking at it? His text comes in just as I'm climbing into the car that was sent for me. *I guess it's a good thing we're forbidden to eat from it.*

You're already there? I text back.

Yeah. I'm always too early on the first day. First day nerves and all.

I can understand that. I've been known to be sick my first days of a shoot.

I can't wait to see you, he texts again, and my heart does a little flip in my chest.

I'm on my way, I text back.

I don't live all that far from the studio, but LA traffic is always horrible, and it takes twice as long as it should to get anywhere.

When my phone rings, I consider not answering. It's my mother.

But I answer anyway. "Hello, Mother."

"Where are you going? You sound like you're in a car."

This is how much she pays attention to my life when we talk.

"We start production today," I say, and she lets out a long hum.

"Right. With that man you're seeing?" This she remembers.

"Graham. Yes."

"I'm not sure that's the wisest of relationships, do you?"

Yep, I should have not answered the call.

I look out the window and I can see the studio coming into view.

"We're happy, Mother," I say.

"If you were happy, you'd bring him around."

I pinch the bridge of my nose. "I have. He was at the awards ceremony last month, and he came with me to your opening, remember?"

Again, she hums into the phone. "Right. Your father is considering him for a project."

I draw in a breath of annoyance. "I've heard something about that," I say, even though I already discussed that with her too.

"See, he's using you," she says accusingly. "Everyone will use you for your father."

Now the giddy feeling I had earlier has turned into that sick bout of anxiety.

"He's not using me," I say, and then I have to remind myself that the truth is we're both using one another to get the things we want.

I'm the one that seems to be forgetting that we aren't dating. This is all an organized plot for public display and to get something we each want for our careers.

"Just be careful," she says. "You don't need the gossip shows talking about you."

I guess she missed how we got into this mess in the first place. Besides, she must not pay too much attention to the gossip shows, because they've already been discussing Graham and me regularly.

"Mom, we're pulling up to the studio. I need to get focused. I'll talk to you later," I say.

"Grand opening in San Diego next week," she says, even though I told her I had to go.

"I can't make it."

"I need you there, Christina."

I wince. "I'll see what I can do, but—"

"Be smart," she says and then disconnects the call.

I steady myself as the car pulls through the security gate and drives through the lot.

I'll need to make sure to screen my calls and not answer my mother's all the time. My job is as important as hers and my father's, and they wouldn't welcome my distraction, so there is no need for me to entertain theirs.

Penny is waiting for me the moment the car stops.

I gather my things as she opens the door.

"Good morning," she says cheerily as I step out.

"Good morning," I say. "Thanks for being here so early." I'm going to continue to make that conscious effort to make sure she knows how much I appreciate her.

"Of course." She tucks her lips between her teeth as if to keep a smile from surfacing. "Your trailer is ready. Jean-Claude has a few items he's going to come and talk to you about." She hands me a packet of papers. "Here are the rewrites for today."

I look down at the scene we're starting with.

"Nothing like jumping in, huh?" I ask, noticing that the first scene we're going to film leads to the bedroom scene.

"It's a good way to start a week, don't you think?" Graham's voice comes from behind me, and I turn to see him walking toward me.

His eyes are locked with mine, and the corner of his mouth turns up.

I lick my lips as he comes closer. He lifts his hand to my cheek and eases in, pressing a gentle kiss to my lips, which lingers. I breathe it in and let it surge through me.

"Good morning," he says softly.

"Good morning," I say, looking up into his eyes.

He shifts his glance from me to Penny, who I realize is standing there with her eyes wide.

"Good morning, Penny," he says as he slips his hand into mine, and I have to remember that even though we've forged a friendship, Graham is still vying for a movie role. He knows everyone everywhere is watching us. I can't get sucked into this fake relationship with my heart. I need to remember I'm using him, too.

Penny clears her throat. "Good morning. I think Jean-Claude is waiting for you both."

Graham nods as if he knew that. He takes my bag from my shoulder and carries it.

Well, I guess this is the real start of it. It's time to act for my job and those jobs I want outside of streaming television movies.

Graham Crowley is my ticket. I need to keep that in mind.

CHAPTER TWENTY-SIX

GRAHAM

And the text that Jean-Claude sends to Graham's agent says, "I don't know what the hell is going on with those two, but they better not fuck up this stupid movie."

Jean-Claude narrows his eyes at us as we walk toward him. He motions for everyone else to leave us.

We haven't started filming yet, and the director seems to already have a problem.

As he stands, he looks at our joined hands.

"This is still a thing?" he asks, motioning between us.

I raise a brow. "Yes. Is this a problem?"

He puckers his lips. "I'm just trying to figure out what the hell is really going on. But aside from that, this better not affect our production."

No matter what this relationship really is between us, I don't like that Jean-Claude is using it as if it's going to be the demise of this movie. We film for three weeks. This isn't an enormous commitment to any of us.

"There's no problem here," I say curtly, and I feel Christina's hand tighten in mine.

He nods, turns and picks up his script, and eyes each of us coolly. "Get ready. We start in an hour," he says before turning and walking away.

I let out a long breath to steady myself.

"Why does he keep assuming that we're going to ruin this?" Christina asks. "Is our screaming and yelling at one another more conducive to production? Especially a romance?"

I chuckle at that. "I wonder that too." I turn to Christina and watch as she lifts her head to look up at me. She's in flats, which makes our height difference quite a bit more noticeable than when she's in heels. "I'm not going to do anything to sabotage this movie or the others we're contracted for."

"Me either," she confirms.

"We're a team."

She nods. "We are."

"You're all in, right? I mean, we've decided to be friends. We can make this work for both of us."

Christina blinks hard as if maybe we're not on the same page as I thought we were.

"Right," she finally says. "We can make this work for both of us."

She takes a step back and reaches for her bag, which is still on my shoulder. "I'll see you on set," she says through a forced smile.

I watch her walk out of the building and toward her trailer. Something just transpired there, and I'm not exactly sure what it was.

The rewrites are minimal for the scene we're about to film. The scene is in William's executive office, and it's when he finally moves in to kiss Yvette.

I pull on my suit jacket and my makeup is retouched before I step out of the trailer and head toward the set.

I notice Christina and Penny walking out of her trailer. She's in a dress with a blazer. Her hair is pulled back into a sleek bun at the base of her delicate neck. We look like two business professionals—uptight and goal-oriented.

A few months ago, I would see her walking toward set and not even take a second look. But knowing the woman now, I can't help but take in the sight.

There's an elegance to her that is natural. She glides when she walks. She glows when she smiles. She seeks approval from everyone she meets.

This movie is an office romance, and though it has a lot more intimacy in it than the other movies we've done, it's also a romantic comedy. It should give her a chance to prove herself to Penelope Mondragon. In this moment, I realize I want that for her. Christina Malloy deserves something of her own—something she's worked for. Something she's recognized for that has nothing to do with her parents.

I grin as I head toward the studio door, thinking about what scene we're shooting this morning. There should be lots of kissing, and I don't have one bag of Doritos in my possession. I don't even have the desire to sabotage this for her—or me.

In fact, I've become fond of kissing Christina, sans any obstacle that I might use to annoy her.

My entire day is all about me kissing Christina. I can feel my grin grow wider. This should be the easy part. It's when we film the scenes that pull emotion of the other kind that might become tricky.

This will be a complete change from how we normally function. Usually, our fight scenes are spot on. It doesn't take much for Christina and me to go at each other with words, or even coffee mugs flying at one another.

The love scenes, or kissing scenes in the cases of these watered down, made-for-TV movies, are harder for us to wrap our heads around. We act when we "fall in love" for the camera. But I don't think I'll have to act this time.

This time, there is something between us that I didn't expect. There are feelings I didn't even know I harbored inside of me.

Though we've become friends, and we've spent some time together, I feel as if I'm leading the narrative between us, and Christina is only following. I've been the one to kiss her and invite her over to my place, and me to her place. We text and call each night, but I'm feeling things I don't know what to do with. I'm just not sure she's feeling the same things.

This is a game. The danger comes in how we play it. We've already heard that those who were happy to report the rumor that we were together now wonder why they haven't seen us. They're already saying that our relationship is in trouble.

As if there is a relationship.

But suddenly, I want more than just tasty pictures online or on a TV entertainment show. I want another night at my house with pizza and my dog—and Christina. I want to sit on the couch and hold her until she falls asleep against me. I want to carry her to my bed and wake with her the next morning.

I want it all.

"Graham, they're looking for you," Penny calls to me from the studio door.

I give her a nod, realizing I've just been standing there thinking about Christina, who ducked into the building a few minutes ago.

Head in the game, Crowley, I say to myself as I smooth out my tie and button my suit jacket.

It's time to give all my charisma to William, the CEO of a huge company, and charm the daughter of my competition, Yvette, Christina's character. But feelings are stirring now. Can I keep William and Graham separate? Is this what Jean-Claude is worried about? Is this why it's better when Christina and I don't get along? We do our work, and we go our separate ways? I'm not usually consumed with knowing how her mouth softens under mine, and what her tongue feels like when it sweeps against mine.

Shit! How am I supposed to do this now? I told her no stage kiss would be the same, but now I can't kiss her like I really want to.

This is uncharted territory for me.

For the first time ever, I think I'm going to have to act. It won't just be something I do. I'm going to have to work at it.

There is a bead of sweat rolling down the back of my neck.

I have to loosen my tie a bit as I walk toward the studio door.

Jean-Claude looks up from his conversation with Christina and narrows his gaze on me as I walk on set. He can see it. He knows I'm sweating this. God, this should be the good part. This should be the sellable *we love one another* part for our characters, and because I'm suddenly feeling things I've never felt before, I'm going to screw this whole thing up.

Christina looks my direction and begins to walk toward me.

"Are you okay?" Her voice is full of concern, and she searches my face.

I take her hand and pull her to the side, down a shadowed hallway.

"You're freaking me out," she says, and I turn and cup her face.

"I am freaked out. I don't know how to act like I have feelings for you."

Her eyes go wide and sad all at the same time, and I realize that came out completely wrong.

"What I mean is, I've never acted with you and cared this deeply for you."

Her gaze softens, but her lips are curled in as if she's having to hold back an emotion. And I can't tell if she's going to cry or laugh.

I lean in and press a kiss to her mouth.

"Listen, I need to tell you something," I say and notice that she begins to worry her bottom lip, but then must have realized her lipstick would need to be fixed.

"What do you have to tell me?" she asks.

I take in a breath. Who would have thought I'd ever be having this conversation with Christina Malloy?

"I have feelings for you that I can't explain." I lay it out there. It either makes or breaks this. "I have to reel this all in just to act as if Yvette and William are just now falling in love."

She blinks hard and eases back from me. "You have feelings for me? Real feelings?"

Does she look disappointed, or surprised? I can't decide.

"I do. And not just feelings that I'm pretending to have in public."

"Because we're friends now?"

This time I pull her to me and kiss her deeper—screw the lipstick. She has to know what I'm talking about, right?

When I ease back, her cheeks have pinked brightly enough that I can see their change in the dimly lit hallway.

She takes a moment to open her eyes, and when she does, I study them. Christina looks intoxicated by my kiss, and I wonder if I look the same to her, because it's how I feel.

"More than just because we're friends," I say.

Christina presses her fingers to her lips. "Oh."

I don't know if she feels the same way, but shit, now I've put myself out there.

"You don't have to feel the same way," I begin to explain. "In fact, I don't think you should say anything at all. We can discuss this later. Just know, William isn't me. Yvette isn't you." I'm explaining it as if she's a child and needs to understand the balance between real life and fiction. "But I'd like to bring my dog over tonight and really sit down and discuss this with you when we're done."

She nods slowly, and I can hear Jean-Claude yelling for our presence. This isn't a good way to start our production. But if Christina and I can figure out what's really happening between us, then maybe it's something bigger than a rumor.

CHAPTER TWENTY-SEVEN

CHRISTINA

And the woman at the craft services table sends a photo of Graham and Christina kissing to her friend. "I guess she's not going to throw things at his head this time."

Blocking is done and noted. We've run the first scene of the day ten times and gotten the close-ups of each of us. After we break for lunch, we'll come back to it and film the moment that William moves in and kisses Yvette.

I understand the need to film a script out of sequence, but today, of all days, it's messing with my head.

Then again, it might be what Graham said to me that's messing with me.

Perhaps this would all be better if we were filming the scene where our characters meet and there is a battle of wills. A war is waged where the best person gets the job—where words, hurtful words, are used. I'd feel more comfortable starting there.

. . .

Penny has my ordered lunch set up in my trailer. We sit to go over the schedule for the next day when there is a knock at the door. We both look up to see Graham let himself in. He's carrying his own lunch.

I can't help the smile that forms on my mouth.

Penny stands up, picking up her plate of food. "I'll let you two have some privacy," she says, but Graham shakes his head.

"No. Sit. I just thought I'd join you both. I don't have any company in my trailer."

I move over on the bench I'm sitting on, at the table in my trailer, and Graham sits down next to me. I wonder why he's not using this downtime to write his book. Instead, he's in my trailer sitting next to me, grinning at me.

"You could use some protein on that salad," he says, looking at the enormous plate of lettuce in front of me.

"In a couple of weeks, I'll eat more," I say.

"Does she eat like this always?" he asks Penny.

She looks at me for confirmation, but I just roll my eyes.

"She's careful about what she eats," Penny confirms as she takes a bite of her own salad.

"I think she could still eat healthy and eat something more filling."

I nudge him. "Give me a break," I say, and take a large forkful of lettuce.

"You'll eat more when we're done filming?" he asks.

"Yes."

"Then I'm going to take you out for a big meal," he says with a wink before turning his attention toward Penny. "So, how do you think it's going?" Graham asks her.

Penny lifts her eyes to him. "I think it's going fine."

"You've been around when we've worked with Jean-Claude before. Do you think he's being a little harsher than normal?"

She worries her bottom lip as she considers. "Not really. I just think he's confused by the two of you being nice to one another."

Graham laughs. "Is this really so strange?" He looks at me for an answer.

"Yes," I say laughing. "Remember, he called me out for throwing a mug at you last time."

"Yeah, but you're not going to do that again, are you?"

I narrow my gaze on him. "I don't plan on it. But then, I didn't plan on it then either."

"Good to know," he says, leaning in and kissing my cheek. "I'll be good."

I can feel my cheeks heat and Penny's eyes are wide again.

She knows we're "faking" it.

I know he has feelings.

I have no idea what I feel.

I have no idea what to tell Penny, either.

I thought I was confusing reality and publicity. I thought I'd worked that out for myself. But when he said he was having feelings, well, that just did me in. What he said went further than the friendship we'd agreed on.

Doing our scenes, I had to focus on Graham's character, and not on him. It wasn't easy. Maybe I need to figure out how to get him out of my system so this isn't so strange to me.

We finish our lunches and Penny excuses herself. She's off to map out the rest of my day.

I realize then that Graham doesn't have a personal assistant. He shows up, does his work, and goes on. I've had an assistant my entire life. It started with a nanny, then I had a tutor added, and a cook that only cooked my meals when my parents were out of town or not home for the evening. Now I have Penny who is always one step ahead of me, making sure I have nothing to worry about.

I pinch the bridge of my nose. What a spoiled brat I am. It's no wonder I spend my evenings alone and that Graham Crowley never thought much of me.

I think about how he treats Penny. He includes her more as if she's my friend than my employee.

I consider that I owe her a few more cups of fancy coffee.

Could I do it all without Penny? Probably. But would I want to? She's become, well, my only companion. That is, until Graham began spending more time with me.

His arm comes around the back of the bench behind me, and I'm suddenly aware of how alone we are.

"You're thinking too hard," he says, and I realize I have my hands pressed flat to the table.

I blink and look up at him. "Yeah. I think I am."

"I just got a text. They want us back on set in twenty."

I nod. I'll need to go to the makeup trailer and get my makeup touched up.

"I'll walk over to makeup with you," Graham says, and now I wonder if I said that aloud or if it was just running free in my head.

He slides out of the bench seat from behind the table and I follow, only to stand and be pressed up against him.

His arms come around me, and my hands go to his chest.

"I think we should practice what's coming up," he says with his lips hovering over mine, and his breath warm against my mouth.

"Graham—"

"Shh." He rubs a finger over my lips. "Can you tell me you don't feel this?"

My breath is unsteady. I don't know what I feel. Chaos. I feel a lot of chaos inside of me—that's it.

I lick my lips and I notice that he's watching my mouth.

Oh, God, I could just sink into him. The problem is, I don't trust him. I don't trust myself. We're standing alone, wrapped up in one another, and we're playing a role. There's the real us—the ones who can't stand one another. There's the new us—the ones who promised to be friends. There's this uncharted us—the ones who kiss now, I guess. And there's the acting us—the ones who play roles of characters who fall in love and live happily ever after.

It's pure chaos in my body.

"Let go, Christina," he says, and again, I wonder if all of that is in my head or if I just told him I didn't trust him. "Let's enjoy this."

His mouth moves over mine, and I lean into him. I let him gather me up and deepen the kiss. I let my knees go weak. I let my heartbeat ramp up. I let myself feel.

I've kissed this man hundreds of times, but when we're alone and he kisses me, it's different. It's so different.

Why can't I believe that he really does have feelings for me?

When am I going to admit I have them for him?

I guess I just did.

His lips linger on mine, and he's smiling against my mouth. "Do you always think this hard?"

I ease back and look up at him. "You confuse me," I say on a jittery breath.

"I'm confused too."

I swallow hard. "This is real to you?"

A line forms between his brows but softens. "Yeah. It is."

"You're not just confused by our circumstance?"

"I was," he says, lifting his hand to my cheek and brushing his thumb over it. "But the more time I spend with you—the more times I kiss you—the less confused I become."

I nod slowly.

What the hell.

What do I have to lose?

"I think I have feelings too," I say, and his grin widens.

"Wow," he lets the word hang there. "Okay, then." He brushes my lips with another kiss. "My dog and I definitely want to spend some time with you tonight to discuss this."

CHAPTER TWENTY-EIGHT

GRAHAM

And the memo at the network reads, "Numbers on Malloy/Crowley views are up. We need to market their relationship and get them to the next fan event. This is gold."

―

William and Yvette have gazed into one another's eyes all day.

William has used his charm.

Yvette has played into his arms.

William takes Yvette's face in his hands, orchestrated by Jean-Claude himself. William tilts his head to the right and moves his lips over Yvette's—closed lips of course.

For the first time, after all the movies we've made together, I feel Christina ease against me. She's not rigid, even though she keeps her lips from parting, her mouth is soft.

Jean-Claude shouts, "Cut!" and we ease apart, only slightly.

"That was different," Christina whispers.

"We have chemistry," I say.

"Who knew?"

. . .

The scene is filmed another dozen times and the kiss just gets better and better—well, for me it does. I can see irritation beginning to brew in Christina.

When she's had enough of something, there is glassiness that coats her eyes. Her breath comes in short puffs. She scratches the back of her neck. And though she's quiet, the energy around her becomes dark.

She's sitting in the chair with her name on it, beyond the cameras. She has a lemon water in one hand and her script in the other.

Her trim legs are crossed and her foot bounces.

On any other day, this would just be the norm and I'd catch it out of the corner of my eye. I'd be much too busy talking to those around the sound stage or sitting in my trailer working on my novel.

Today, I want to defuse this bomb that is Christina Malloy.

As I walk toward her, Penny is handing her pills from a bottle. I've been around enough people in this industry to wonder what she takes, but then I notice the bottle says Tylenol and my shoulders release a bit. I've also been around enough people to know Christina would never take illegal or unnecessarily prescribed drugs.

What she needs is some protein. I haven't seen her eat since lunch, and that was just lettuce.

My chair is next to hers, so I sit down and pull a bag of Doritos from the pocket of my suit jacket.

Her eyes go directly to the bag and then lift to look at me. Penny is gathering things and shoving them into Christina's bag as if she's going to make a run for it.

"Are you kidding me with those?" she blurts out the words so sharply, spit flies.

I grin. "Did you want some?"

She eyes the bag again and takes a breath. I think if she had a coffee mug...

"I most certainly don't want any. And you're an asshole if you're going to eat those before we're done."

My smile widens as I look at her. Once upon a time, I would have opened that bag and poured the entire thing into my mouth just to get a reaction from her. Then, when she was steaming mad, I'd have walked away.

Now, I study her. This has nothing more to do with the Doritos than it has to do with me. She's tired. She's hungry. She's worried that she's upset Jean-Claude, without merit, mind you.

She needs a good, deep kiss, a protein bar, and a cuddle from a dog that seems to adore her.

I reach into my other pocket and pull out a granola bar. I hand it to her.

"What's this for?" she snaps.

"You're in need of fuel. We have at least three more hours of this. Do your body a favor." I nudge her with my hand until she takes the bar.

"You're really not going to eat those Doritos, are you?"

"No, sweetheart. I'm not." I lean over the arm of the chair and kiss her softly.

The icy demeanor melts and she smiles. Even Penny's shoulders ease.

"I was just teasing with the Doritos," I say, handing them to Penny. "Put them in her bag for later," I tease.

Penny purses her lips to keep from smiling as she drops the chips into the bag.

Christina's eyes are on me. She wants to lash out at me. She wants to curl up in my arms. There's a fine line of emotion that swims in her gaze.

I take back the granola bar that I had handed her, and I open it.

"Seriously, sweetheart," I say the word from my heart. "Fuel your body." I hand her back the opened granola bar, climb from my chair, and stand in front of her.

With my hands on either side of her, leaning in on the arms of her chair, I press a kiss to her taut lips, holding there until hers go pliant under mine.

I can feel her dissolving back into the Christina that trusts me.

"Need anything else?" I ask.

She eases back a bit, her eyes still closed and her tongue brushing over her lips.

She slowly opens her eyes and looks at me. "I think I'm good here," she says.

"I'm going to go see what's holding us up. I'd like to get to my dog."

The corner of her mouth curls up. "I'd like to get to him too," she says.

My chest squeezes at that. The later we go today with filming, the less time I'll have with Christina and Loki. That would be the norm for production weeks, but today, I want that time.

I watch her watch me, and I can't believe this is where this little farce has led. I want to spend time with this woman, kiss her, feed her, take care of her.

I want to be the one she can lean on.

I want to be the one she can trust.

I want her to be herself, and sometimes when she's alone with me, I think she lets down that guard a bit.

The call is made for us back on set, and Christina lets out a breath.

"I guess we're back on," she says.

"Eat the granola bar. You have plenty of time."

She nods and takes a tiny bite. It's not enough to keep her going, but it's something.

"I'll meet you on set. I'm going to go find a bag of Funyuns," I say, and Penny snorts out a laugh and quickly reels it back in when Christina's eyes go wide on her. Then Christina turns those wide eyes on me.

"Seriously?" There's heat in her cheeks again, and I smile at her.

"No, not seriously. Now eat that granola bar and let's go. I have more kissing to do with you today."

She takes another bite, her eyes never leaving mine.

Yeah, she heard that right. I didn't just mean the rest of this scene. I have a lot more kissing planned.

CHAPTER TWENTY-NINE

CHRISTINA

And the fourth story on the news was about a fire in LA. No one cares about rumors tonight.

Graham's eyes are closed and his head rests against the back of the seat in the SUV that is driving us to his house.

The plan is to get Loki and head back to my house.

Maybe it would be best if I just had the driver take me home, and Graham could spend his evening relaxing.

I look out the window as the city settles in for the evening. Today was probably the best day I've ever had on a set, and it wasn't only because I kissed Graham all day long. Admittedly, his attention was nice.

He didn't sabotage our scenes, even if he teased about doing so. He was attentive and asked questions that only made the scenes better when Jean-Claude agreed with him. He made sure I was fed and had water, and he took care of Penny's needs, too.

Usually between takes, I wouldn't have seen Graham. Today, he was by my side, as if we had a connection.

I look back at him, easily asleep and peaceful.

We do have a connection.

Why did it take some stupid rumor to make us come together?

The car slows in front of Graham's house and comes to a stop. Graham's eyes flutter open and he draws in a deep breath.

"Sorry," he says. "I guess I fell asleep."

I smile at him. "Why don't I have him take me home. You're tired."

He shakes his head as the driver comes around to the back of the car and opens my door.

"That was just a little break," Graham says as the driver then opens his door. "Let's get Loki and head to your house. I won't stay long, but Loki needs some time out of the house, and I could use some time one-on-one with you."

I press my lips together to keep them from turning up into a smile. He wants to spend more time with me when we've worked together all day.

My stomach flutters at the attention he's giving me. I know he doesn't have to do that. It's not part of the agreement. But he'd said he had feelings for me, and didn't I then admit the same?

Graham steps out of the car, and I step out of my side. He thanks the driver and waits for me to clear the car before taking my hand and walking toward his house.

I can hear Loki's welcome from behind the front door, and it makes me smile. What a wonderful thing, to have someone waiting for you when you got home.

"Why don't you take him to the set?" I ask as Graham slips his keys into the lock.

"He wouldn't behave."

"You don't think so?"

"Oh, I know so. That's why I don't take him. We've tried before. He gets too much attention and then starts to look for it," he chuckles as he pushes open the front door and Loki bounds toward him.

We step into the house and Graham crouches down to accept the welcome from his dog.

"Hey, boy," he says, nuzzling his face against the dog's fur. "I'm happy to see you too." He kisses the top of Loki's head. "Look who I brought."

Graham steps to the side, and I watch Loki's head lift to look at me before he rushes past Graham and to me.

He jumps up, his paws coming to my shoulders, and I lean in to hug him.

"Hi, sweetheart," I say as I take a moment to hug on the dog that stands as tall as I do on his hind legs.

Loki sets himself down and runs a few circles around the living room, where I notice Milo lounging on the couch watching TV.

He looks up at us, shifting his glance between us. He's leery of what's going on between us, and I'm sure he's spent the past few years being a sounding board for Graham's feelings about me, so I can't blame him.

"He was snoring a few minutes ago," Milo says with some humor. "Now he's all riled up."

Graham slaps a hand on Milo's shoulder. "We're going to take him with us. You can relax in silence."

Milo sits up. "Are you taking him all night?"

Graham shifts a quick look in my direction. "I'll be home in a few hours. We're going to eat and relax for a bit."

Milo nods slowly. "How was your first day on set?"

"Best one yet," Graham says, shooting me a soft smile. "Have a seat. I'm going to change and get Loki's stuff together. I'll just be a minute."

I nod and sit down in the oversized chair next to me.

As I sit and cross my legs, Loki comes over to me and rests his head on my lap.

I think I'm as taken by the man's dog as I am with the man.

I run my hand over Loki's head and look up to see Milo studying us.

"Loki doesn't usually take to women like he has to you. Mind you, he only usually sees Graham's mother, and he likes her. But you're different," Milo says.

"Why do you think?"

He scans a look over me and Loki. "I don't know. I guess any woman I bring home doesn't spend a lot of time with him."

"What about the women Graham brings home?"

Milo's brows draw in, and I realize that a girlfriend wouldn't put it that way.

"I mean that he used to bring home," I amend.

Milo puckers his lips. "Graham doesn't just bring women home. The man always has a sea of women pining for him, but he's not that kind of showman, if you know what I mean."

That flutter that had started in my belly moves up into my chest.

Graham is tall, dark, and handsome. He's smooth and smart. I can't believe he hasn't shared that gift with all the women in state —in the world.

"Well, I'm honored to get to be around Loki then," I say, and the dog lifts his head to look at me before turning and trekking down the hall to Graham's room.

Milo leans his forearms on his knees. "I hope you don't think I'm prying, but this thing between the two of you is a bit surprising."

Don't I know it.

"I mean, he hasn't really had a lot of good things to say about you working together," Milo continues.

I swallow hard, uncross my legs, and rest my forearms on my knees to match Milo. "We're all a mystery, aren't we? I mean, we change how we think, dress, and eat all the time. We like one political candidate until they do something we don't like, and then we change our perspective. Sometimes you take a moment to get to know someone you didn't care about, only to find out there's something there."

Milo nods and sits back on the couch. "I guess you're right. For the record, he's been really happy the past month. Maybe this is a good thing for the two of you."

I shrug and sit back in the chair.

I'm just hoping I defused that doubt.

Graham and I might be starting to have feelings for one another, but we're still in this for selfish reasons. And, after today, and listening to Jean-Claude bark orders because he thinks streaming movies are beneath him to create, I'd really like to work on a Penelope Mondragon movie.

CHAPTER THIRTY

GRAHAM

And the text between Sal and Penelope Mondragon says, "Let's set up a meeting and discuss Malloy."

~

We make a salad for dinner, but I don't allow Christina just a pile of lettuce. The salad is filled with color, and I convince her that if we shred up a chicken breast, it will keep us fuller.

As I toss it all together, she reaches her fingers into the bowl and pulls out a slice of carrot and nibbles on it.

"Did your mother teach you to make that?" she teases.

"Why, yes she did," I say, picking up the bowl and carrying it to the table. "Vegetables are great, but they can taste good too."

Christina picks up our glasses of wine and carries them to the table.

We each take a seat, and I dish out the salad.

Loki is lying by the patio door on a blanket that Christina set on the cold floor for him. He's at home in her space.

"Milo says Loki doesn't usually take to women," she says as she lifts her wine to her lips and watches me from over her glass.

I look over at Loki and back to her. "I suppose he's right. He's usually curious, but then goes on his way. With you, he gets excited to see you and snuggles up to you."

"So, you didn't say all those nasty things about me to him like you did to Milo?"

The fork full of salad that I just put in my mouth will choke me if I try to swallow now.

I chew mindfully and follow it with a sip of wine.

"Did Milo say that to you?" I ask.

She shrugs as she takes a bite of her salad. "He mentioned that this thing between us is weird because you've made comments about us working together in the past, like maybe it was difficult."

I sip my wine again. "I've said that." It gnaws at me now. "I'm sorry."

Christina shakes her head. "Don't be sorry. My mother thinks you're using me to get to my father. She's not on board either. I haven't been too kind about what I say about you, it seems."

"I never should have talked about you to anyone. I guess if I had a problem with you, I should have talked to you about that."

The corner of her mouth curls up. "Then we wouldn't have been enemies, would we?"

"I guess not."

"I like this better," she says, then pulls her bottom lip through her teeth.

"I'll never talk bad about you again," I promise.

"No matter what, we're friends?"

Oh, I want so much more than that now. I don't know why this change has come over me. All I want is that part in her father's movie.

No, that's all I *had* wanted.

I hold out my hand to her, and when she takes it, I pull her from her chair and guide her toward me. I ease her down on my lap and wrap my arms around her.

She steadies herself with an arm around my shoulders. Her

chest rises and falls with her breath. I've surprised her by making this move, but it excites me to have her here.

I lift my hand to her neck and graze the tender skin with my fingertips as I lift them into her hair and guide her to my mouth.

Her eyes close as her mouth opens to mine. Christina slides her tongue against mine and the taste of wine intoxicates me more than drinking it.

Her fingers wind up into my hair and this kiss steals my breath.

Without releasing one another, or lessening the kiss, Christina moves from sitting on my lap to straddling me. Her skirt rises up her thighs and I can feel her warmth against me.

My fingers grip her hips as she bites down on my bottom lip.

I flinch and Christina pulls back.

"I'm sorry. Did I hurt you?" she asks breathlessly.

"No. You just surprised me."

"I should—" She lifts from my lap as if she's going to climb off, and I ease her back.

"Don't move," I whisper my words against her neck before I brush my lips across her throat. "I want you right where you are."

My mouth finds hers again, and the warmth of her, all of her, makes my body ache.

I slide my hands up the outsides of her thighs until my fingertips are under the hem of her skirt. Her tongue sweeps my mouth, and I can feel the moan that escapes her.

I press her to me, my erection straining beneath her.

Christina's mouth pulls from mine, and her head falls back, aligning me with her breasts. The V-neck of the dress accentuates the swells of softness, which she guides my head toward.

I pepper kisses over the soft skin as Christina moves against me, making that erection she's created twitch beneath her.

My grip on her ass gets tighter, and I maneuver us so that when I stand, she's wrapped around my waist.

Her mouth comes back to mine, and I carry her to the couch in the living room.

I ease us both down, her dress now up around her waist, and her legs parting to make room for my body.

I bury my face against her neck. "God, Christina," I say as she wraps her legs around me. "I don't know how long I can last with you."

She moves to look at me. "I'm okay. We can do this."

I smile at her desperation, and then I consider it.

Her body moves beneath me, but I can't take her now. I can't just have sex with her because my dick is uncomfortable in my pants.

She presses up against me again, finding my mouth and dragging me under with hers. I can't imagine ever tiring of kissing her.

With her mouth on mine, I'm drowning in her. The thought that we got here because we were discussing what I'd told Milo about her sends a sharp pain through my chest.

A month ago, I dreaded seeing this woman, and now she's consuming me as she grinds against me.

I want this. God, do I want this.

But it can't just be me taking her on the couch.

This woman has never been important to anyone, but she is to me now. If I'm going to have sex with her, it needs to mean something. She needs to know that she's special. I need to make her feel special.

My thoughts are distracted when I catch a glimpse of Loki walking by. His collar and tags clank as he walks through the room.

I ease up, and Christina turns her head to see him.

The heat between us begins to settle.

A smile forms on her lips, and she looks up at me. "I forgot he was here," she whispers because I think that's all she has breath for.

"Yeah," I say, sitting back and looking at her beneath me.

The lace of her bra peeks out of the dress that has been bunched up. Her panties are delicate lace that begs for me to remove them.

I adjust myself before climbing off the couch and reaching for her.

Her brows are drawn in and worry masks her face.

"What's wrong?" she asks as she takes my hand and stands.

"I should take him home."

"You can stay," she says. "I'm okay with all of this."

Pressing my forehead to hers, I breathe in to calm my body. Though touching her, smelling her, makes that calm fight me.

"I want to." I groan. "You have no idea," I say, but she knows what I'm fighting below the belt. "This isn't how I want to do this. You deserve better."

Christina lets go of me and takes a step back from me. She fixes her dress and hugs her arms around herself. "I guess you're right. We should think more about this."

"I think it's a good idea. Don't go getting into your head that I don't want to do this. I just don't want to take you on the couch while my dog roams through your house."

She looks at Loki and then back at me. "It's fine."

I reach for her, but she moves again. "Christina, don't shut down on me."

"Maybe it's time for you to go. I mean, you did tell Milo that you'd be home." She bats her eyes and I wonder if she's going to cry. "Besides, I have to get to the set early tomorrow. We're filming outside, and they want to catch the light."

I nod and move to her. This time she lets me touch her.

"I'll see you in the morning," I say, and she nods. "This changes nothing."

I lift her chin with my finger and direct her gaze to me.

"This is real. You know that, right?" I ask, looking for her confirmation.

She studies me before she nods. I worry that she's as confused as I am, but I know what love and respect feel like. She doesn't. She's going to worry that I'm just playing with her.

I need to make this something she'll never forget or question. As far as I'm concerned, I'm all in now. Sure, I want that role in the movie, and I want that extended contract for the network, but I want Christina too.

CHAPTER THIRTY-ONE

CHRISTINA

And the girl at the donut shop tells the hair stylist next door, "I don't think Graham Crowley is really dating Christina Malloy. I mean, what does he see in her? He's much too hot for some plain-Jane like her."

The door to the SUV slams back at me since I've pushed it open too hard. I manage to pull my leg back in before it hits me.

Penny opens the door from outside the SUV and looks at me.

"Are you okay? Did that hit you?" she asks, concern lit in her eyes.

"I'm fine," I say. "I'm fine."

I hand her my bag and my purse. Then I realize my phone is on the seat and I grab for it as I set my foot on the ground. As I step out of the car, the heel of my shoe slips and I fall back against the car, catching myself.

Penny's eyes grow wide. "Christina!" She moves to me, but I shake my head. I caught myself. I'm not hurt. I'm just out of sorts.

It's dark out still and I have on my sunglasses. I'm afraid that makeup is going to have to do a lot of work to get the bags under my eyes not to show.

"I'm fine," I say again. "Is there coffee?" I ask.

"I'll get you one as soon as we get inside. Do you need breakfast, too?"

I press my hand to my stomach as we walk toward my trailer. We never finished dinner last night, and I fell into bed the moment Graham and Loki left.

"Something easy on my belly," I say as we step into the trailer and Penny holds open the door for me.

She nods at my instruction.

I take a few moments to collect myself as Penny runs off for coffee and breakfast. At this point, I don't even care what she brings me. I'll eat anything.

The timer on my phone goes off, and I startle. I have to be in the makeup trailer, and my day needs to begin. It's going to be a long one. I'm hungry. I'm sleep deprived. I was rejected.

A sob escapes my throat and I suck it back in. I cannot fall apart because of Graham Crowley. It's fake. It's all fake.

I get Penelope Mondragon at the end of it all and this *thing* with Graham is fake!

I breathe through the tears that want to flow, and when I have control, I slide on my sunglasses again, and head out into the dark to have the makeup artists do their magic.

Within the hour, I'm fed, caffeinated, covered in makeup, and standing on the outdoor set. Jean-Claude wants the light just right, and since this scene is only of me, hopefully I can give him what he wants, and we'll only need a few takes.

The April morning air is still nippy. I have on the coat I'm supposed to wear in the scene, and Penny holds a larger blanket for me for between takes.

Getting back to work without worrying about Graham feels

right. I need to stop letting him kiss me. I need to stop spending time with him outside of the set. I need to never straddle his lap and feel him beneath me like that again.

All this runs through my head as I get set for the next take.

Penny takes the blanket from me, and they fix my hair and makeup as Jean-Claude gets set.

It's then I see Graham and Loki standing on the outskirts of the set among the crew. He waves and smiles as if last night hadn't rocked his world as it had mine.

I don't move from my mark.

He's holding Loki's leash, but Loki is sitting like a well-behaved boy at Graham's feet.

Jean-Claude gives me my direction, gets into position, and I'm off when he commands it.

I'm simply walking down the street with extras moving past me. I stop and look in the window to a store. A car pulls up, and I hail the taxi that drives down the street. As soon as I reach for the door to the taxi, Jean-Claude yells, "Cut!"

He comes from his chair toward me.

"We're good. Go get warm," he says, patting my cheek with his hand.

I walk toward Penny, who holds out the blanket to me and wraps it around me.

She hands me a travel cup of coffee, and I sip, but I'm shaking. I'm not sure if that's from the weather or from my nerves because I can see Graham moving toward me.

When Loki sees me, he pulls against the leash, but Graham keeps a hold of him.

I crouch down to cuddle the dog.

"Hey, boy. Are you taking a field trip today?" I ask as I rub Loki's head, and he presses into my hand.

"He's going to spend the next few days with his grandparents, so he wanted to say hello before he heads over there," Graham says.

I look up at him. "Why isn't he going to be with you and Milo?"

The corner of his mouth turns up. "Milo has a conference, and the next few days for us are busy." He holds his hand out to help me to my feet, and inches me close to him. "And I want some alone time with you," he says, and I feel the breath rush from my lungs.

"Why?"

His grin is full now and his eyes soft. "Because you're my girlfriend," he says matter-of-factly.

I press my free hand to my forehead.

"Christina?" Graham says and I look up at him. "Everything okay?"

I take a breath to question his motives. My head and my heart are so confused, but I don't get anything out.

"Crowley, the dog?" Jean-Claude shouts in our direction.

"Just visiting. He's headed out," Graham says, grinning at me and never looking in Jean-Claude's direction. "I'm going to take him to my mom, and I'll be back in a bit. By the way, you look beautiful this morning."

Graham leans in and presses a gentle kiss to my lips.

I watch as he smiles at Penny, and then he and Loki head back toward the trailers.

"He's a really nice guy," Penny says.

I swallow hard, watching him walk away, saying hello to everyone he passes.

I have to agree with Penny. He does seem to be a nice guy.

Shit! I'm so confused about how I feel. I don't know what to think about Graham Crowley.

CHAPTER THIRTY-TWO

GRAHAM

And the entertainment reporter says, "Charles Malloy is at it again. There are whispers that his next movie will top the budget of his last one. You know what that means: more explosions, more car chases, and more love scenes."

~

Loki's barking probably worked better than if I'd rung my mother's doorbell.

When she opens her front door and pushes open the screen, Loki takes off for her. Just as Christina had done earlier, my mother kneels to accept the love Loki is offering.

"Well, there's my boys," she says, nuzzling the dog, but looking up at me.

"I'm beginning to feel as if he loves everyone more than me," I tease, unhooking his leash as he moves past my mother and into the house.

My mother stands and pulls me in for a hug. "He loves you most," she assures me. "Do you have some time?"

I look at my watch. "I don't have to be on set for a few hours. They're doing Christina's outside shots this morning."

She nods, and I walk into the house. "I just made some coffee."

I follow my mother into the kitchen, moving to the back door to let Loki out so he can run through the yard.

"How's filming going?" she asks as she fills two mugs of coffee.

"It's only the second day."

"Oh, I lost track, I guess."

I sit down at the island as she puts a mug in front of me and takes the stool next to me.

"And how are you and Christina?" She smiles over the rim of her mug as she sips her coffee.

I sip from my mug. "Interesting."

"Things aren't good?"

"I can't say that. It's just that we haven't really clicked for years. I mean, we weren't friendly before. Now that we're into this, there are some hiccups getting on the same page."

Her brows draw inward. "I would have thought you figured all of that out, and that's why you were together."

I chew on the inside of my cheek. I could confide in my mother. I could tell her all about what's going on, but Christina can't. I guess that's not fair, so I don't let my mother in on our secret.

"Attraction is strong," I say, and my mother smiles. "So sometimes when we talk about things, it gets bumpy."

With her mug between her hands, she watches Loki through the window, running through the yard. "But you're trying to work on it? I mean, it's not easy when you're working together."

"Yeah, we're working on it."

"And what does Loki think of her?"

That makes me laugh. "He loves her."

"Well, he's a good judge of character," she says before she sips her coffee again.

I look out the window at the dog chasing a bird. She's right. Loki is a good judge of character, and he does like Christina a lot.

I'm hoping that being alone tonight, we can explore these new feelings. I never expected this would be the outcome, that's for sure. I just wanted the movie deal.

~

I was hoping to catch a few moments with Christina before we started filming, but by the time I get to the studio, I am whisked away to makeup and expected on set.

As I sit in the makeup chair, Sandra walks into the trailer, a large smile on her face.

I turn in the chair, the makeup artist following my moves to keep working.

"Hey," I say. "I didn't expect to see you."

"Yeah, I need like five minutes of your time."

I look up at the makeup artist as she applies powder to my face. She gives me a nod, removes the protective paper from my collar, and I stand and follow Sandra out of the trailer.

"So, what's up?" I ask.

"First of all, I'm hearing great things about you and Christina. You both are really going all in, huh? I mean, it's not news like it was a week ago, but there is still a happy buzz among your admirers."

I look around to see who is close by. Luckily, we seem to be as alone as possible on a working set.

"We are actually seeing each other," I say and watch as Sandra processes it.

The line between her brows deepens. "What do you mean, you're actually seeing each other?"

"I mean, we're dating. We're a couple."

Sandra bites down on her bottom lip. "You're dating?"

"We are."

"That wasn't the plan, Graham. You just were supposed to take a few pictures, be seen in public, and not throw things at one another on set."

"And in the meantime, we found out we really like one another. I mean, I like her—a lot."

"Well, I didn't see that coming," she says. She looks down at the packet in her hands. "I was bringing this by for you."

She hands me the packet and I look inside. *Malibu Money / a Charles Malloy Production.*

I lift my eyes to Sandra. "Seriously?"

"He wants to meet with you on Saturday at the club."

"At the club?"

She rolls her eyes. "His country club."

"Oh," I say as I look back down at the packet.

"All of the information is in the packet. This is what you wanted, Graham. This is what you've been working for. And this is what this little game has gotten for you."

I purse my lips. "It's not a little game."

"This is her dad, Graham. Do you really want to be dating her and working for her father?"

"There are millions of couples out there where one of them works for their partner's parents."

"Partner?" she asks, and I eye her coolly. Sandra shakes her head. "Just meet with him. Don't bring up the dating his daughter thing. I'm sure if there's something to it, he'll talk to you. Just talk business."

"And what about Christina? Can I share this with her?"

Now Sandra's eyes go wide. "Nondisclosure form, top of the packet."

I nod. "What if her father tells her about it?"

Sandra shrugs. "Graham . . ."

"Seriously. What if Christina comes to me and tells me about this?"

She worries her lip. "Then you go to her father and ask them to cancel the nondisclosure or rewrite it."

"I'm not going to stop seeing her," I say, because all the sudden I feel as if tables are turning. Though I know it's just my insecurities.

"Not for me to decide," Sandra says.

I look toward the set and see Christina receiving notes from Jean-Claude.

I hand Sandra the packet. "Will you drop this into my safe in my trailer?" I ask.

She nods. "I really thought you'd be more excited about this."

"I'm excited," I say, but there's more at stake here. I don't want to keep secrets from Christina. I want her to be excited for me too.

CHAPTER THIRTY-THREE

CHRISTINA

And the music plays as the commercial starts. "At Ella Malloy Spas, you'll be pampered and stress free."

Graham holds my hand as we drive toward his house. He's been quiet today. I think it threw Jean-Claude for a loop too.

I didn't expect Graham to want to spend time with me after we wrapped for the day. Last night hadn't gone very well. But I guess since he decided to take his dog to his mother's house, he wants to try again—whatever that looks like.

I don't know if Sandra's presence at the studio had anything to do with his distant attitude today. He hasn't said anything about her visit. Not that I expect him to say a lot. I'm not sure when that part of a relationship is supposed to kick in. This is new to me. And isn't that about the saddest thing I've ever thought?

When Graham stops at a stoplight, he shifts a glance toward me. "You were amazing today, by the way," he says.

"Thank you, but I didn't do anything different than I ever have."

He chuckles. "I notice now."

I chew my lip. "Why?"

"Why?"

"Yeah, why notice now?"

He inhales as the light turns green. "I see you now."

"Because you have to? I mean, you have to pay attention to me because we agreed on it?"

He shakes his head. "I think you know better than that now. Maybe it's what got me into this, but it's different now. I see you different now."

Graham lifts my fingers to his lips and presses a kiss to them.

"Don't you feel differently?" he asks.

I do feel differently, and I want to believe that this is all real now. But, like he said, I grew up in this town, in this industry, and everything is fake.

No one is genuine.

No one talks kindly, except to your face.

There are exceptions, but I haven't been privy to that too often. My own mother is one of the biggest gossips. I can't even confide in her.

"I do," I finally say, answering his question.

"Why don't we stop by your place first?" he suggests.

"Why?"

"I'd like you to stay the night. The whole night," he says.

Even though I guess I anticipated staying with him tonight, hearing him say it sends flutters through my body.

"If you're sure."

He turns to look at me and smiles. "I did make sure my dog wasn't around so that we could finish what we started yesterday. And even if that doesn't happen, I'd love to wake up with you."

I've never had anyone say such things to me. I mean, I'm no virgin, but I sure don't have a lot of experience. The very thought of spending a night with a man—with Graham—makes me warm all over.

"Just pull up to my place," I say. "I'll run in quickly."

Graham laughs. "I can come in and wait."

I shake my head. "No. I don't want to chance us losing track of our night," I say, smiling at him. I think he understands me.

It takes me less than ten minutes to put a bag together. Luckily, I have a travel bag that's always ready, and I add a few outfits. I make sure to get the clothes I borrowed from Graham so I can return them.

When I return to the car, Graham is FaceTiming, so I slide into my seat as quietly as possible.

"Don't let Dad feed him too much," Graham says.

"You're a worrywart," a woman's voice says. "Was that her?" the woman then asks.

Graham slides a look in my direction. "Yes," he says.

"Well, don't be a pain in the ass. Introduce us."

Graham turns the phone toward me, and I see the face of the woman he'd been talking to. I recognize her from the photo he has in his living room, though gently aged twenty years.

"Mom, this is Christina," he says, and the woman smiles as Loki jumps into the picture and she laughs.

"Hello, Christina," his mother says, trying to calm the dog and hold the phone. "He heard your name."

"Hello, Mrs. Crowley. It's nice to meet you."

"Oh, call me Anna," she says as she kisses Loki's head. "I think this is your biggest fan."

Loki barks, and Anna hushes him and shoos him off.

"Graham says the first few days of filming have gone smoothly," Anna says.

"They have," I agree.

"I'm glad to hear it. Well, I should let you kids go. But

Christina, Graham's brother will be in town this weekend, and we're planning dinner on Friday. If your schedule works out, we'd love to have you join us."

I shift a look toward Graham, sure to keep the fear I'm feeling from showing on my face.

"You and Graham discuss it," Anna says. "Honey," she says, and Graham adjusts the phone back to him. "I'll talk to you tomorrow."

"I love you, Mom."

"I love you, too. And Christina," she says, and he shifts the phone again. "It was nice to meet you."

"Likewise."

They say goodbye, and Graham puts his phone into the cupholder. He's grinning, and I wonder what he's thinking.

"Ready to go?" he asks, and I nod.

He pulls from the parking space and heads out to the street.

"Sorry. That was probably an awkward way to meet my mother," he says.

"Not anymore awkward than you being around my mother multiple times and she doesn't even acknowledge you—or me."

He takes my hand. "My mother is still a midwestern woman. She's lived in California now for twenty years, and she's still baking pies and volunteering."

Graham smiles when he speaks of her. What I wouldn't give to have just a little of that.

"And your dad?"

"He's ex-military, so a little tougher. But just a little bit," he chuckles. "When we moved out here, he started as a driver for a service. When he could, he dropped my name here and there." His smile widens. "Remember the Wonder Glow Magic Sounds Keyboard?" he asks.

Now I laugh. "I do. I wanted one so bad."

"They were like ten bucks."

"Yep, and cheap, and silly, and not worth me having in their house," I say and notice that Graham's smile fades. "But, anyway, what about them?"

He takes a moment before the smile returns and he continues. "My dad was driving some exec who had come into town and happened to be talkative. He told him about his son who played Chip, and I got the commercial."

I turn in my seat. "With the girl with the long, red hair?"

Graham looks at me and laughs. "You remember that?"

"Oh, I wanted hair like that. I even asked my mother if we could dye my hair to look like that."

He doesn't say anything but squeezes my hand.

I know what all of this is. He's not the first person to feel sorry for me because of my upbringing. That starts with me. Penny reacts to my parents, too. She hurries around me all the time when they're near, as if to give me all the attention.

Though, I think I just realized that.

I bite down on my lip and turn in my seat to look at Graham. "Glow Stick Pencils!" I nearly shout, and Graham barks out a laugh so loud that even I jump.

"Yes, I was also the Glow Stick Pencil boy," he admits.

Still laughing, I ease back in my seat, our hands still clasped together.

Who knew I'd been so enamored by Graham Crowley for so long?

CHAPTER THIRTY-FOUR

GRAHAM

And the text message from Sandra to Sal reads, "They're dating. Did you know that? They are actually dating. Charles Malloy is going to have a fit. This isn't going to work."

When I'd offered to stay at Christina's house, she said she wanted to stay at my place and not hers because my place has personality.

And while I throw together something for us to eat, I can hear her in the other room playing *Ms. Pac-Man* and laughing to herself.

I rest my hip against the counter and listen to her make those all too familiar sounds when you're fighting ghosts, dots, and the joystick, and I smile.

There is a deep-seated need in me to give Christina as much compassion as possible, because it has become very clear she's never had any—therefore, she never gave any.

But even in the past month, I've seen that change a bit.

I've seen her bring Penny coffee and engage in conversations with her, where before, Penny was just there to be at Christina's beck and call.

She's still laughing as she walks into the kitchen.

"Did the ghosts get the better of you?" I ask.

Christina smiles as she walks to me and wraps her arms around my waist.

I wonder if my face shows my surprise at that. Until this very moment—okay, minus her straddling me—I've made all the moves in this weird relationship.

"I suck at video games," she says with some pride.

"You just need more practice," I say, brushing my hand up into her hair.

"Maybe I do."

She looks at the thrown-together charcuterie board I've put out for us and then back at me.

"That's transportable," she says.

I look at the board. "I suppose it is. Where did you want to go?"

Something shifts in her eyes. They grow dark, and I swear the heat in the room climbs ten degrees.

Christina steps back and picks up the tray. "Milo is out of town?"

All I can do is nod.

She starts down the hallway with the tray. "Are you going to follow me?" she calls back to me.

I look around the kitchen as if it's going to give me answers. Then I pick up the two glasses of wine that I'd poured and head toward my bedroom.

The tray is set on the top of my dresser, but Christina isn't in the room.

I notice that the bathroom door is half open, and the light is on.

"Did you want to watch something?" I ask as I set the glasses on my nightstand.

A moment later, Christina steps out of the bathroom, her hair now pulled up into a bun on the top of her head. Wisps of hair frame her face.

The front of her dress is unbuttoned and opened enough I can see a lacy pink bra peeking out.

She walks toward me, and I'm damn glad I set those glasses down.

She slips her arms around my waist again, and I wrap my arms around her. Our bodies are pressed together, and I realize, even through that make-out session the other night, we weren't pressed together this tightly.

"I want you to know, I was all in the other night," she says softly.

I lift my hand to brush back one of the wisps of hair and tuck it behind her ear. "I don't you want to regret anything," I say. "But I was all in too."

She lifts on her toes and wraps her arms around my neck. "We're not pretending anymore, right?"

My heart is hammering in my chest, and I wonder if she can feel it. "We're not pretending."

"Good. Take me to bed, Crowley. I desperately want to be your girlfriend."

I swallow hard as I let that sink in. This woman has a way of making me feel things I never have, and I don't want to feel them with anyone else—ever.

Lowering my mouth to hers, I hoist Christina to my waist, and her legs wrap around me as her tongue sweeps through my mouth.

There's no way she can't feel my heart, because I can feel hers.

I turn us toward the bed and ease her down beneath me. Christina's hands come to my chest, and she begins to unbutton my shirt with nimble fingers that are eager to touch me.

My hand slides up her thigh, taking her skirt, bunching it up at her hips.

Christina's hands press to my bare chest, and my erection throbs as I press myself between her legs.

"God, Christina," her name come out on a breath. "You're going to kill me."

She grins up at me. "I'm going to make you never forget me."

I chuckle. "I can promise you that I will never forget you."

I press my hand to her warm, wet panties, and her back arches, pushing her against me harder.

"I want to touch you," I say. "I want to explore you."

She shakes her head. "Later."

"Later?"

"I don't want to take our time with this. Not this time. I can't wait," she says, wrapping her legs around me, pulling me tightly to her. "Please, Graham. We have all night—the rest of our lives—to explore."

"You're sure?"

"I've never been more sure," she says, reaching between us and cupping me.

"Oh, yeah," I groan.

We are at each other in that moment. She's pulling my shirt from my body, and I'm pulling those pretty lace panties from her thighs.

Our mouths tangle in a kiss, stealing breath, but giving us life. Christina works my belt and the buttons of my pants, and I lift her dress up and over her head, exposing that pink bra that she'd teased me with.

"Fuck, Christina. You're lovely."

The smile that turns up the corners of her mouth lights in her eyes. "I am?"

"You are," I say, pissed that she questions it. She should know how lovely she is. "Everything about you is lovely."

She lets out a little laugh as she runs her fingers down the length of my back and into the waist of my pants.

I can see it in her eyes. She questions what I've told her. It's hard for her to believe that I would think that—that anyone would think that.

I lower my mouth to her throat and feast on her tender flesh as she claws at my back. She doesn't want to take our time, but I have to know she's ready for this. This changes everything.

"Are you sure you want to do this?" I breathe the words into her ear.

"Yes." The word comes on a sigh.

"It changes everything," I say.

"I want it. I want this. I want it all to change." She moves so that she's looking me right in the eye. "I want you, Graham. I want you."

I stand and step out of my pants, then move to the nightstand, opening the drawer and pull out a condom.

Christina is watching me appreciatively, and for that I'm grateful.

I lay back on the bed and roll on the condom.

"I'm glad we came here," she says. "I don't have any of those at my house." She bites down on her lip.

"I'll always take care of this part. I promise."

Her eyes bat quickly. "Don't think I'm weird, but I've only done this a few times."

I admire that. No one in this town can say that—or at least that's what I'd thought.

"We can wait," I offer.

She shakes her head. "I don't want to wait. I want all of you right now," she says, maneuvering herself until she's straddling me.

"I'll be gentle," I say, gripping her hips as she poises herself right over me.

"You don't have to be," she says.

"I'll always take care of you," I say, because it's in my heart and it's what I feel. "Let me love you, Christina. Let me show you just how special you are."

CHAPTER THIRTY-FIVE

CHRISTINA

And the intern on set posts a picture to Instagram of Graham and Christina kissing in private. "For you naysayers, here's some hard proof. They don't actually hate each other. I guess she's done throwing things at his head."

I hate that I cried, but I did.

Graham pulled me to him and held me. He didn't question me. He just held me.

Wrapped in his arms, I found a comfort I've been searching for. When my tears were dry, we did it again—and again.

The entire night was spent pleasing one another. I've never had a man touch me in such gentle and erotic ways, and he let me explore what it is to pleasure a man I care deeply for.

"You need to go to sleep." His breath is warm in my ear. "We have to be on set in a few hours."

His arms are wrapped around me, and I'm happy. I'm so very happy.

"Jean-Claude is going to kill us when he sees the bags under our eyes," I say softly with a quiet laugh.

"So fucking worth it."

Graham pulls me in tighter, and my eyes close.

I want this to work, I think quietly to myself as I feel my body begin to settle. I want to spend the rest of my life waking up in this man's arms.

~

Flirty smiles pass between us in the kitchen as we drink coffee. Shared soft kisses are irresistible as we get ready together, and this is all new to me. I've never shared a bathroom with a man.

I've never cared for a man like this.

I can't believe I feel this way about Graham Crowley.

"Do you think you can make it to dinner at my parents' house on Friday?" he asks as he sprays on his cologne.

I watch him add his cologne and then look in my bag for my atomizer.

"Are you sure you want to introduce me to your family?"

He moves to me. With his hands on my waist, he eases me against the bathroom counter. "I'm very sure," he says as he moves his lips to my neck. "You're going to love my family, and they're going to love you."

I press my hands to his chest to ease him back. "I'm not under the impression that you didn't say negative things about me to them."

Graham cups my face in his hands. "My family doesn't think that way. My mother is looking forward to getting to meet you. She'll make her own judgements."

"Does she know about the deal we made?"

He shakes his head. "I haven't told anyone. Your parents?"

I shake my head. "I can't tell them anything. I can't even trust my mother with news like that. It would be spread everywhere."

His eyes go sad. I don't want him to feel sorry for me. I do enough of that.

"We should go," I say, turning back to the counter and dropping my atomizer into my bag.

Graham pulls it from my bag and holds it out to me. "Aren't you going to put this on?"

I wrinkle up my nose. "You don't like it."

He lets out a breath, and his shoulders drop. "I'm sorry I said that."

"You wouldn't have said it if it wasn't true."

He takes my arm and sprays the perfume on my skin. "I've learned to appreciate it," he says with a smile.

"Are we making a big mistake with this?"

Graham wraps his arms around me. "No," he says reassuringly. "It was just a strange way to get to this point."

He's not wrong. I certainly didn't think I'd ever be in Graham Crowley's bathroom getting ready for my day after a night of amazing sex.

∽

Jean-Claude certainly is not on board with our relationship. And now that we've taken it to this next level, we can't stand to be apart.

I feel like a teenager, only I get to wake up with Graham next to me each morning.

The makeup team continually has to fix the dark circles under our eyes, or the lipstick that Graham keeps kissing off my lips each time we come back from the trailers.

Usually, I wouldn't want anyone upset with me, or to cause delays, but sneaking away between scenes with Graham has made it all worth it.

The whispers as we walk around hand in hand, or with our arms around one another, have been accompanied by smiles this week. There are often whispers when Graham and I are working, but now that we're together, it feels different—and no one is ducking, assuming a miscellaneous prop will fly through the air.

I know this is some kind of honeymoon phase, but the past few days have been magic, and I don't ever want to lose this feeling.

～

As Graham drives toward his parents' house, I scroll through my phone.

"Someone on set isn't following their contract," I say.

"How's that?"

As he pulls to a stoplight, I turn my phone to show him a picture of us kissing outside of my trailer.

"Interesting," he says, grinning, and then turning his attention back to the light as it turns green. "We certainly want to make sure we pull the blinds closed in my bedroom tonight."

I drop my phone to my lap. "That's not funny."

He's laughing. "It is a bit."

"That's stalking."

"It's not going to happen."

I chew the inside of my cheek. "Maybe we should start staying at my place. I mean, I do have security."

Graham reaches for my hand. "I don't care where my dog and I stay, as long as I continue to wake up with you—every day."

I can't help the smile that forms on my mouth, or the flutter in my chest.

This little publicity stunt is more than Graham getting into one of my dad's movies, or me working with Penelope Mondragon. What's happening between us is life-altering, and I'm afraid I'm falling in love with this man. If there is a crash at the end of all of this, I'm going to be devastated.

CHAPTER THIRTY-SIX

GRAHAM

And the morning news anchor says, "Oh, I had the biggest crush on Chip, the next-door neighbor from *The House on the Corner*. What I wouldn't give to be Christina Malloy!"

When I take Christina's hand to walk to the front door of my parents' house, she's shaking.

"Are you going to be okay?" I ask, lifting her hand to my lips and pressing a kiss to her knuckles.

"I have never gone to meet anyone's parents before."

I grin down at her. "Never?"

Panicked eyes look up at me. "Never. I'm not kidding."

"I thought you'd dated before."

Her tongue darts between her lips before she pulls her bottom lip through her teeth.

"I've never had a relationship like this before."

"I don't know that many have," I tease, but her eyes are pleading now.

"Graham..."

"I'm sorry," I say.

"Any relationships I've ever had were short-lived, or someone I knew, and I knew their family too. Or it was a relationship to just get at my parents."

Her jaw trembles now, and with her words, my stomach flops. Well, shit! Isn't that all I'm doing, really? That's how this started. But she was in on it.

My mind is spinning now. Are we still using each other?

I take both of Christina's hands in mine. "This is different. You know that, right? You and me, we're different."

She nods. "I know."

"So, it's just another first for us. I've met your parents, now you meet mine."

Christina barks out a laugh. "But have you met them? Did they extend you any attention?"

Now I chuckle. "Your father shook my hand."

She rolls her eyes in obvious disgust. "Just don't have a lot of expectations," she says, but she's grinning now. But it makes me think of the meeting I have with her father tomorrow—the secret meeting.

My stomach clenches again. I don't want to keep secrets from her, but what choice do I have?

"Are you going to stand outside all night?" My mother's voice comes from the front door.

I lift my head and smile at her. "We were just trying to decide if we wanted to head to the airport and jump on a plane to Tahiti," I say, and Christina's eyes go wide before she nudges me.

"Seriously, Graham. If you do that and don't take me and your father, what kind of son are you, really?"

I love my mother. She's quick with the wit too.

I can feel Christina ease, and I fold one of her hands into mine, and we walk toward my mother.

"Mom, this is Christina," I say as we approach her.

She holds out her hand to Christina, who takes it, and then my mother wraps her other hand around Christina's.

"It is nice to finally meet you in person," she says. "I've enjoyed your work for years."

"Oh, my. Thank you," Christina says. "And it's wonderful to meet you as well."

"Please tell me this boob is treating you well," my mother says, shooting me a quick glance with a wink before turning her attention back to Christina.

"He's delightful."

My mother lets out a hum. "I've trained him to be a gentleman, so if that ever changes, you just let me know. I'll throw him over my knee."

Christina laughs, and my mother grins in my direction. I shake my head.

"C'mon," my mother says, taking Christina by the hand and leading her into the house. "Graham's father and his brother Brian are out back waiting for us."

My mother shoots me one more smile before she disappears with my girlfriend.

I follow them through the house that I grew up in, and I can see Christina trying to take it all in as my mother walks her through. There are family photos and trinkets mixed with flawless decorating taste.

My mother often considered becoming an interior decorator, but she was dedicated to raising my brother and me, and now taking care of my father in his retirement.

As Christina and my mother step out onto the back porch, my father and my brother both stand, but Loki runs between them and right to Christina.

She sturdies herself to accept the dog's affection.

"Well, we know who he likes best," my father says as Christina stands and Loki saunters over to me.

"Boys, this is Christina, Graham's girlfriend," my mother says, and again it hits me.

This was all supposed to be a scam, and yet, it's not. She might not have been in relationships, but I have been. And this one is different in so many ways. I've never felt for anyone the way I feel for Christina.

I watch as she shakes the hands of my father and brother, and then my brother zones in on me. He moves to me and wraps me in his enormous arms.

"Hey, big bro," he says and laughs at our size difference.

"Showoff," I tease as I hug him with a pat on his back. "You're lookin' a little small around the neck," I say, and Brian laughs.

"Trying to look more like my famous bro."

"Sure you are." I laugh as he steps in. "She's beautiful," he whispers in my ear, and I only nod. She sure is.

I step back from my brother and take Christina's hand again. There's an ease to her now, and that's a credit to my family.

I've been with her and her parents. This ease doesn't exist between them.

***

My mother, the hostess that she is, brings dinner out to the patio. The table was set, wine is poured, and I'm the subject of conversation as they fill Christina in on my past, my strengths, and of course any embarrassing event that ever happened to me.

"It totally paid off to have the older brother who was cute 'ole Chip on TV," Brian says as he takes a bite of his bread. "I was never lacking for female affection." He playfully raises his brows.

My mother shakes her head, but my father is grinning as he cuts his pork chop and takes a bite.

"You're a pig," I say to my brother with a wink.

"Dude, I had to get something out of it. I was going to public school, and you had that hot tutor."

At that point, my mother chokes on her drink.

Brian laughs, and I notice Christina's lips flatten as if she's trying not to smile.

Gesturing with his butter knife, Brian looks at Christina.

"The tutor they had on set for the kids for school—blonde bombshell," he says.

"No one says that anymore. That's reserved for Marilyn Monroe," I argue.

"Dude, she was Marilyn Monroe-esque." Brian gestures with his hands in a wide, grand fashion in front of his chest.

I shake my head. "She was nice."

"She was a size two with DDs," Brian adds.

At that point, my mother grabs Brian's arm, her eyes wide. "Son . . ." she says in a low, calm, yet threatening tone.

It's then that my father clears his throat. "Bombshell," he says to Christina.

I can't help but laugh then, and my mother, who is smiling, shakes her head at the nonsense going around.

"Christina," my mother redirects the conversation. "What about you? Were you tutored on set?"

Christina wipes her mouth with her napkin. "No. I went to private school, but I wasn't working a lot when I was younger. I only did a few commercials and was an extra in a few movies, but nothing that took me away from school except my stint as Annie in a touring company."

My mother's eyes widen. "Annie? Oh, that's one of my favorites."

"Mine too," Christina says.

"Annie," my mother says again, her smile wide as if she's never been prouder to have someone at the table.

My mother takes a sip of her wine and composes herself. She still fangirls from time to time.

"It was a surreal event, Graham getting that part and all of us moving out here." My mother reaches for my hand. "It was the best thing, but there were times when we wondered if it was best for our boys."

"Trust me," I say with my head tilted toward Christina. "They kept me grounded. I had curfews. I had rules. I had chores that didn't pay anything."

My mother slaps my arm playfully. "I didn't want my little boys to be tabloid fodder."

Oh, if only she knew that would backfire so many years later —but in the most fantastic way.

"Yep, I've never done drugs. There are no pictures of me drunk on the Sunset Strip. And I've kept my affairs in order," I tease, but I notice that both my mother and Christina stiffen at that.

"See why I joined the military?" Brian picks up his glass of wine and sips. "I had to move around the globe just to get to have some fun."

That causes my mother to laugh and rest her head on my brother's shoulder.

"Says the man who goes into other countries to help them."

Brian shrugs. "I have to look good, so if my big bro's mug ends up on those tattler shows, and they come after me for a story, we can focus on my humanitarian agenda."

I reach for Christina's hand under the table, and she lifts her eyes to me.

She's smiling and her gaze is light. I'm not a bad guy, and now she knows the influences I've had. These people made it so that I walked the straight and narrow and understood hard work.

My parents are a model couple, and my expectations of love are based on their relationship.

Looking at the beauty who is smiling back at me, I think we could have that kind of relationship. With her hand wrapped in mine, I know that I want to try.

CHAPTER THIRTY-SEVEN

CHRISTINA

And the guy who cleans Sal's office walks through the door to dump the trash. "That Malloy gal is some looker, huh?" he says as he looks at her picture on Sal's wall of actors he represents. "Who wouldn't want to be Graham Crowley right now?"

Sal grunts. "They'll fuck it up."

∼

I don't remember when I've laughed or enjoyed the company of others so much.

Before we left, each member of Graham's family hugged me. I can't even remember the last time my mother hugged me, and I'm not sure my father ever has.

I could have cried when his mother not only hugged me, but she did that little squeeze and rock back and forth thing that I've seen people do, and then she did the same thing to Graham—her own kid. She treated me like she treated her own kid!

I almost cried. How could I not?

I wish I'd never hated him. I see now that his meanness was really playful banter. The angrier I'd get at him, the more he turned it up. Maybe that's how siblings work. That's how he and Brian came across. Brian would jab, Graham would jab back—and they'd laugh. Was I supposed to laugh back then? Was I supposed to one up his Doritos game instead of getting mad?

"What are you thinking?" Graham asks as we drive toward his house, Loki pacing across the backseat ready to go home with us.

"I love your family."

He smiles wide. "I knew you would. There's just no one like my mother. I mean, I hit the jackpot there. And my dad, whew, he's just a great guy. The Marines have reined in my brother," he says and laughs. "Humanitarianism is right, though. If he wasn't a marine, I think he'd be a doctor or a teacher. He just helps people."

The joy of the night bubbles through me, but it creates a deep cut too.

My mother is selfish and a gossip, and uninterested in me.

My father, he's more selfish than my mother. He has an entire apartment in his office. And what that means is he doesn't have to go home—sometimes he didn't—doesn't. It's no wonder that he's been associated with other women. I suppose if I let my mind wander, I'd realize there were more than two women that he'd been involved with.

I swallow hard. The thought makes me sick.

Real marriages are the ones like the Crowleys'.

Graham is made of that kind of stock—I'm not.

I realize I'm going down a dark path when Loki pokes his wet nose into my ear.

Jumping, I turn to look at the dog, who looks so proud of himself, and I realize in that moment, I'm as in love with the dog as I am with the man.

My breath hitches.

I'm in love with Graham. I thought I was before. I mean, the thought had crossed my mind, but after meeting his family, I know it.

I want what his parents have.

Watching the man with his family, it only made him more delicious.

I can't even imagine what came over me and made me turn to him. "I love you," I say.

Graham's eyes go wide, and he shifts a quick look in my direction, and then back to the road.

"Oh, well..."

Shit! I've made a huge mistake. I can't believe I said that.

Sinking into my seat, I wish he'd just take me home, and that's when my phone rings. It's my mother.

For the first time in my life, I'm happy for her distraction.

"Hello, mother," I say, pressing my phone to my ear and letting my gaze settle on the lights outside.

Loki's breath is on the back of my neck, and Graham reaches for my hand.

There is so much going through my head, I'm not sure it won't explode.

I'm listening to my mother go on and on about her pickleball partner canceling on her. There is something about lunch, and tomorrow, and I hear my voice say, "I'll be there. I can be your partner."

She agrees with an "Uh-huh," finishes her story, gives me a time, and hangs up. There is no I love you, or thank you, I'll see you tomorrow, or goodbye. When she was done talking, she hung up.

I lower my phone to my lap, and Graham squeezes my hand.

"Is everything okay?" he asks, as if I hadn't made everything awkward a few minutes ago.

"Yeah," I say, dropping my phone into my purse. "Her pickleball partner dropped out on her. She needs me to play."

"Like in a tournament?"

I shake my head. "For social status."

"Oh," he says, but I hear the confusion in it.

It doesn't matter, and there is no need to go on with the conversation further.

Graham pulls into his driveway and parks his car in front of the garage. "The garage door is sticking again. I'm going to open the door and then park in the garage. Do you want to take Loki into the backyard?"

Loki is pacing the back seat and then barks. He knows he's home, and he's ready to run.

"Yeah, I'll take him," I say, just needing to get out of the car and get some air.

I open my door and step out into the driveway as Graham gets Loki's leash on him.

I walk around the car and take Loki's leash. He's pulling against me, but Graham is standing here looking down at me. His face is shadowed by the lights on the garage behind him.

"Is everything okay? You seem out of sorts," he says.

Did he miss what I said in the car? Did I not say it?

"I'm fine. Fine," I say, and I step around him and walk toward the back gate with Loki leading me.

Once we're in the back yard, and the gate is closed, I take off Loki's leash and let him run free in his own space. I can hear Graham opening the garage door, and that's when the first tear rolls over my cheek.

I pull my phone from my purse and text Penny.

I hate to do this to you. I need a ride. Can you pick me up at Graham's?

I'm surprised when she texts me back immediately.

I happen to be a mile from his house. I'll be right over.

I thank her, drop my phone back into my purse, and wipe my eyes.

The gate opens and Graham walks through.

Loki rushes to him and he bends over the dog and kisses his head.

I clutch my purse close to my chest.

"What's going on?" Graham asks walking toward me.

"Penny is coming to pick me up. I'm going to have her take me home. All my pickleball gear is there."

He nods slowly. "Are you playing tonight?"

"No. I just think I should go."

The sound of a horn in the street has me stiffening. She wasn't kidding. She was close by.

Graham reaches for my hand. "Don't go."

"I think I need to."

"Did I do something?" he asks.

I bat my eyes to ward off the tears that threaten. "I need some space."

I can hear him inhale in the dark yard. "Christina, I lo—"

Pressing my fingers to his lips, I shake my head. I can't hear him say the words.

CHAPTER THIRTY-EIGHT

GRAHAM

And the entertainment report during the evening news didn't mention Christina and Graham, but the reporter said, "Olivia Chase is rumored to be seeing a man who is a decade her junior. The A-lister is also known to be a bit of a party girl and hard to work with. That seems to be the norm, but who would want to invest in a movie that she stars in if she's that much trouble?"

Coffee isn't cutting it this morning. I'm sure that I was awake all night long, tossing and turning.

I texted Christina to make sure she'd gotten home okay, and she replied that she had. But the texts I sent after that went unread and unanswered.

I didn't expect that she'd leave after we got home last night. I didn't expect her to tell me she loved me, either.

With my elbows on the counter, I rest my head in my hands. What did I do? How did I screw this up?

Loki nudges me with his nose. Even he's not very happy this

morning. "Did I do something wrong?" I ask him, but those eyes looking up at me make me even sadder.

Okay, so the night was overwhelming for her. I have to remember that. Something triggered her between leaving my parents' house and coming home. She blurted out the words *I love you* and then everything fell apart.

I wonder if she's ever told anyone that before. And by anyone, I wonder if her family ever said those words to her.

Rubbing my hand over my chin, I realize I need to shave. I have to meet Christina's father at his club, and I can't even tell her what I'm doing.

Sandra turned in the nondisclosure document they'd asked for.

For the first time in a very long time, I don't feel in control. Even when this whole scam started, I knew that I could make or break it. There was some control there. But now, I can't focus on anything but Christina. And I'm going to have to withhold this information from her. Hopefully it won't be for long.

~

Pulling up to the club, my stomach tightens and my chest aches. Just the selection of cars that are valeted around the drive makes me realize that I'm still a kid from Ohio.

The valet hurries to my car and pulls open the door after I put it into park.

"Hello, sir," the man says.

"Hi. I'm meeting Mr. Malloy here," I say.

"I think he's right inside, in the lounge."

I stand just outside the building, take off my sunglasses, and draw in a deep breath. This meeting is everything I've ever wanted. Charles Malloy waits inside for me. Romances, though they got me here, will soon be a thing of the past.

This is it.

I hook my sunglasses on the front of my shirt, push back my shoulders, and walk into the club.

Eyes scan over me as I walk to the lounge. No one here is starstruck seeing me, but some of the faces I see cause me to be starstruck. I nod silent hellos to those I know in passing, or others whose eyes I've caught.

Just as the valet had said, Charles Malloy is sitting at a corner table in the lounge with a man whom I know to be his assistant.

When his assistant sees me, he nods toward Charles Malloy, who then turns his head and stands.

He doesn't move toward me, instead he stands and waits for me to move to him.

"Mr. Malloy," I hold out my hand to him and he shakes it.

Charles Malloy takes my hand, and he's scanning a look over me, even though his eyes are shielded by dark sunglasses.

"Mr. Crowley. Please have a seat," he says.

I take the empty seat at the table, and Charles Malloy nods to his assistant, whom he hasn't introduced, and the assistant stands and walks to the bar.

"Thank you for meeting me," he says.

"My pleasure, sir."

He eases back in his chair. "How's filming going?"

"We're a week into this project, and it's going well," I say, and he nods slowly.

"Jean-Claude is an idiot," he says flatly. "The man doesn't understand direction. That studio suffers when he works."

I find myself chewing the inside of my cheek to keep from reacting. Sure, Jean-Claude's vision never matches mine, but I'm there to act, not to direct. And he's no fan of me, Christina, or the platform on which we work, but I'm not going to comment on that.

Charles Malloy's assistant returns with two glasses and sets them on the table before he takes his seat.

Charles moves one of them in front of me and takes a sip

from his. "You look like a whisky and Coke kind of guy," he says, and the corner of his mouth curls up as he nods at the drink he's offered.

I pick up the drink, very aware that it's only eleven o'clock in the morning. I take a sip and try not to wince. I'm anything but a whisky and Coke kind of guy.

"Let's get right down to the reason I asked you to meet me here," he says, leaning his forearms on the table. "You've been brought to my attention, and your work is good."

"Thank you, sir."

"I have a new project filming in Italy. It's an action film, and I think you'd fit the bill of the main character."

Every nerve in my body is firing. What I hear is, *you're the next action hero star.*

"I'm honored, sir."

He laces his fingers together. "I assume you read the sample of the script I sent."

Of course I had. I'd read it in my trailer while they were filming Christina's single scenes, and then I tucked it back into my safe.

"I did. It's intriguing."

"Are you interested?" he asks with a rise of his brow that peeks up behind his sunglasses.

The man has some power to send a partial script, have a secret meeting in a public place, and simply ask, *are you interested?*

"I am."

He nods slowly and sits back again, picking up his drink and taking a big sip. "Alister will work with your agent to get you in for a screen test with the other actors," he says, pointing to his assistant, who nods as if he's taken in the information.

"I appreciate it, sir," I say.

"Now," Charles Malloy sits back in his chair and steeples his fingers. "Let's talk about my daughter."

CHAPTER THIRTY-NINE

CHRISTINA

And the caption read, "Awkward family gathering."

My mother is a grown-up toddler. We lost. We lost fair and square, and sure, I'll take some of the blame for that. I'm rusty. I don't play all that often. But my mother—*my mother!*—was more worried about her appearance on the court, so that she nearly got a ball to her face, which started the feud, which ended with the loss.

To say I'm embarrassed is an understatement. I wish I knew where the backdoor to this place was. What if someone sees me with her?

"MaryEllen needs to understand her place," my mother says as we walk through the club. She's not quiet about it either. She wants to be heard, and I want to not be seen. "Oh, look. Your father is here," she says and begins to walk toward the lounge with a pace and gait that I'm not used to seeing her use.

At the same instant that I see who my father is sitting with. Graham lifts his head, and his eyes go wide.

"Sweetheart," my mother says as she sets her hand on my father's shoulder. "I didn't know you'd be here this morning."

He looks up at her, his sunglasses on, and nods. "I had some business to do. You know Graham Crowley?" he asks, and my mother holds her limp hand out to Graham.

Graham stands and shakes her hand. "It's nice to see you again, Mrs. Malloy," he says.

"It's Ella," she says almost curtly. She hates going by my father's last name.

Graham nods and lifts his eyes to mine.

"Good morning, Christina," he says with a smile.

"Good morning," I say, but I don't move toward him. I don't know what to do in this situation.

With his family, it was easy. They accepted us. They sat around a dinner table and smiled when Graham would hold my hand, whisper in my ear, or kiss me gently. His family welcomed us at the door with hugs and kisses and sent us home with the same.

My mother doesn't accept our relationship. Nor would she ever accept any relationship I might be in.

I'm not even sure my father knows about our relationship. He doesn't know anything about me at all.

"Are you dining here?" My father asks my mother.

My mother wrinkles her nose. "Of course not."

"Then we'll see you later." He turns his attention back to Graham, who is looking up at me, lost for what to do or say.

I give him a smile and follow my mother out of the club.

"Why does he do business here? Then it's in everyone's ears," she says as we wait for the valet to pull our cars around. "What are they discussing?"

"I don't know."

She looks up at me, her eyes shielded by a dark pair of Chanel sunglasses.

"You don't know? Don't you and your boyfriend discuss this kind of thing?"

"No, we don't," I say, because I'm equally confused as to what Graham is doing at the club with my father. He didn't mention that he was meeting with my father.

Why didn't he mention it?

There's a lump in my throat that's choking me. A heat rises through me, and I feel dizzy. I press my fingertips to my forehead and draw in a deep breath.

He's getting what he signed up for. No doubt my father is talking to him about a movie deal.

I grip my purse to me tighter. If he's getting his movie, then what we have is over, right? That was the deal.

And since he didn't stand up and move to me, hug me, or kiss me, there's something wrong. I told that asshole that I loved him, and in the presence of my father, he couldn't even show affection to me.

What did I expect when I agreed that this wasn't just some scam anymore? I'd give anything to be part of the Crowley family, but the same will not hold true for anyone wanting to be part of my family. I'm stuck in this hell by myself for the rest of my life. I'll never find a man who doesn't just want to use me to get to my father, but who won't stay to be part of my family.

My mother's hand on my arm has me sharply turning, and I realize I'm nearly hyperventilating.

"What's gotten into you? Is it that man?" my mother says.

"No," I spit out the word. "It's not the man. The man is fine. His name is Graham, and wouldn't it be nice if you remembered that," I say as my car is pulled into the drive and parked.

Without another word to my mother, I walk toward the car, tip the valet, because God knows that my mother probably won't, and I head home.

Home, where nothing is expected of me, and nothing waits for me.

I'm bent over in down dog when my phone dings. Sweat drips on my mat as I ignore the text. When it dings three more times, I finally look at it.

I'm outside. Let me in?
Christina?
Sweetheart, can I come in?
Please?

They're all texts from Graham.

Picking up my towel, I wipe at my face as I stand and hurry to the door. When I open it, I can see him out at the gate on the street.

I don't have any idea what he's doing here, but I'm going to venture to guess he's here to tell me that this little thing we're pretending to have is over because he got what he wanted.

I might as well get it over with.

I buzz him in, and he hurries toward me. There is an urgency in his eyes.

He grabs my arms and moves me back into my condo, but a moment later, he's kicking the door closed and pushing me up against it.

His mouth is on my mouth.

His body is pressed firm against mine.

I lift my arms around his neck, and he hoists me to his waist. My legs wrap around him as he presses me to the door harder.

When we need air, we break apart, and his lips move down my throat, which only makes it harder for me to breathe.

When he reaches the swells of my breasts in my tank top with his lips, I let my head fall back against the door.

Graham moves us from the door and carries me down the hallway to my bedroom, his mouth back on mine, my legs still wrapped around him.

When his legs hit the bed, he lays me down on it. His fingers move right to the waistband of my pants, and he pulls them from my body.

I wrap my legs around him again to pull him down to me, but he shakes his head and begins to unbutton his pants.

This sexy silence makes me forget all of the things that were filling my head earlier.

Graham is here, and as he eases his pants down, he kneels in front of me, between my legs. The moment I feel his tongue lap at me, my body goes pliant to him.

I love this man. Whatever I'd been thinking before, I was wrong. I love him.

CHAPTER FORTY

GRAHAM

And the psychic lays down the tarot card in front of Ella Malloy. "There is about to be great loss."

"I'm going to lose something?"

The psychic lays down another card. "Great loss for someone in your life. Your daughter maybe."

"Oh, she has nothing to lose. She's fine."

There is a fine line between savage and gentle, and I can't seem to find it.

With her taste on my tongue and her sweet moans in my ear, I might just explode.

I finish kicking out of my pants and open the drawer to her nightstand for a condom. I know they're there because I put them there. Since the moment we tumbled into this physical relationship, we haven't kept our hands off one another, and last night was the first night we've spent apart.

It's not the sex. It's the connection.

But I've made sure that that connection has protection—in

our bedrooms, trailers, cars, her purse, my wallet. You can't be too safe.

Handing Christina the condom, she tears it open as I rid myself of the rest of my clothing. She hands it to me, and as I sheath myself, she pulls the sports bra she's wearing up and over her head.

Those dark eyes look up at me, and the flush of passion is pink in her cheeks. She told me she loved me. Women tell me that all the time, but this one—I believe her.

As I ease inside of her, and she arches beneath me, I have to push away the conflict that's tearing me up inside.

This thing between us was never supposed to be more than a sham, but it's more. It's full of feeling. It became physical. It became personal.

Christina pulls me tightly against her. Her breath pants in my ear. Her skin is slick beneath mine. Her heart beats so hard I can feel it in time with my own.

Fingernails claw into my back.

My fingers grip her tender skin as we move together.

Simultaneously we spill over, that sensitive quake of nerves shaking us both.

I collapse against her, and she wraps herself around me. I can feel the need from her. She's holding on for dear life as if she knows what's eventually coming.

I press my lips to her ear. "I love you, Christina. I love you," I say, because she can't stop me from saying it now. "I love you."

Her arms wrap even tighter around me, holding me in place against her. I can feel her move beneath me, but I'm afraid it's the quake of tears that has her shaking.

Easing back, I look down at her, but she turns her head.

I roll to the side of her and reach for the edge of the comforter to bring up and around us. The air is cool on damp skin.

When I look down, I see the streaks of tears on her cheeks, and I wipe them away with my thumb.

"Did I hurt you?" I ask, because that might kill me if I did.

"No," her voice is soft.

"What happened?"

"You said you love me," she says, her breath hitching.

I can't help but smile down at her. "I do."

"No one—no one—has ever said that to me."

Swallowing hard, I take in what that means. She's not saying that a man or a lover neglected those words. She's telling me that no one has ever told her they love her.

Fuck!

"Christina—"

She presses her fingers to my lips. "You said it. It'll stay with me forever," she says, as if she knows what's coming our way.

∼

After eating lunch, some frozen meal in Christina's freezer, and a shower that started an afternoon that landed us back in her bed, we decided to drive back to my place and get Loki. I swear this damn dog loves this woman as much as I do.

We drive up to Griffith Park to take Loki for a walk.

I'll never admit to Christina that I'm hoping someone will post pictures of us, and my dog, looking happy and in love. I want that narrative to continue. I want her father to see that we are happy, and this won't get in the way.

"Are you going to ask me about this morning?" I finally ask Christina as we walk the trail.

"No," she says, her head lifted as she takes in the view of the city below us.

"Maybe we should talk about it."

Christina stops and turns to me. "I know what it was. I just hope it's everything you want. But this isn't where we should talk about it." She rises up on her toes and presses a kiss to my lips. "I love you. That's all you need to know," she says as she takes the leash from my hand and starts walking with my dog.

I run my hand over my mouth as I watch her walking.

Charles Malloy has offered me exactly what I want. He has a trilogy of movies with a new action hero, and he wants me as the face of that hero. This is an iconic moment. This is what makes me a legend.

He's offered to buy out my contract at the Love Is in the Air network. We will film through Italy, London, and Paris.

Movie premieres will be worldwide, not just some small theater with a staged red carpet to make it appear bigger.

The money is outrageous.

The opportunities endless.

The caveat is crushing.

The woman, who is now running ahead with my dog right in stride next to her, can't be part of it. Her father added that little tidbit right before she and her mother walked up to us.

I can have my name synonymous with the next greatest role in the history of movies, but I can't have the producer's daughter in my life.

Christina stops and turns back to look at me. Loki barks as if he's calling out to me.

"We have today, Graham," she calls back to me and it rips my heart in two.

I don't know what she knows, but she's an intelligent woman. No matter what her father may or may not have said to her, she knows.

I will break that confidentiality if it means she understands. What I don't know is if I can take this role and lose her.

CHAPTER FORTY-ONE

CHRISTINA

And the Twitter post with a photo of Graham and Christina walking Loki on the trail at Griffith Park says, "That's one hella lucky dog and man to have Christina Malloy to themselves."

Until he tells me it's over, I'm going to hold on as tightly as I can.

Making dinner in his kitchen, music playing, the dog moving in and out between us, and Milo yelling at a game from the other room, I feel comfortable—at home.

As I stir the Alfredo sauce, Graham wraps his arms around me and brushes his lips against my neck.

I close my eyes and absorb the feel. "You know I don't cook. So entrusting me to stir this while you do that is risky," I say on an airy breath.

"I trust you," he says, lifting my shirt just enough to touch the skin on my abdomen.

"Graham..." I lean against him.

"I love you," he whispers in my ear.

"Are you trying to seduce me?"

"Is it working?"

I grin as I turn my head to look at him. "Yes, but this won't keep."

He hums his understanding. "Just know I love you, and that's never something that will go away."

I swallow hard, and Graham moves from me to begin to set the table.

I have to bat my eyes to ward off the tears. His goodbye is going to break me if I let it.

"Shit, that game kicks my ass every time," Milo says as he walks into the kitchen. "That smells good."

"Well, someone is going to have to tell me when to stop stirring," I say.

Milo looks over my shoulder. "Not quite yet," he says.

"Thank you."

Milo kisses me on the cheek, and I catch the look on Graham's face. The sentiment was innocent, and I know he knows that, but it disoriented him.

Milo heads for the backdoor, and Loki follows him.

While stirring, I watch Graham open the wine and set it on the table.

"Are you sure I should still be stirring this?" I ask just to fill the silence.

He walks back over to stand next to me. "I'll get the bowl of pasta and we'll be ready."

Before he moves from me, I reach for his arm with my free hand.

He turns, his eyes searching for something.

"I love you," I say. "Are we okay?"

Graham leans in and presses a kiss to my lips. "Yeah. We're okay."

. . .

Milo convinced Loki to go to his room with him when we all decide to turn in for the night. No doubt he knows something is wrong and that Graham and I need time together.

When I walk out of the bathroom, Graham is sitting up in bed, scrolling through his phone.

I pause in the doorway a moment and take in the sight of him.

One of his long, toned legs peeks out from the sheet he has pulled up to his waist. His face is illuminated by his phone, and the lines of his jaw are sharp.

He hasn't said anything about his meeting with my father, except to ask if we were going to talk about it.

Graham lifts his eyes from his phone, and they settle on me.

"You are beautiful," he says, and his voice washes over me.

"I'm naked."

His mouth curls up into a wide smile, and he lays his phone on the nightstand. "Even better," he says as he holds out his hand to me.

I move to him, easing myself down on the bed next to him. His arms come around me and tuck me under him as his mouth moves over my jaw.

"I'll never tire of having you in my arms," he says, and I bite down on my bottom lip.

"Then never let me go," I whisper before pulling him to me and taking his mouth. I don't want to give him time to think about it, react, or say anything.

∼

I've managed to direct conversations to not include my parents for the past two weeks. As far as I know, Graham hasn't met with my father again, and he hasn't mentioned the movie deal. Perhaps it fell through.

We've spent time with his parents, having dinner at their

house, or the time we had them over to Graham's for a barbecue in the backyard.

Admittedly, there's some jealousy that I'm dealing with. I don't begrudge him having amazing parents. They accept me, and love me—but my parents, we will never have that kind of relationship with them.

I mean, even though he's never mentioned it, I wouldn't put it past my father to have some nondisclosure signed so that Graham can't even talk to me if he talks to my father.

In our downtime, I've had Graham and Milo help me decorate my house so it's warmer. It's a shocking reminder that I don't have friends who I share memories with—therefore there are no photos. And in searching on my phone, there isn't a single family photo that I didn't pull off some entertainment site or that doesn't have my family posing in front of some background promoting one of my father's movies, or an entertainment venue.

Luckily, in the past two months, I've taken a ton of selfies of Graham and myself, and of course, Loki.

Sure, at times those selfies were taken to post for the good of our public relationship, but there are plenty that we took because we love each other.

As I watch Graham and Milo move the sofa in place, after they put down a rug that Milo thought would be perfect for the space, I lift my phone and capture the moment. Maybe I can add this to the photos that I've had printed for frames. I can remember this moment forever.

"I do think this place finally looks warm and inviting," Milo says as Loki curls up on the carpet they just set in place.

"Dude, don't diss my lady's home," Graham says.

"I thought I was complimenting." Milo looks in my direction. "Sorry."

"Don't be. I think you're right," I say.

Graham moves in next to me and wraps his arm around my waist.

"Loki just makes himself at home," he says.

"He is home," I say, hoping that he understands I want him and his dog around.

Milo looks down at this watch. "Are you sticking around?" he asks Graham.

"Yeah."

"I have a date. I have to go," he says, heading for the door.

"Did you forget?" Graham laughs.

"Dude, she just texted me." Milo scrolls through his phone and turns it toward Graham. "Hottie, huh?"

Graham growls. "Maybe you could use a real relationship. She looks like the cocktail waitress who's the wannabe actress."

"Shit, if I wanted something else, I'd have to move towns." Milo looks toward me. "You'll get him home and to work tomorrow?"

I shift my glance up at the man next to me, the one that makes my heart flutter every single time he touches me. "I'll take care of him and his dog."

Milo nods and heads out the door.

Loki lifts his head, as if he's only noticed that one of them left. He looks at us, perhaps making sure we're not leaving too.

"What do you say we go sit out on the patio and have some wine?" Graham says.

"We have to be on set early in the morning. Maybe we should go to bed."

"Not yet. I just want some time with you."

We wrap filming this week. I know we've taken this publicity thing too far and considered it real. But after this week, we won't see each other like we do now—unless this is real.

Why am I questioning it?

Graham takes my hand and laces our fingers together. He leads me through the kitchen and out to the patio.

"Sit. I'll come back with some wine."

I nod and take one of the seats.

I'm shaking now as I listen to him move about the kitchen.

When he returns, he hands me a glass.

"This is champagne," I say, looking up at him, the glow from the kitchen at his back.

"It is," he says. "I'm celebrating."

My chest aches. This is it. This is where he tells me he got the movie. This is where he tells me this thing between us is over. He got what he was waiting for.

Loki walks out onto the patio, brushing past Graham. Pacing a small circle, Loki looks up at me, and then rests his head on my lap.

"He's totally trying to take my spotlight," Graham says, chuckling.

"Why do you say that?" I ask.

He moves toward me and kneels in front of me, just as his dog had.

"Because I wanted to make this moment special."

"Special?" My voice squeaks as I say it.

Graham takes my glass and holds it up to the light cascading from the house. The bubbles float to the top, but it's then I notice something in the bottom of the glass.

"What is that?" I ask.

He offers me a sip of the champagne, and I sip wearily. Then he takes a long sip and laughs.

"I thought this would be more romantic," he says before reaching his fingers into my glass. He pulls the item out of what's left of the champagne and clasps it in his hand. "Now it's just sticky."

"Graham, what are you doing?" I ask, and even Loki lifts his head to study him.

"I hated the idea of us being part of this publicity stunt, but seriously, I couldn't imagine that I'd fall in love with you. I thought the dislike was pretty strong."

I pucker my lips. "Thanks?"

"I mean, I knew how to not like you. I just didn't know I already loved you."

"Graham..."

He sets the glass on the ground next to him and eyes it before looking back up at me.

Graham opens his hand, and my shaking hands move to my mouth.

"Christina, this isn't some stunt anymore. I know what I feel." He holds up the diamond ring that he'd fished out of the glass. "I know they said we didn't have to get married, that we just needed pictures of us in public," he says, laughing. "But I do want you in my life forever. I want you to be my wife. Will you be my wife? Will you marry me?"

My jaw trembles, and my eyes fill with tears. I can't believe this is what he's doing. I've been waiting for him to tell me it's over—to take the role—to walk away.

My breath is stuck in my lungs, and all I can do is nod, because the words won't come out.

Graham slips the sticky ring on my finger and then rises to place his hands on my cheeks.

"Christina Malloy, I love you. I will never stop loving you."

He presses a kiss to my lips.

"I love you too," I manage. "I will always love you."

Loki lets out a howl of approval, and we both pull him in to us.

This is my family. This man and this dog. He chose me.

CHAPTER FORTY-TWO

GRAHAM

And the news anchor laughs as she tosses her hair over her shoulder. "Have you seen the pictures coming off the set at the new Love Is in the Air movie? There seems to be something big and sparkly on Christina Malloy's finger."

Christina sleeps.

Loki snores on a blanket next to the bed.

I'm wide awake considering what it is that I have done.

My arms are wrapped around Christina, and the diamond I put on her finger catches the bit of moonlight coming in the window.

I haven't signed anything with her father but the nondisclosure agreement. We've only talked about the opportunity—well, he talked about the opportunity. I didn't say much in our short meeting.

Charles Malloy told me he wanted me. He told me what would be expected. And only a minute before his wife and daughter walked up on us, he'd told me he'd heard rumors that I was dating his daughter, and that she would not be getting involved with anyone in the industry, and that we wouldn't be having a relationship.

There was no time for me to tell him about the publicity we were gaining from the relationship, or the fact that we were no longer pretending.

And now, we're engaged.

What can Charles Malloy do about it now? Won't this be better? We'll be family now, and I won't have to give up Christina.

I understand it's a gamble. I might have just lost the biggest role of my life—but I'll get the girl.

Christina shifts in my arms and rolls to face me.

"Why are you still awake?" she whispers, her breath warm on my chest.

"Just thinking," I say and then kiss the top of her head.

"Jean-Claude is going to flip."

I run my hand over her hair. "We're almost done with him. Besides, it should be good for this film, don't you think?"

She lets out a low hum. "I don't care. The only thing I care about is that I have you."

I pull her to me a little tighter. That's right. We have each other.

~

Loki is going to the set with us this morning. With only a week left of filming, they're just going to have to deal with him.

As we walk back into the condo, after Loki's morning walk, as the sun comes up, Christina is packing up her day bag.

She smiles at us as we let ourselves into her home. It's comfortable to be in her space now and have the codes to freely come and go through the gates.

"I packed up his blanket," she says, pointing to a bag by the door that leads to the garage. "I thought it might make him more comfortable on set."

I move to her and place a kiss on her cheek. "I love you."

She smiles up at me. "I love you too," she says, resting her hands on my chest.

I notice her hands are bare, and I take hold of her left hand.

"Where is your ring?" I ask.

"I put it in my safe. I don't think wearing it to the set is a good idea."

I shake my head. I need her to wear it. This needs to be the next rumor, even before she tells her parents.

I had the conversation with my parents about proposing a week ago. My mother cried, though she promised they were happy tears. My father shook my hand and pulled me in for a hug, but he didn't say anything.

Milo picked up the ring from the jeweler. With my mother's help, we'd picked out something suitable for Christina, but something she could customize later.

I knew if I walked out of a jewelry store, she'd know about it before I had the chance to pop the question.

Ideally, I would have waited. I've known her for years, and this affection, though it always simmered behind the crude comments, is new. But if I'd waited—well, I'm afraid I would have lost her.

"I have a safe in my trailer. You can leave it in there while we film," I say, lifting her fingers to my lips and kissing them. "I want you to wear it."

The corner of her mouth curls up. "If I wear it, someone will see it."

"I don't have anything to hide," I say.

Her eyes are wide and bright as she considers it before she walks to her bedroom, and a few moments later, returns wearing her ring.

She holds up her hand, and the ring sparkles on her finger.

I take her hand and pull her to me. "I can't wait to marry you," I say.

"I suppose we'll need to talk about that. You know my mother will turn this into a circus."

I chew the inside of my cheek, considering that for the first time. "I'd marry you in a drive through chapel in Vegas."

She laughs easily, and I'll never tire of the sound.

"And wouldn't that be a spectacle of its own?" she says, moving into me and placing a warm kiss on my mouth.

∽

Penny is the first one to notice the ring when she meets Christina at the car to take her bag. She doesn't say anything, but her eyes go as wide as saucers, and she looks at me.

Christina is talking about the day ahead, but as I get Loki's leash on him, I give Penny a smile and a small nod to let her know that what she's thinking is true. The love of my life, Christina Malloy, said she'd marry me.

I don't know who else noticed the ring on our walk from the car to our trailers, where Christina tucked it into my safe, but Jean-Claude has been alerted to the engagement, and the fact that I brought Loki for the day.

He is pacing when Christina and I make it to the set to start filming.

"Are you kidding me?" Jean-Claude shouts, and the entire set grows quiet and stills. "You're engaged now?"

Christina reaches for my hand, and I give hers a squeeze to let her know we're in this together.

"I don't see that there is an issue that should include the entire crew," I say.

Jean-Claude moves to us. His face is red, and his hands are fisted at his side. "You're fucking this up for everyone."

"Anything between me and Christina isn't anyone's business.

If you have a problem, let's take it somewhere private. Your shouting at us is only giving this the attention you don't want us to have."

Jean-Claude's jaw tightens as he looks between us. He leans in toward Christina.

"Your father won't have this," he whispers to Christina.

"It's not my father's decision," she says firmly, and I wonder if everyone in this town knows Charles Malloy's policy on who his daughter can and can't date.

The grip she has on my hand tightens.

"We need to finish this shoot," Jean-Claude says. "This crappy movie isn't going to help any of our careers."

Jean-Claude marches back to his chair, and everyone on set begins to move about, going back to their tasks.

"This isn't about us," I say softly. "He's just unhappy."

"Yeah, but now my father is going to know before I can tell him. I don't know what deals he's made with you, but your involvement with me won't help you."

Her eyes have gone sad. I can't even tell her what her father said to me.

"You're more important than anything your father could offer me," I say.

Christina worries her bottom lip. I don't think she believes me.

"I love you," I say as Jean-Claude calls everyone to get into place. "Don't worry about your father."

She nods, lets go of my hand, and walks onto the set.

I realize I might have fucked this up for both of us—career-wise that is.

I brush my hands over the suit jacket I have on, and I straighten my tie.

We're about to film the scene where our characters go to blows in a corporate meeting after they've been intimate. It's beginning to feel a bit surreal.

CHAPTER FORTY-THREE

CHRISTINA

And the trade paper says, "The new Charles Malloy film might have a surprising new star. Olivia Chase is slated to be the film's leading lady."

～

Every blind in my trailer is closed. Soft ocean sounds come from the speakers, and I'm lying on the couch with a warm compress over my eyes. Graham took Loki for a walk, and I'm trying to relax for a moment.

We've been running that scene most of the day.

The lighting wasn't right.

The sound wasn't right.

I honestly think the director isn't right.

We're almost done with filming, and I have every intention of having Sal work on my behalf so that I never have to work with Jean-Claude St. Paul again.

But the banter between the characters has given me a headache.

This used to be where Graham and I shined the brightest. Any opportunity we had on set to yell at each other and call one another names, we were right at home with that kind of dialogue. But now, it takes work, and it's exhausting.

There is a tapping on the door, and I let out a little moan.

"Christina, it's Penny," the voice calls out.

"Come in," I say reluctantly.

Because it's Penny, I don't move from the couch, or take the compress off my eyes.

"Can I get you anything?" she asks.

"I'm fine. I just needed a few minutes."

"I think it looks good," she says, and that has me moving the compress from my eyes to look at her.

"You're kidding, right?"

"No. I mean it. I think Jean-Claude is just bitter, and he's being an ass."

Penny never talks like that, so it has me sitting up and grinning at her. "You think so?"

"Yes. He's just jealous that Graham is getting attention from your dad, and Jean-Claude can't even get a meeting with him."

I chew on my lip as I take in what she's saying. "Who said Graham was talking to my dad?"

She raises a brow, pulls her phone from her pocket, and scrolls. When she's done, she holds up the phone.

It's a picture of Graham and my father at the club the other day.

"So? They were having a drink. Graham is my boyfriend, and he's with my dad. I saw them there."

"Maybe he was asking if he could propose to you," she says, as if that would explain their meeting.

"I don't suppose so. But Graham hasn't said anything about the meeting."

She crinkles up her nose. "Of course not. He makes everyone sign nondisclosure agreements."

"My father does?"

"Well, yes. He uses them for everything," she says matter-of-factly. "You didn't know that?"

I rub my fingers over the bridge of my nose to ward off the headache that's been festering there.

"You were in that room. You know that the deal was to make everything sweet enough that Graham would get a Charles Malloy movie, and I'd get the Penelope Mondragon opportunity."

She nods. "They also said you just had to pretend, and you didn't have to marry the guy."

That was when my phone began to ring with my mother's tone.

"They want you back on set in twenty," Penny says as she lets herself out of the trailer.

I groan as I pick up my phone and answer.

"Christina Abigail Malloy, don't you dare tell me that you're engaged to that man!" My mother is shouting into the phone. "I see it on some random Instagram post? You have got to be kidding me. Tell me that's not true. Tell me!"

I should have left the ring at home.

"Mother—"

"Seriously, Christina. It's like I don't know who you are."

"First of all, I'm almost thirty years old. I can make my own decisions on who I date."

"You know your father and I have tried to keep you from getting involved with anyone in the industry. This is a horrible idea. He's a horrible man."

I'm not even sure now if she's talking about Graham or my father.

"Graham is an amazing man," I say, figuring that's who I'm defending.

"As if I've ever heard you say something nice about him."

Lesson learned. Never talk poorly about any of your coworkers. You never know when you might fall head over heels in love with them.

"Things change," I remind her.

"Your reputation—"

"Won't be hurt by loving Graham Crowley," I say.

"But you're not engaged, right? That's a misunderstanding."

I purse my lips and realize I need to cut this conversation short and get to makeup.

"Mother, I need to—"

"Christina! Answer me, dammit."

"Yes!" I shout it out. "Yes, we're getting married," I say, and then wince that I did so in such a way.

"Oh, no, you're not."

"Oh, yes, I am. And I'm old enough that it doesn't matter what you say, or Dad says. I get to make these decisions on my own."

"And what about our reputations?"

How in the hell is this woman my mother?

"Are you kidding me? Dad's done enough damage to both of your reputations. Me marrying a man that I love isn't going to do that."

"I hope to hell you're alone when you're talking to me like this," she scolds.

All my life, I've been the dutiful daughter. I show up to openings and premieres. I was raised by nannies and caretakers and shipped off to private schools.

I've mostly stayed out of the tabloids, and honestly, even now that I'm in them, it's nothing shameful. I haven't hurt anyone, or myself. I'm not drunk, stoned, and out spending Daddy's money. I work. And I'm proud of my work.

And I'm in love with a man who loves me back.

"I need to get back on set, Mother," I say, gathering my binder and heading toward the door.

"Your father is going to be furious."

"Then he can take it up with me. It's not going to change anything."

Again, she hangs up without even a goodbye.

The other day, Graham's mother called me to invite me to lunch. When the conversation was over, she said she loved me, and when I hung up, I'd cried. I think the fact that Graham comes from great people only makes me want to marry him more.

As I walk toward the makeup trailer, I notice Graham walking toward his trailer with his manager, Sandra. There is an ache in my chest.

I want to be a part of anything he's doing going forward. Will I get that chance? How do we make this work?

CHAPTER FORTY-FOUR

GRAHAM

And the post on Instagram said, "Sebastian Yates is Penelope Mondragon's newest crush when it comes to her characters. Who would be the perfect match?"

"This is the most asinine thing I've ever seen you do," Sandra isn't holding back. "You don't go and fucking propose to her. This was for publicity. Where did you get it in your head to propose?"

Her cheeks are red and the cigarette she lit in my trailer is nearly gone because she's taken such long drags from it. I don't know how the woman hasn't choked.

Loki has tucked himself in the back room on my bed, and I can't blame him.

"You need to break it off," she says before snuffing the cigarette out on the inside of a coffee mug by the sink.

"I don't need to," I argue back. "I love her. And no matter how this started, this is how it's ending."

"You're fucking up your career!" she shouts again. "Charles

Malloy wants you in this film. Olivia Chase!" She throws out the name and my stomach tightens.

"If he wants me in the film, then he'll have to do it as my father-in-law. And I couldn't give two shits about Olivia Chase."

Sandra lifts her hands in the air. "Christina Malloy is disposable."

That has me coming to my feet. "She's not. And I won't have you or her father talk about her like that. Christina is so much more than just a trinket to be danced around in front of a crowd for her parents' amusement."

I run my fingers through my hair, fully aware that they're going to have to fix that before we begin filming again.

"You know, there are thousands of producers with big budgets. There are thousands more action scripts that I could read and produce my damn self. If he won't have me, well, fuck him," I shout.

"You've been working since you were fourteen. Do you want to give that all up?"

"You seriously think that some ensemble actor is worried he won't ever work again because he married his co-star? Shit, Sandra, this is how legends are made. I have six more of these movies contracted. I have a fan event next month. These people want me. If I don't get a fucking Charles Malloy film because I'm head over heels in love with his daughter, then I don't need it."

She shakes her head. "I can't believe we're even having this conversation."

Sandra picks up her bag and hikes it up on her shoulders. "Charles Malloy wants an answer by Friday. I'll have the contracts in my office. If you want this, you lose her."

"You're the one that put us together," I remind her.

"So that you could get this. You have it. Cut her loose."

"I'll let him know my decision by Friday."

Sandra closes her eyes and takes in a deep breath. "Don't give it all up for her, Graham. No woman is worth it."

. . .

I'm still jittery from my conversation when I leave hair and makeup. I don't understand the need for Christina and I to have acted on that stupid rumor and create some publicity stunt if it can't work in the end. But then again, without the publicity stunt, we wouldn't have each other. And without the publicity stunt, I wouldn't have the opportunity to star in one of the biggest movies Charles Malloy ever produced.

I almost choke myself with my tie as I straighten it while walking to the set.

As I walk on set, I notice someone else is sitting in Christina's chair. A woman with a notepad, and she's writing things down.

Christina is running a scene with Justin Cartwright, who happens to play her assistant in this movie, but has been her love interest in the movies in which I'm not.

There's a playfulness between them, and for the first time ever, it gnaws at me. When we were on set together, we'd say snide things and throw things at each other. Where in the hell did a rumor start that we were a couple? Watching her interact with Justin, and how easy she is with him, it would have made more sense to have them put together as a couple.

I wince at my own thoughts.

It's my ring she'll wear home. She's my fiancée.

Christina notices me from the corner of her eye and turns her bright smile in my direction. She says something to Justin, but heads toward me. This is proof I can let these negative thoughts go.

She moves to me, rises on her toes, and kisses me. "Did you see who's here?" she asks with a giddy giggle as she adjusts my tie, which I must have messed up on my walk.

"No. Who?"

She moves her eyes in the direction of her chair and the woman who is sitting in it. I study the woman for a moment.

"Is that Penelope Mondragon?" I ask.

The corners of Christina's mouth turn up into an even wider smile. She maneuvers us so we are facing the other way.

"She's watching me and taking notes. She introduced herself and told me that she's writing a screenplay for me. For me," she emphasizes.

"Honey, that's wonderful."

"It is. I mean, that's all that's been said. I haven't heard anything else, but . . ." Christina draws in a breath, places her hands on my chest, and looks up into my eyes. "I'm going to get what I wanted. You're going to get what you wanted. And we're going to get each other. Who would have thought this was how this would all play out?"

"Who would have thought?" I repeat her sentiment, but without the same excitement.

"Let's get ready, people," Jean-Claude shouts and Christina steps back.

"We're almost through this scene," she says.

"Almost."

"I'm going to take a moment and work up hating you," she says with a wink. "I have to make it seem real now, don't I?"

I nod and she walks away.

I suppose I could tell her that her father will only give me the movie if I dump her. That surely would make her loathe me again, wouldn't it?

Justin moves in beside me and crosses his arms in front of him as he watches the crew assemble. "Everything okay?"

"Sure."

"You and Christina seem happy. I didn't think there'd be a day when she didn't throw something at you," he says with a laugh.

"Things change."

"You saw Penelope Mondragon was here?" he asks quietly.

"Yeah. I saw."

"Sebastian Yates," he says the name, and it has me turning to look at him. "Mondragon is writing it for Christina and Sebastian Yates," he clarifies.

I swallow hard. Sebastian Yates has stature like Brad Pitt or George Clooney. He's got to be at least twenty-years older than Christina, too. Fuck!

I hate all of this. I get what I want. She gets what she wants. We lose each other—and she gets paired with Sebastian Yates.

"Let's shoot this," Jean-Claude yells.

I'd rather take my fiancée and run for the hills.

CHAPTER FORTY-FIVE

CHRISTINA

And the trade magazine says, "Charles Malloy has an eye for talent. There is no actor who wouldn't want to do a movie he chooses to produce."

When Jean-Claude was satisfied, or tired of the scene, he walked off set, and that was that.

At this point, I have called Graham an idiot more than I ever had when I didn't like him.

We've been in one another's faces all day, yelling and threatening. My character pushes his character. They throw papers off a desk and scream some more.

My throat is becoming raw, and the angry line that forms between my brows has deepened.

I haven't seen Graham since he walked off the set when we were done. No doubt he needed a few moments to decompress too.

Penny and I walk back to my trailer. I just want to get out of wardrobe and into my clothes.

As soon as I'm changed and have handed Penny my items that need to go back to wardrobe, my phone rings. It's not a ring tone I hear very often—it's my father's.

When Penny has left the trailer, I finally answer his call.

"Hello, Daddy," I say, leaning against the counter and rubbing my fingers over my forehead.

"I have a car waiting for you at the studio."

"I came with Graham this morning," I say, not sure why he would send a car for me.

"The car is there. You'll come to see me, and you'll come alone."

I chew on my bottom lip. "We just wrapped, and I'd really like to—"

"Christina, you will get in that car and come see me in my office. I don't have time for any of your antics. Just do as I say," he says and ends the call.

I don't understand why my parents can't freaking finish a phone call. Is it so hard to say goodbye?

I grip my phone in my hand. I want to throw it. I want to chuck it at the wall, but I won't.

He's probably heard that Graham and I are engaged. This is where the shit hits the fan, and instead of talking to us as a couple, he's going to reprimand me in private. Lovely.

Fine. I'm almost thirty years old. I can handle my father.

As I step out of my trailer, Graham and Loki are walking toward me.

I don't suppose I'll ever tire of seeing the man and his dog.

"Tough day, huh?" he says as if he's completely defeated.

"Yeah. Wasn't so pleasant."

Graham nods. "Are you ready to go?"

I hike my bag up on my shoulder. "My dad just called. He has a car waiting for me. He wants me to meet him to talk."

Graham winces. "About the engagement?"

"I can only assume."

"I'll go with you," he offers, and the sentiment squeezes at my heart.

I move to him and wrap my arms around him. His body is stiff as he wraps his free arm around me.

"I'm okay. I'll go and talk to him. I'll have his driver take me back to your place," I say before lifting on my toes to kiss him softly on the lips.

"I love you. Deep inside, I feel as if you need to hear that over and over from me to know it's true."

I ease back slightly. "I know you love me. I have your ring," I say, holding up my hand and wiggling my fingers at him.

"I'll be waiting for you," he says as Loki brushes up against my leg. "He'll be waiting for you too."

I kneel and give Loki a hug around his neck. "I'll see you soon, boy."

When I stand and look at Graham, I see something I haven't seen in the few months we've been spending so much time together. There is deep seated worry in his eyes, and I wonder if there is something behind this meeting with my father that Graham knows about.

No, I don't want to start second guessing my fiancé.

I'm my own woman. If I want to marry this man, then I'm going to marry him. There is nothing my father can say that'll change that.

∽

I'm irritated that it's seven o'clock at night, and my father is having me meet him in his office. Seriously? He couldn't let me just go to their house and hear what he has to say?

Is he keeping this from my mother?

Is this business?

There is a security guard poised at the entrance to the building when the driver opens my car door.

I don't even thank him as I step out and walk toward the building.

When the guard opens the door, I move past him and right to the elevator that will take me directly to the top floor, where my father keeps his office.

As the elevator door opens, I step into the grand entry. *CHARLES MALLOY PRODUCTIONS* greets me in grand gold letters that hover over a waterfall wall.

Just like his sunglasses being worn inside, this screams attention-getting, and I've never liked it.

My father opens the large glass door that leads into the offices.

"Christina," he says in a low voice. His eyes are narrowed on me.

"Dad," I say and step through the door.

Without another word, he walks toward his office, and I follow.

There are a few people still in the office, and that makes me sad too. Is there so much that has to be done that he has employees still working into the night?

Why I even consider that, I don't know. I know he has people working all the time. The man has always been all about business. Family didn't matter.

When we reach his office, he moves behind his desk.

"Close the door," he says as he sits down.

I do so and look around.

The walls of his office are lined with photos of him and hundreds of A-list actors and actresses. There are news clippings that have been framed, some movie posters, and a cabinet of awards that I know don't mean a damn thing to him.

What there isn't is a family picture on the wall or on his desk. Even Graham has family pictures in his home. His parents have walls of photos of them all. My father has an office that showcases the names he can drop, but not one photo of his daughter or his wife.

There is a door to the side of his desk that leads to the apartment he keeps. I wonder why he won't take me, his daughter, in there to discuss whatever he has to talk to me about.

I twist the ring on my finger with my thumb and then fist my hand. What I wouldn't give for my parents to be excited about what's coming in my life.

"Sit," he says, pointing to the chair in front of his desk.

I take the seat, cross my legs, and rest my hands on my knees —ring on display.

He looks at my hand and then up at me.

"Penelope Mondragon has a new project with Sebastian Yates," he says.

I study him as he clasps his hands on the top of his desk. No mention of the ring on my finger. No mention of me being engaged to Graham. Does he not know?

"Okay," I say. "And?"

"She wrote the script with you and Sebastian in mind. He's already signed on."

There is a flutter in my stomach when he mentions the script. Penelope hadn't mentioned that she had anyone else in mind, or that the script was ready to go.

"I thought she was still writing the script. I talked to her today."

He nods. "She's still working on the final." He pushes a script in my direction.

Cheers to the Happy Couple, a screenplay by Penelope Mondragon.

I reach for it and notice that when I lift it, my hands are shaking.

This is it. This was what it was all about. Won't Graham be so happy to know I got my promise too?

I thumb through the first few pages and then flip to the very front where she's added a synopsis.

My father leans back in his chair and watches me with his arms crossed in front of him.

This movie is everything I could ever have imagined it might be. It screams cult favored rom-com. If I do this movie, I'll be among the rom-com royalty that I've dreamed of.

I know better than to get giddy over it or to show my excitement.

Keeping my smile inward, I slide the script back toward my father.

"She's magical," I say. "I think this is going to be an amazing film." I study him for a moment. "Why do you have it?"

My father sits forward, resting his forearms on his desk again. "I'm producing it."

I blink hard and the smile surfaces. My father is producing the movie. Does this mean he believes in me? He wants me to have what I've always wanted?

"It's a rom-com," I say, but there's still a hint of excitement in my voice.

"And was written for my little girl."

I don't even know how to react at this moment. I could jump across the desk and hug him, but then how would he react? I mean, he called me his *little girl.*

Instead, I just smile at him.

"What do you think? Are you in? Do you want to sign?" he asks.

Now the excitement breaks through. "Yes!"

He nods and slides another stack of papers in front of me.

This is about to change my entire life.

Before I can pick up the contract and put my name in ink, he lays his hand on the top of it.

"There are some caveats to this," he says. "Let me see your left hand."

CHAPTER FORTY-SIX

GRAHAM

And the Ella Malloy Spa manager adds a note to the schedule, "Olivia Chase and Graham Crowley are coming in for a couple's massage. Is this under the right name?"

I took Loki for a run. When Milo got home, we hit the gym. By ten o'clock, I had begun pacing the house, and by midnight, I decide to call Christina to see why she hasn't arrived.

My call goes unanswered.

Loki is standing right next to me. I have the feeling he's worried about her too. Maybe I should head over to her house and check on her. She was probably exhausted from today and just headed home. I know I'm exhausted. I don't remember fight scenes between us taking so much energy.

Just as I decide to grab my keys and head out, my phone rings.

"Hey, are you okay?" I answer quickly having seen her name pop up on the ID.

"Yes," she says, but it's curt and quick.

"Why didn't you come over? I was just heading to you," I say, moving to the bowl by the door to get my keys.

"No. Don't. I don't want you to," she says, but the words are choked. "I'm fine. I'm going to bed."

"Christina, is everything okay?"

"Fine," she says, but again, it's laced with something dark.

"I'm coming over," I say with Loki on my heels as I start for the door.

"You will not," she shouts through the phone. "I don't want you here."

"Honey—"

"Just don't," she shouts again. "I have to go."

"Wait," I shout back. "C'mon, what's going on?"

"Goodbye, Graham," she says, and the line goes silent.

I stand there with my trusty dog, keys in hand, looking down at my phone. What in the hell just happened?

I can't let it go like that, so I text her. *Just tell me you're okay and safe.*

A few moments later, I get a text back. *I'm fine. Goodnight.*

I stare down at the screen on my phone. "Well, I guess we'd better just go to bed. I'm not thinking her evening went well."

Loki turns his head up to me and lets out a whine. He's feeling this as a loss too.

I run my hand over his head to give each of us some calm. I turn off the lights and we head to bed.

~

Loki and I are at the set early. I'm hoping to find Christina before we get started. I have to know what happened last night after her meeting with her father.

Instead, I have Jean-Claude headed my way. His lips are pursed. His eyes are narrowed. His fists are tight at his side.

When I see him eyeing my dog, I manage Loki behind me a

bit. He's a docile dog, but if this man comes at me with fists, I can't guarantee my dog won't attack.

"I told you not to fuck this up!" He shouts at me, and I wonder what it is that I've done to have everyone angry with me. "We have three more days of shooting!"

I hold up a hand to ward him off.

"I have no idea what you're talking about."

He snorts out a laugh. "Get your shit together," he says through gritted teeth as he passes by me.

My jaw is tight, and my heart is racing now. Instead of heading toward my trailer, I start for Christina's.

As we approach, Penny steps out of the trailer, and her eyes go wide.

"Hi, Graham," she says, her eyes moving between me and the trailer. "I was just headed out to find you."

"Where is she?"

Penny purses her lips, but she doesn't answer.

"Penny, I need to talk to her."

She winces at that. "She says she'll be on set on time."

"Is she here?"

Again, Penny's mouth tightens before she hands me a manila envelope. "She wants you to have this."

I take the envelope and look back at her. "What is this?"

"I need to go," she says, turns, and hurries off.

There's a throbbing in my head, and I look up at Christina's trailer. I don't know if she's in there or not, but she's made it quite clear that I'm not welcome.

"C'mon, boy. Let's get settled."

We turn to walk toward my trailer when I see Sandra hurrying my way.

She's the only person who has smiled at me.

"Good morning, handsome," she says before she hands me a cup of coffee in a Styrofoam cup, and then takes a sip of the one she has in her other hand. "I looked at the call board. You're not even expected for another two hours, but I figured you'd be here." She shifts a look at Loki. "He's friendly, right?"

"Sure," I say, but I'm not sure what realm I woke up in this morning. He might turn on me too.

"What's that?" She nods to the envelope in my hand.

"I have no idea."

Her smile widens. "I think I know. C'mon, let's go inside and chat."

There is nothing I want less, but I follow her back to my trailer. As she steps inside, I see the door to Christina's trailer open. Both Christina and Penelope Mondragon step out, and Sebastian Yates follows.

What the actual fuck?

"Graham, let's talk. I have more meetings," Sandra says.

I watch Christina walk away with Sebastian Yates close behind her. I'm sick—physically sick.

"What are Penelope and Sebastian doing here?" I ask as I smell the scent of Sandra's cigarette lighting.

"They're talking business, just as we are."

I turn to her. "I didn't agree to anything yet. I have a few days left."

"And why didn't you sign to begin with?"

"You know why. I can't sign if I'm attached to Christina. Her father was very clear. I get the movie if I break up with Christina."

Sandra leans up against the counter and takes a long drag from her cigarette. Loki pulls against the leash, so I take it off, and he hurries to the back, into the bedroom where I know he'll hide until she's gone.

"He told you to break up, so you proposed?"

"I don't want to lose her. It shouldn't be either/or," I argue.

"What's in the envelope, Graham?" She nods and I wonder how much of this she already knows.

I pick up the envelope and drop the contents on the table. A packet of papers slides out, and then something bounces on the table and into the bench seat. When I go after it, tears immediately fill my eyes.

I pick up Christina's engagement ring and hold it in my fingers.

"What the fuck is this?" I ask, raising my eyes to Sandra.

The corner of her mouth curls up. "It's her decision," she says, and in that moment, I know Sandra is part of this. "Christina signed to do the Penelope Mondragon movie."

I bat my eyes. "Same clause?"

"Of course. Her father is producing it."

I narrow my gaze at her. "Her father is producing it? He doesn't believe in the genre. Why is he—"

"Really, Graham? He's a control freak. If you want that part, then you accept this. She has."

I shake my head. I don't buy this. This isn't how this ends.

CHAPTER FORTY-SEVEN

CHRISTINA

And the fortune cookie read, "One bad chapter doesn't mean your story is over."

~

I should have waited three more days, but my father had wanted an answer.

There is a buzz on the studio lot and especially around the set. I'm sick. Every part of me hurts—but mostly my heart.

Graham deserves the movie my father offered him, and the only way he'll get that is if I let him be a free man. I hate that my father has the ability to make or break him as an actor who is easy to work with. My father might not be able to squash Graham's entire career, but I'm not willing to be the reason that might happen.

I love him too much to take this away from him.

When I watched him and Loki stop and talk to Penny, and then walk into his trailer with Sandra, everything inside of me broke. He has his ring now. He has the script and the contract. And the lucky son-of-a-bitch has his dog to comfort him.

I have Penelope Mondragon, and that's all I had wanted before that stupid rumor started that put me and Graham into one another's path.

Sebastian touches my shoulder. "Are you doing okay?" he asks because he's a decent guy.

"I'll be fine. Just a lot going on right now," I say, and he nods.

"I've never had something come together so quickly, have you?"

The corner of his mouth is turned up, and the excitement of this opportunity radiates through him.

Sebastian Yates is famous not only for his amazing looks, but for his kindness and humanitarianism. Much like Graham's brother, he's just an amazing human.

As an actor, Sebastian is synonymous with rom-coms, action films, and dramas. The man can do anything. The fact that he's giddy to be working with Penelope too, well, I can't help but feel a little of his excitement. Though, I lose everything else to have it.

I lose the man I truly love.

Sebastian's eyes widen on me, and I realize I haven't answered his question. "No. You're right. This was a very quick process."

"I can't wait to get started. I guess I'll see you around soon," he says, taking my hand and giving it a squeeze in a gesture of friendship, even though I've only met the man a few times.

Graham and I only have one more scene to shoot together. The rest of the scenes are without one another. I only wish this had all come down after we had wrapped.

I nearly scream when someone grabs my hand and yanks me toward them.

It's Graham, and he's pulling me away from the set and down the same hallway where he told me he had feelings for me.

When he lets go of me, he runs his hands over his hair and paces a tiny circle in front of me, obviously collecting his thoughts.

"What in the hell, Christina?" He scrunches up his face, and I notice he has my ring on his pinky. "I mean, what the actual fuck?"

"You don't have to talk to me like that," I say, on the verge of crumpling onto the floor in a pool of tears.

"At least I'm talking to you." He moves in closer. "Do you want to tell me what's going on?"

I bat my eyes up at him. "It's over, Graham. This was stupid."

"This is real." His voice has softened and I'm going to choke trying not to cry.

"It was a rumor that got out of control. We were using it to get what we wanted. Well, we got that. You have the movie my father offered, and I got a Penelope Mondragon movie. We should be happy."

He bats his eyes, and I can see that they've gone moist. "Christina, I proposed because I want you, too. I love you."

I swallow hard, sure that the lump in my throat is going to strangle me. "But do you really? I mean, you get a three-movie deal, and Olivia Chase."

Her name burns on my tongue.

"Screw all of that. I want you."

I shake my head. It would be so easy to fall into his arms and walk off into the sunset, but that's not the right thing to do. He needs this. He wanted this. He deserves this. I can't be what stands in his way.

"Graham, we know this was all a mistake. We got wrapped up in it. You're free to do all the big things you want to do."

He shakes his head. "This is your father talking. What did he make you do?"

God, I have to spin this so he takes the role. I read the script, and if he doesn't take it, he'll regret it for the rest of his life—I'll regret that I held him back.

"He didn't make me do anything."

"Bullshit. I'd only get the role if I wasn't dating you. So now that he's producing the Mondragon movie, he made you the same deal, right? Right?" His jaw ticks. "Because none of this shit makes sense, considering that they wanted us to play this up to get this far."

Composing myself is getting harder. "I want this," is all I can say, but it's bitter on my tongue.

Graham shakes his head. "He's holding you back, just like he always does."

"How can you say that when we're both getting what we were promised?"

"Things changed."

I'm going to pass out if I don't breathe!

"Graham, we're not meant to be. Look at your life and look at mine. It was never going to work."

He twists the ring on his pinky. "You're wrong. God, you're so wrong. If you really think that I did all of this for this role—" He scrubs his hands over his face. "This is what you want? You want to have the movie that was promised and walk away from us?"

"We were a rumor."

"I don't believe that and neither do you," he's shouting now. "I didn't peg you to be so selfish."

My jaw goes slack. "Me?"

"Yes. I'd give this all up to be with you, and here you are, giving it all up to be with Sebastian Yates!"

The tears are dry now, and my hands come to Graham's chest, and I shove him back. "This has nothing to do with Sebastian, and you know it."

"He's already walking out of your trailer."

"Are you kidding me with that? So was Penelope. At least I haven't slept with my co-star. I'll bet you'll be super cozy on set."

Now his eyes go wide. "What in the hell are you talking about?"

The set behind us has grown quiet. This was a mistake, but I'm in it now.

"I saw how she talked to you and clung to you at the awards.

C'mon, I'm not stupid. I was raised in this town. Only women who know what you can offer them act like she did."

"You've lost your fucking mind!" he shouts. "God, I really thought that I was the bigger asshole. But you proved me wrong."

He moves past me, and I can't even help myself when I turn and say, "Where are you going?"

"What the fuck do you care? But just so you know, I have a movie to finish so I can go be some big action star, because my fiancée just dumped me. Maybe I'll go get drunk and stoned too. Oh, and if Olivia Chase is free . . ." he shouts, and now I can see everyone's eyes on us. Shit!

Only because I see Penny sprinting toward me, I don't fall against the wall and slide to the floor in a heap of tears.

She wraps an arm around me and leads me into a small office, away from prying eyes.

Shit!

Shit!

Shit!

CHAPTER FORTY-EIGHT

GRAHAM

And the woman peering out of the makeup trailer snaps a picture on her phone and texts it to her sister. "Something is going down on the set. I think they broke up."

I can't fucking believe it. This is total bullshit!

I'm screwed no matter what I do. If I take the role, I lose Christina. If I don't take the role, and keep Christina, I don't get any other roles.

But I guess she's made our decision.

I walk back to my trailer and lock the door. Loki rubs up against me, and I flinch. I don't even want his comfort right now.

The contract is sitting on the table, right where I left it.

A Charles Malloy film will set me up for a long career.

A movie with Olivia Chase, who is hands-down one of the hottest names in the industry to be associated with, even if she's the biggest bitch I've ever met, won't hurt my box office totals.

Having my contract with the Love Is in the Air network bought out, well, it'll hurt. I enjoy this job.

But above all else, I thought what Christina and I had was real. Who would have known it would be her that thought so little of it? Then again, what does she know of commitment and love? She's never had anyone love her like I love her—loved her.

Fuck!

I pick up a pen and sign my name to the contract. What's done is done.

Move over aging action stars, there's a new man in town, and he just gave up everything to share in the stardom.

I throw the pen back down on the table, walk to the back of the trailer, and drop down on my bed. Loki jumps up and moves in next to me.

He's going to miss her too.

~

Our last scene together is a nightmare. Not only that, it's a sweet and soft scene.

The universe hates me.

The number of people surrounding the set has increased. No doubt, they're all there to see if we can handle this, because as I found out while I was walking to set, our breakup is already front and center on the news.

I take my mark and I can see Christina, her back turned, taking hers.

Jean-Claude is already beside himself with irritation at the entire mess we're in.

Sandra is here, and so is Sal. They're not here unless there's reason to defuse a situation—and I suppose that's what they're expecting.

Well, they won't get it on my end.

I'm going to be professional.

Though, I'm sure most of this is because of how I handled the conversation earlier, and not so privately.

Penny is chewing on the side of her thumb and clutching a notebook to her chest.

"Let's get this over with," Jean-Claude says, and everyone gets into place.

Christina turns around, and I wonder how we're ever going to shoot this scene. Her eyes are red. I can see her entire body shaking.

This isn't what she wants.

It's not what I want.

What's done is done.

"Take your marks," Jean-Claude shouts and the extras get into place, and so do Christina and me.

She won't lift her eyes to me.

I can't breathe.

They roll. They set the marker. Jean-Claude yells, "Action!"

At that moment, Christina lifts her eyes to mine. She's not even in there. This is all Yvette.

"I can't be your business partner," Yvette says to William. "I can't see you every day and know that we have a history."

I swallow and take the choreographed step toward her.

"Then I quit," I say, hoping that I'm portraying William, because I feel this line resonate through me.

"You can't quit. The investors—"

William interrupts Yvette's words by stepping in, pulling her to him, and gazing down at her before he presses a soft kiss to her lips.

"It's all or nothing, Yvette. But I want it all—I want you."

I watch as her throat works, and I know that Christina has broken through for just a moment. Then her eyes change.

"You want me?"

"More than any promotion or job title. I love you," I say, and William is long gone. This is me talking.

"What if—"

"No, what ifs. I love you. You're all that I want."

Christina's tongue runs over her lips, and I'm shocked Jean-Claude hasn't yelled cut yet.

"I love you," she whispers, and it twists in my gut. That's for William, not for me.

"Marry me," William says, and I feel as if I added a bite to the words. I can't say them without feeling as if I'd been punched.

"But what about the contract?" she asks, and I realize how much this movie is mirroring our lives.

"To hell with it."

Yvette smiles at William, lifts on her toes and wraps her arms around his neck. "Yes! Yes, I'll marry you. I love you so much," she says.

Christina presses her mouth to mine, and this is no longer acting. She trembles under me, and I hold on for dear life.

This is goodbye, no matter how many times we have to do this scene—she's saying goodbye to me.

"Cut!" Jean-Claude yells, and Christina eases back, sadness swimming in her eyes.

She doesn't say anything else.

Much like we did on other projects, she kisses me and then walks away.

I stand there, still on my mark, waiting to start over.

"That was good!" Jean-Claude yells.

I turn to him. "One take?"

"It's perfect."

"You didn't get all the angles."

He narrows his eyes at me. "I got what we need. Let's move on, people."

I look back at Christina, who is walking away with Sal and Penny.

That was it. That was the last time I'll ever act with her.

That was our last kiss.

I suppose being an action hero will be a challenge, but at the end of the day, I get to blow things up and punch people. And right at this moment, I feel as if that's warranted.

~

Loki keeps pacing by the front door. I suppose this is why people don't introduce those they date to their children, if they have them. They get attached.

"She's not coming," I say to him for the tenth time in an hour. "Give up."

Loki whines and walks back to me, resting his head on my lap.

"I can't fix it. It's too late."

I run my hand over his head, and he looks up at me with those eyes that made me bring him home in the first place.

"It's for the better," I say, but it hurts. "She's getting her chance, and she'd never have gotten it any other way."

Saying the words out loud makes me understand what happened just a little bit more.

She had to do what was best for her, and I get that. Without this movie, Christina will be stuck at the network for the rest of her life. And though I know she enjoys it, she needs something bigger. She deserves to be the starlet she is.

"Dax Brown, huh?" Milo walks up the back stairs and into the living room, plopping down in the chair.

I study him. Dax Brown is the name of the character I've signed to portray. "Who have you been talking to?" I ask.

He shrugs. "No one. It's on that entertainment network's feed on Instagram." He looks down at his phone. "Graham Crowley has signed on to be Dax Brown in Charles Malloy's next movie opposite Olivia Chase as Francesca Cross."

I blow out a breath. That hadn't taken but a hot minute to become news.

"This comes on the heels of Crowley's public breakup with

Christina Malloy, the producer's daughter," he continues, and I wish he'd have stopped with just the announcement.

Milo lowers his phone. "Parents got involved, huh?"

I snort. "You could say that."

"You could always see her on the side," he says, and I smile at his optimism.

"Christina made her decision. She broke it off."

He nods. "Proposing didn't fix it, huh?"

Who was I fooling in thinking it would? Even Milo saw right through it.

CHAPTER FORTY-NINE

CHRISTINA

Five Months Later

And the entertainment news announced that an A-list actor had donated money to a charity. No one mentioned Christina and Graham anymore.

The warmer hues of my bedroom make it cozy, and harder to get out of bed. As I look around, I still can't believe I'd lived here as long as I did without it being homey. I guess I didn't know what homey looked like until I'd met Graham.

Dolly, my yellow lab, which I got as soon as we wrapped the last Love Is in the Air movie, moves to the side of my bed and rests her head next to mine.

"You're ready to go out, huh?" I ask, raising my hand to rub between her ears.

She's been my savior, and I often wonder how Loki is. I'm sure he's on set with Graham.

But wouldn't it be nice to get them together for a playdate?

I sit up, push back the covers, and drop my legs off the side of the bed. I haven't opened the drapes yet, and the room is still dark.

Dolly makes me get up every morning, and not wallow in my own pity—which I do often.

It's been five months since I've seen Graham and Loki, and I miss them both.

I have it under good authority that Graham is in Italy with my father. For some reason, instead of just throwing money at a project, my father seems to be very invested in that film with time, too.

I've stayed away from TV or news shows, because I know there have been pictures of Graham and Olivia on the beach together. I want to think they're staged, but so was our relationship—so was ours.

Dolly paces the bedroom as I pull on my yoga pants and a sweatshirt, then slip my feet into a pair of shoes before I take her outside.

The air is crisp as I let Dolly out into the yard, but it feels good on my skin. I think I'll take Dolly to the dog park. I have the need to be around people, which is a new feeling, too. Though, since I've had Dolly, I find I'm more comfortable going out alone. Maybe she's my protector.

After I get ready, and have my morning coffee and protein shake, Dolly and I head out just as my mother calls.

I've been very selective of the times in which I take her calls. I've also been standoffish and cold, she tells me, but I'm still in recovery mode.

I haven't spoken to my father at all.

"Good morning, Mother. How are you?" I say as Dolly and I walk toward the dog park a few blocks away.

"I'm achy," she whines. "It's cold out."

I sip my coffee from my travel mug and think about how easy it would be to stay in bed, and before Dolly, I would have. My mother is right. It's cold out, but there is no excuse.

"It's not so bad. Dolly and I are out walking."

She tsks me. "I don't know why you have that dog. Really, Christina..."

She doesn't even finish with the reasons she's so against it. But Dolly is my family now. Everyone else got taken from me—no, I gave it up so Graham could have exactly what he wanted—what he deserved.

"We need to go to Miami. I have a grand opening next week and—"

"Mother, I'm in the midst of filming. I won't be going to Miami," I say with great pride and a bit of bite. I no longer need to be paraded around as her shiny object that keeps her grounded.

"You know, since you dated that man, you've had a mouth on you."

I grin as we turn the corner to the dog park. "Well, you might imagine I have some hurt feelings. But Dolly and I are at the dog park. We're going to run now."

"Christina—" she calls out.

"I'll talk to you later. Bye," I say, which is more than she would say to me.

As soon as we are in the fenced area, I take Dolly's leash off her, and she runs off. Even she's made some friends at this park.

But it's then I see a black lab running toward me.

I brace myself, but he comes right up to me, pauses, and then lifts his head.

"Loki?" I say, and that's when he jumps up on me.

I hug him as if he is a long-lost person I haven't seen in ages. "Hey, pal," I say as Dolly comes back to investigate.

"Dolly, this is my friend Loki," I say as the two dogs sniff one another.

But then I realize Loki didn't come alone. My heart begins to pound in my chest and my breath is labored. I look around, but I don't see Graham anywhere. Nor do I see Milo.

"Loki!" a woman's voice calls to him, and I turn to see Graham's mother running toward us. "I'm so sorry. He just got away from me, and—" she pauses. "Christina?"

I can't help the smile that forms on my mouth. Thank God I have on dark sunglasses. My eyes have welled with tears.

"Hello, Mrs. Crowley."

"Anna," she corrects me as if things hadn't gone horribly wrong between me and her son. Then, when I stand, she pulls me in for a hug.

She eases back, her hands on my arms, and she looks me over. "Milo is out of town, so we're dog sitting," she says as Loki and Dolly decide to take off. "It looks like they've become friends. Or did you have him before?"

"Her, but no. I've only had her a few months. Her name is Dolly."

"She's beautiful," she says, watching the two new friends chase one another around the park. "Do you have time to sit a moment?"

I've missed this. I've missed her.

In the few short months that Graham and I were a couple, she was kind and enthusiastic about what was to come for us. And even now, she's still kind.

"I do," I say and Anna nods to an empty bench.

We walk to the bench and sit down.

She laughs as Loki and Dolly walk side by side, as if maybe they're having a conversation too.

"I'm glad we came down here today," she says. "The dog park by our house has a few unruly dogs. Loki isn't a fan."

"We come to this one often," I say. "It's close to our condo."

She nods and then turns to look at me. "How have you been?"

Do I tell her I'm in therapy because I miss her son so much? Do I tell her that I haven't spoken to my father since I signed on to do the Penelope Mondragon film, because what he expected wasn't fair? Do I ask her if the news is right, and Graham moved on with Olivia Chase?

"I'm doing good. We started filming last week. The good part is it's mostly all being filmed here on the lot. We'll go to Minnesota next month and do some outdoor shots in the snow."

"Penelope Mondragon is a genius," she says. "She writes a lot like Nora Ephron did in the eighties."

My smile widens. "Very true. I'm in an elite group of women doing amazingly written rom-com."

"I'm so proud of you," she says, resting her hand atop mine.

Well, shit! Now I am going to cry.

My mother, or father, have never—*never!*—said that to me.

Loki and Dolly walk back to us, and each of them rests their head on my lap. The tears are gone, and I set my coffee mug on the bench, and lean in to love on both of them, before they decide to run off and play again.

"Fast friends," Anna says, watching the dogs take off.

She lifts her phone and takes a picture of them, and I swear they pose for her.

A moment later my phone pings, and when I look down, she's sent me the picture.

"I have him all week. Maybe we can meet up tomorrow so they can play," she offers.

"I would love that. I have to be to set by ten."

"Seven-thirty?"

"We'll be here."

CHAPTER FIFTY

GRAHAM

And the interoffice email in Sandra's office read, "We will answer no more questions to the press about Graham and his relationships outside of his current movie."

Action hero work is grueling.

I'm in the best shape of my life. I was in training the moment I signed on. There's been weightlifting, cardio, weapons training, and strict dieting. This has been my life for five months.

Italy is beautiful.

The beaches are different than they are in California.

The food, so much better.

And the countryside—it's glorious to wake up to each morning.

But, when I wake up, I'm always alone. No dog. No Christina. No hope.

We've been filming since six o'clock this morning, and now I'm off to the trailer full of gym equipment to work with my trainer for two hours. Then, it's back to filming.

Olivia has been a bear on this film, and I'm sure that the director and Charles Malloy are second guessing their choice in using her.

She's lazy.

She drinks too much.

She goes out and parties with the locals, and I'm seriously not too sure of the ages of the men she keeps company with. That's always been a trait of hers. Men much too old or much too young.

Yesterday, we had to cut filming short because she was so stoned, she could hardly keep her eyes open. The physical aspect of this movie is grueling, but the emotional aspect of having to keep up with Olivia's drama, that's exhausting.

But, when the film is done, it's going to be a masterpiece. That is, if we ever get through it.

As I walk into the gym trailer, my phone pings with my mother's text sound.

I look down to see that she's sent a picture.

Loki made a new friend at the park today. Her name is Dolly.

The picture has me grinning. I miss that dog. I can't wait to get home to him.

They look happy, I text back, grateful to have seen this today.

Her owner and I sat and chatted quite a bit. We're going to meet up again tomorrow.

Leave it to my dog to make even my mother a new friend.

Before I can text again, my mother sends another photo. I stop my advancement into the trailer. My trainer watches me.

There on my screen is a picture of Dolly, Loki, and Christina. She's kneeling, and loving on both the dogs.

"Are you ready? They called down and gave me a timeframe in which to get you back," my trainer says.

I chew my bottom lip. No, I'm not ready. My world was just rocked.

Olivia is so out of it that me screwing up all my lines is overlooked. I can't focus. My mother and my dog are spending time with Christina, and here I am filming a movie I sold my soul for, and I hate it. I hate every minute of it.

"One more time, folks," the director cries out from his position next to the camera.

I draw in a deep breath and look toward Olivia.

She's sewn into some dress, half ripped and half singed. I'm in a torn tuxedo, and the only part about this that I glean any enjoyment from is that someone told me I look like James Bond. I don't even care which James Bond. I'll take the compliment.

We both are harnessed to a crane that will lift us up. The ocean is our backdrop.

The scene is one where a car speeds by spraying bullets, and I grab Olivia, and we jump off the bridge. They'll add the car later, but they have a huge fan that blows dust up at us as if the car is speeding past. Our stunt doubles will be the ones jumping off the bridge and landing in the water.

The director yells, "Action!" and Olivia grabs my hand. A moment later, the fan blows at us, dust clouds my vision as I scoop her up with one arm around her waist, and we jump over the bridge.

The scene is cut, and we dangle from our harnesses. Only Olivia, who usually pushes away from me, is still pressed against me. My arm holds her in place, but her head has dropped back.

"Olivia?" I say, and I realize the weight of her against my arm as I hold her. "Olivia!"

I lift my hand to her chest. She's not breathing.

Shit!

"Get us down! Get us down, now!" I shout.

"It'll take two minutes to reset. Hold on. We'll—"

"She's not breathing!" I scream down, over the noise of the fan, to the crew below us.

I keep shaking her, but there is no response. I can't hold her and do CPR on her while we hang in the air.

I lift her head and cradle it, so it doesn't fall back again. Just as I decide to try and blow air into her mouth, they begin to lower us back to the bridge. I can hear an ambulance coming close. There's always one just on the edge of the set for when someone gets hurt, but this isn't what I'd have expected.

As soon as our feet hit the ground, I wrap both of my arms around Olivia to hold her up. Her body is limp.

The paramedics move in, along with the stunt coordinators and technicians, to get her unhooked and laid on the ground. One paramedic is bagging her, and another begins to do CPR. My knees have gone weak. The blood is draining from my head. The only thing keeping me upright is this fucking harness.

An assistant walks up next to me and hands me a bottle of water.

"Drink this," she says, signaling to another stunt coordinator to remove my harness.

When I'm freed, she takes my arm and eases me to the ground. "Are you okay?" she asks.

I blink hard. "I'm fine. She just went limp," I say with a shaky voice.

The assistant sits on the ground next to me and we both watch as they move Olivia onto a gurney, the paramedic still doing compressions on her.

It's all a blur as they load her into the ambulance and speed away.

The entire crew is silent. The set is still. No one knows if Olivia Chase is dead or alive.

Eventually, people start to move about, but it's as if they're all in slow motion.

"Why don't you go back to your trailer and rest. I'll come get you when we have some news or know what we're going to do," the assistant that came to my rescue says.

I nod, and then stand. My legs are still shaky, so I take a moment before moving.

The trailer is just beyond where we're working, but it seems as if it's taken me an hour to just walk toward it.

Did she die up there with my arm wrapped around her?

What did I do?

No, I didn't do anything. I can't go putting blame on myself. Olivia has a solid reputation for drinking and doing drugs. No doubt that played into it.

My phone dings the moment I step into my trailer. It's sitting on the table right where I left it.

It's a text from Sandra. *This looks cozy,* she says and sends a picture of me holding Olivia close up on the wire.

Fuck! This is such bullshit that this kind of stuff goes on and all the sudden there is an instant rumor. I'm done with rumors.

I start texting back, but I stop. I'm not going to say anything until I know what happened. I'm not going to feed this rumor mill.

Instead, I call my mother. And when she answers, I start sobbing.

CHAPTER FIFTY-ONE

CHRISTINA

And the note from Penelope Mondragon to Sal said, "Christina Malloy is gold! I'm already working on another script for her. What are the chances of getting Graham Crowley to commit, do you think?"

∼

Sebastian eases back from me. His hand is still on my cheek and my lips tingle from whatever lip plumper he used before he kissed me.

"I love you," he says before kissing me again. "Don't ever forget me."

"Cut!" The director moves toward us, a grin on his lips. "You two are box office gold. Do you know that?"

I smile as Sebastian eases away from me.

"I don't know if I was feeling it. Tell me what you want. I can do it again," Sebastian says, and the director shakes his head.

"We got this one," he says and moves on.

"Did you think it was good?" Sebastian asks me, and this is the norm, I have found out.

"I think it was great."

"Good," he nods. He stands from where we are seated on a bench and walks away.

I shake my head. There is no confidence in this guy, and it makes me chuckle. Sebastian Yates, with his gorgeous face and his to-die-for physique, has no confidence.

I think of how different he is from Graham. Graham was all confidence, and wasn't that what had turned me off him to begin with? He was so sure of himself that I had found him arrogant and annoying.

He's been on my mind a lot the past week, especially since I've spent time with his mother and Loki at the dog park, and then we went to lunch on Saturday.

Anna says Graham is excited about the film, but he's homesick. I'm sure he misses his dog.

Penny walks toward me with Dolly at her side. I have to admit, I had selfish reasons for getting Dolly, but she brings joy to Penny, too. And to Loki, I consider. They're friends now.

Penny hands me a bottle of water.

"That was really good," she says, but she's twisting her lips.

"Was it, really? It felt like I was watching a train wreck."

A laugh escapes before she clamps down on her bottom lip with her teeth.

That causes me to laugh, and Penny sits down next to me as Dolly lays at my feet.

Penny looks down at her phone and then hands it to me. "I assume you've seen this?"

She shows me a photo of Olivia and Graham dangling in one another's arms between takes.

"I saw it," I say, trying to keep my voice light, but it shakes. "My mother shared the photo and the news about how close they are."

A line forms between Penny's brows. "Is that the only place you get your information? From your mom?"

"Mostly. She loves to gossip."

Penny looks back down at her phone. "They just put out the press release this morning. Olivia Chase overdosed and went into cardiac arrest while they were filming. He's not holding her intimately. He's holding her because she went limp on the wire."

I blink hard and look at her. "She overdosed?"

"They had to do CPR on her and everything."

"Did she die?"

"Well, yeah, if you consider they had to do CPR on her to get her back. But she's alive. She survived."

Now my heart is racing, and I wonder why my mother hadn't had that bit of news to share? Surely, she got it from some gossip show and not my father directly.

I tighten my jaw.

"I'm sure that was devastating for them all," I say, and Penny nods.

"Looks like they'll have to shut down production. I'm not sure they'll want her back on set."

"I'll bet that will hit my father right in the pocket."

Penny's eyes go wide when I say that, but she doesn't respond. I don't wish Olivia Chase any ill will that she doesn't bring onto herself. But that stupid movie cost me everything. And here I am, living my dream, and Sebastian Yates is a lot of work to be around. I'm supposed to be swooning over him, and to be honest, when he kisses me, he hums out a count of how long the kiss should be.

It's had me pondering the kisses Graham and I shared back when I didn't like him. Even though they were staged kisses, and he'd eaten an entire bag of Doritos to irritate me, my knees went weak when he'd kiss me.

I swallow hard.

"There's a new fan event coming up, too, and they want you to be on a panel, do a meet and greet, and sign," Penny says, looking at the schedule on her phone.

I nod. I'm already cast in the next Love Is in the Air movie, which will start as soon as we wrap on this Penelope Mondragon movie. Justin Cartwright will be my love interest, and though we are friends and enjoy one another, I just don't think we have the same chemistry as Graham and I had.

But those days are over.

Graham's contract was bought out by my father. He won't be back to the Love Is in the Air network. He's an action hero now, just as he'd wanted to be.

I hear a phone chime with a text, and Penny pulls my phone from her pocket and hands it to me.

I look down at the screen. There's a picture of Loki, but it's not a number I have in my phone. *Any chance you're going to the dog park today?*

Who is this? I respond, looking at the photo, but there is nothing that distinguishes where it was taken.

Sorry. It's Milo. I grin down at the phone, and I know Penny is watching me. *Anna said you'd been meeting up at the park with your dog. I think Loki would like to see his friend.*

"You're smiling a lot," Penny says, and I show her the picture of Graham's dog. "Is that Graham texting you?"

I shake my head. "No. Mutual friend. How much longer do you think we'll be today?"

Penny looks at the iPad she carries and at the call sheet on her screen. "I think you should be done around six."

If all goes right, I could be there by seven. They have lights at the park, so it won't be dark.

Milo sends back a laughing emoji. *We'll meet you there then. Just text if something comes up.*

There's a lightness in my chest that hasn't been there for months. Dolly stands and rests her head in my lap. "I knew you'd bring joy to everyone you met," I say as I run my hand over her head. "What do you and Loki have going on?"

CHAPTER FIFTY-TWO

GRAHAM

And the Instagram feed is filled with pictures of Graham Crowley holding Olivia Chase against him midair. "If Graham Crowley held me that close, I'd faint too," says @GrahamCrowleyFanGurl102.

Jet lag is real. I've been trying to sleep it off for two days.

Production shut down when Olivia overdosed. We'd only been filming for a month. It's up in the air whether we wait her out of detox, go on without her, or they can the whole thing.

What it means is I'm currently contracted, yet not employed. I'm getting a paycheck, but I'm not doing any work.

I'm drained.

Dragging my ass out of bed, I start for the living room, and Loki comes right to my side. He's been very kind to not jump up on me. It's as if he can read my weariness.

I owe Milo big time for taking care of him for me while I was in Italy. Even the past few days that I've been home, Milo's taken him to the dog park.

He never mentions it, but I wonder if he ever sees Christina there. I know he goes at night and my mom was meeting her there in the mornings. But there are hundreds of dog parks. It doesn't mean he goes to the same one my mother did.

I plop down on the couch, and Loki climbs up to sit with me. "So, you've been seeing my girl behind my back, huh?" I ask him as I rub his head. "How is she? Just as beautiful as ever?"

Loki lifts his head as if in a nod and I laugh.

"Or is her girl your new girlfriend? Are you using Christina?"

He lets out a bark, and I laugh harder. I swear he's the smartest dog on the planet.

When I hear the back door open, I turn to see Milo walking in. Looking at my watch, I realize I've slept the entire day away.

"You look like shit," he says.

"I feel like it. Jet lag is no joke," I say as he sits down, and Loki jumps off the couch and walks to Milo. Such a traitor.

"Dude, I just got here," he says to Loki, running his hand over Loki's head. "I suppose you want to go for a walk, huh?"

"I can take him. I should get out of the house for a bit."

Milo chews his bottom lip. "It's no problem, really. I just need to change."

I eye him coolly. "So, you *want* to take him?"

"It's just been our thing."

"I'm home now. He's my dog. I'll take him."

Milo sits on the couch opposite me and leans forward, resting his forearms on his knees. "Shit, man. We kinda have a date."

Now I sit back and study him. "Son of a bitch, you're using my dog to get you a woman." I laugh, but his expression hasn't changed.

"Not really," he says and sits back. "It's his date."

I look at Loki, who is looking at Milo as if he can't wait any longer to get out of the house.

"Oh, my god. You've been spending time with Christina?" My voice is filled with accusation, and my chest squeezes. "Are you seeing Christina?"

"Whoa," he blows out the word, holding his hands up in surrender. "I said the date was his, not mine."

I have to process that. Rubbing my fingers over my forehead, I rub away the ache that is building there.

"You've been going to the dog park so that Loki can see Dolly?"

"Yeah," he says. "That and your mom thought Christina could really use a friend. She's not doing so well," he says, and I consider that.

I swallow hard. She shouldn't need a friend. She should have had me the entire time, even if I was in Italy and she was still here working. We should have been together.

Not being with her, seeing her, touching her—it's left a hole in me for the past five months. And with what Milo has said, I assume the same goes for her, too.

I know she pushed me away, thinking I used her, but that was never my intent, even though we both got what we wanted. Though my prize didn't end up being that at all. Instead, I lost what I wanted, only to get something else entirely, and it was a waste of time.

"I guess you shouldn't keep her waiting then," I say as I stand to walk back to my room.

"Hey, man." Milo stands, and Loki looks between us. "You should take him. She'll be there at seven."

I shake my head. "She won't want to see me."

He shrugs and tucks his hands into his front pockets. "I wouldn't go so far as to say that."

"Why's that?"

A smile forms on his mouth. "You know she doesn't speak to her father?"

"So?"

"So, she doesn't know that you're home. She doesn't know anything other than Olivia Chase overdosed and your movie is on hold."

"I'm not understanding," I say, but that could be the lack of oxygen to my brain at this point.

"I've been meeting her every day for the past week. She's loving the movie she's working on, but more than once, she's made a comment that Sebastian Yates isn't as talented as she thought he would be. And, in a sincere moment, she said that even when she hated you, you still made her knees go weak when you kissed her."

My lips twitch wanting to smile. "Why were you having a sincere moment with her?"

"Christ, man. We're friends. Like I said, she needs a friend."

"Then you should go be that friend."

He shakes his head. "She needs a friend," he restates. "But what she needs more than that is *you*."

"Me?"

"Yeah. She misses you. She wanted you to have everything you deserved."

I lean my hands on the back of the chair. "You're telling me that's why she called everything off?"

"That's exactly what I'm telling you."

I let out a little laugh. "Are you telling me that in a week, you've grown so close that she would disclose that to you?"

He throws up his hands. "You're an asshole, you know. I've been her friend for months while the two of you tried to figure out what the hell you were doing."

"What does that mean?"

"It means I know that relationship started as a fucking rumor, and it grew into something real. I was here, remember? I heard you talk about her before that, and even though you had to work your aggravation out, you just never hated her that much."

I run my hand over my face.

Milo stands and walks around Loki. "She loves you, but she wouldn't go against her father, who wouldn't give you the opportunity you got if you were engaged to her."

"She told you all of this?"

Milo shrugs again. "A friend knows what another friend is saying, even if they're not using those words."

"What do I do?"

"You could take your dog for a walk."

I look at Loki, who is still watching us have this conversation.

"I'm still contracted for the movie," I remind him.

"Which is already a shit show. So, if you're in love with the producer's daughter, what more could go wrong? Your production is already shut down because the female lead overdosed. Now what? You don't even know how long you're home. They can't call the shots forever. This is bullshit. And let me tell you, from someone who lives a normal life and works a normal job, it's not so bad. So, if her dad tanks both of your careers, you both are successful enough to do your own thing. You don't need him. You don't need anyone else in this fucking town. Finish some of those books. Write some movies. Be happy with the woman you love. And, like I said, I've been around, remember? I know that it's so much more than some publicity stunt. What you had with Christina was real, and I know you're still in love with her."

"Do you think she'd want to see me?"

Milo smiles wide. "I know she would. And, to Loki's benefit, if you got back together with Christina, he could be with Dolly."

Loki's head lifts when he hears Dolly's name, and I let out a laugh. "What do you say, boy? Should we go get our women?"

CHAPTER FIFTY-THREE

CHRISTINA

And the tabloid at the grocery store checkout has a picture of Charles Malloy with his hand on the small of a young actress' back.

Things I never thought I would do before I had a dog—walk to a park, in the dark, alone.

Dolly has given me a freedom I have never had. Being selective as to when I talk to my mother has helped too. And therapy—therapy helps.

I'm not alone in a hell that includes the way my parents treat me, especially in this town. At thirty, I understand I was a mistake—okay, not a mistake. My therapist doesn't like that. I was a surprise. An epic surprise.

Then I was a trophy.

I was the daughter of two people who loved to see themselves on the fronts of magazines and on TV. They dressed me up and paraded me around.

I was Annie, for such a fleeting moment, but that held some clout. Okay, sure, they didn't make any effort to see the show more than once, but those are some of the pictures I have on my phone. Those pictures I had to scrape off a website so that I could have a family portrait.

I blow out a breath as I come to the gate of the park.

I'll need to journal all of that when I get home. Journal it into a book that already has that story in it, but as it came up again, it's worth noting and getting it out of my head.

The park is lit up, and dogs run and play. I don't see Loki yet, but Dolly is already tugging against her leash.

"Hold on." I laugh as I open the gate to the park.

As soon as we're inside, I take off her leash, and she takes off to find her friends.

A moment later, I feel something brush up against my leg. I look down to see Loki looking up at me.

"Well, there you are, my friend," I say as I crouch down to pet him, and Dolly hurries over to us. A moment later, they hurry off, and I can feel Milo standing near me as I stand. "Those two are a pair, aren't they?"

"They have a pretty special relationship," the voice behind me says, but it's not Milo's voice.

Pulling my bottom lip between my teeth, I tighten my sweater around me as I turn to see Graham standing behind me.

My mouth goes dry as I take him in.

His face is shadowed by the lights, beard growth, and a baseball hat. He looks different. His shoulders are wider, and his chest harder beneath his shirt.

I lift my eyes to his and drink him in. God, I've missed him more than I realized. Everything in me aches to pull him to me.

"Hi," I say, not sure my voice is even loud enough for him to hear.

"Hi," he says.

It's as if we're frozen here, until Dolly and Loki come at us in a full run, brushing past my legs, and knocking me directly into Graham, who is sturdy.

His arms came up around me to hold me in place, and the dogs stop only briefly to look up at us before running off to play.

Graham doesn't release me. He keeps me folded against him, and I make no attempt to move. It feels different. His chest is wider, and his arms are thicker. But the sensation that it sends through me is the same—love. I've never stopped loving this man that I sent away.

I don't know why he's here and not in Italy. I don't know why Milo didn't come with Loki. All I know is that all the broken pieces inside of me seems to be sewing themselves back together at this moment. This moment was brought to me by my dog—my dog, who seems to be my lifeline lately, all because I lost this man who is holding me.

I can smell Graham. It's not his cologne or soap, it's him, and I've missed him so much.

His arms tighten around me, and mine around him as I step into him—sink into him. Resting my head on his chest, he tucks me under his chin.

I'm afraid I'm going to wake up and this will all have been a dream, but I'll take it. It's all I have left of him.

I feel him press a kiss to the top of my head, and I melt into him more.

"I hope you don't mind that I'm the one who brought Loki," he says into my hair.

I ease back and look up at him. "What are you doing here?" I shake my head. "I mean, why aren't you in Italy?"

The corner of his mouth turns up. "You don't talk to your father at all, do you?"

"I try not to," I admit.

Graham lifts a hand to push back a strand of hair that has come loose from my ponytail, and he tucks it behind my ear.

"Olivia overdosed."

"That I'd heard."

"We closed down production for now," he says. "I don't know when I'll be back to work."

"I guess I'd heard that too. I just didn't know you were back."

His finger traces down my cheek and over my jaw. "I've missed you," he says.

I swallow hard and force myself to take a step back and compose myself. I'm the one who gave back his ring. I'm the one who called it off. I'm the one who made a scene. I can't just be standing here, in a dog park, and forgetting why I did that.

I tuck my hands into the pockets of my sweater. "You look good," I say, and I hope it doesn't sound creepy the way that I said it.

"Thank you. So do you."

"Thanks. I've been getting out of the house with Dolly more."

"So I've heard."

The conversation dies there, and the silence becomes awkward.

Dolly and Loki walk the edge of the park, but on the other side. It's as if they're kids hoping that their parents won't call them to go home right away.

"How about we sit for a bit?" Graham says.

I nod and follow him to a nearby bench.

Again, we fall into a silence, and it's not the same silence we had months ago where we were comfortable in one another's presence.

I guess the moment we had when the dogs ran into me was all we can have. I did this to us. I caused this.

"How's your movie going?" Graham asks as he crosses his legs and watches out over the park as the dogs mingle with other dogs.

"It's good. We're only a week in with months to go."

He nods, but he doesn't look at me.

"What are they saying about yours?" I ask.

He shrugs. "We're shut down indefinitely right now. I don't

know if we'll go back when Olivia is out of rehab, or if they'll replace her, or just shut it down."

I reach for his hand and give it a squeeze, because it feels like the right thing to do. "I'm sorry."

He finally turns to look at me and his eyes are soft. "Thanks."

Dolly comes back to me, and I pull out the water bowl that I have in my bag. I set it on the ground and pour water from the bottle of water I brought into the bowl. Loki looks up at Graham, who shrugs.

"Loki, you can join her," I say, rubbing Dolly's side, and she moves over to make room for her friend.

"She's good for you," Graham says, studying me. "You light up when she's around."

I smile up at him, my hand still on my dog. "She's helped me through the past few months."

Graham runs his hand down his face.

"Christina—"

I shake my head. "I'm sorry. I shouldn't have said that."

I begin gathering the items I had taken out of the bag and toss them back in. When Loki and Dolly run off for one more dash through the park, I dump out the bowl, give it a shake, and throw it in the bag.

"We should talk about it. We never did," he urges, but I shake my head again.

"We got what we wanted."

"No, we didn't," he says, reaching for my hand. "I didn't get you."

I draw in a breath and study our hands. "Graham, it wasn't real."

"And we both know that's the real lie." He releases my hand and whistles for Loki.

As Loki and Dolly walk back toward the bench, Graham stands up and holds Loki's leash in his hand.

My heart is racing. He's right here. He came here knowing I

was here. I'm pushing him away again, but I don't have any choice. He's still committed to my father's movie, no matter what stage it's in. I'm knee deep into my movie, and it's what I wanted.

Graham hooks Loki's leash, and Loki rubs his nose up against Dolly. Will this be the end for them, too?

"For the record," Graham says, looking down at his dog and not at me. "I would have given everything up to have had you. It might have started out as some publicity stunt, but I fell in love with you, and my heart is still broken."

Graham begins to walk toward the gate, and Loki follows.

Dolly rests her head on my lap, and I don't even try to hold back the tears. I should chase after him. I should run and tell him I'm miserable too. I do love him.

"I really messed up, didn't I?" I ask my sympathetic dog as I lower my head to hers. "C'mon. Let's go home."

CHAPTER FIFTY-FOUR

GRAHAM

And the email that goes out to the Love Is in the Air Fan Event ticket holders says, "Due to her filming schedule, Christina Malloy will not attend this year's event; however, Graham Crowley, who was not scheduled to be in attendance, will be there."

When I pull up in front of my parents' house, it's dark. I look at my watch. It's eight o'clock. I can't imagine they're in bed already.

I pick up my phone from the cup holder and text my mother with Loki on the seat behind me, pacing as if he wants to go in too.

Are you awake? I text.

A few moments later, my mother texts back. *What's the matter?*

She didn't answer my question, but she did answer my text. *I'm in front of your house.*

I don't get another text. Instead, I see the living room lights turn on, and then the porch light. Only another moment later, the front door opens, and my mother is standing there in her pajamas.

I chuckle to myself.

I step out of my car and open the door to the back seat. Before he jumps out, Loki studies me.

He has to know I'm conflicted.

I give him a nod, and he jumps out of the car and hurries up the front steps. As I close the door, I watch as my mother crouches down and snuggles my dog, and then they both wait for me—watching me.

"I didn't mean to interrupt you," I say.

"Who says you're interrupting me?"

"You're already in your pajamas. The house is dark."

She puckers her lips, but her eyes are light. "We went to bed early," she says with a rise of her brows, and there's a hint of something that makes my skin crawl. I don't want to know what she means by that.

The look on her face changes to one of concern. "Honey, what's wrong?"

I run my hand over my jaw and let out a breath. "I saw Christina."

Her eyes light again. "You did? She looks good, doesn't she? Did you meet Dolly?"

I let out a snort. "Yeah. She looks great, and Dolly is sweet."

Loki's ears perk up at Dolly's name. Shit, my dog is in love too.

"But you wouldn't be standing on my front porch if it had been a good meeting, now, would you?"

And that's why I'm here. I need my mother.

She steps back to hold open the screen door, and Loki and I pass into the house.

"Go to the kitchen. I'll make us something to drink."

Loki and I head to the kitchen. I sit down at the table as my mother gets Loki's bowl and fills it with water first. Once she sets it down, and he begins to lap at it, my mother takes down the box of dog treats she has, and Loki swiftly moves to her, forgetting his water.

She hands him the treat, rubs his ears, and returns the box to the cabinet while Loki takes up space on the kitchen floor with his treat.

"Christina and I had lunch last week. She said she'd started filming, and that Penelope Mondragon is a genius," my mother says as she turns on her electric kettle and pulls down two mugs and her tea box.

"She is a genius. This is Christina's ticket. She'll be sought after now."

My mother nods as she carries the mugs and the teas to the table and sets them down before taking the seat next to me. "But I didn't take it that she was happy," she says.

"Why wouldn't she be? She has everything she wanted."

Twisting up her lips, my mother shakes her head. "I don't think she does."

"What's missing?"

She rests her hand on my arm. "You."

I want to believe that, and especially since it's coming from my mother.

"I don't think she's missing me."

"I think you're wrong," she says as the kettle signals that it's ready.

She stands and walks to retrieve the kettle. When she returns to the table, she pours water into each mug before she sets the kettle on the table and sits back down.

"Sweetheart, I know what she did. She gave you up so you'd go to Italy and do the movie. Right?"

I study my mother. How close did she and Christina get? Did Christina tell her everything?

"Well, yes. But what do you know?" I ask.

A line forms between her brows and she shakes her head. "I don't know anything. I just assumed that's what she did. She's miserable without you."

This is it. This is where I come clean. "Did you know that our relationship was a PR stunt?"

She blinks hard at me. "I don't understand."

I sit back in my chair and cross my legs, and then my arms. "A rumor got started that we were seeing each other. Our agents thought it was a good thing to run with because the ratings of our movies are higher than another pairing. They knew I wanted the action film, and that Christina wanted the Penelope Mondragon film. With us in the public eye more, it got us exactly what we were wanting."

"So, your relationship was fake?" she asks as she moves the box of teas between us.

I draw in a breath. "Yes."

She resigns to the conversation over the tea and sits back in her chair to watch me. "Wait," she says, waving a hand in front of herself as to erase what I've said and to start over. "I'm very confused. You asked her to marry you."

"I did."

"You did that for a role? Are you kidding me? Were you going to marry her and have fake kids or something?" Her voice rises and her nostrils flare. She's angry.

That makes me laugh. "No. No. The deal was we would post pictures of us and have PDA. That was supposed to be it. But I fell in love with her. I didn't know it would be possible, but I did."

My mother's face softens. "Graham," she says as she presses her hand to her chest.

"But I think it was one sided."

She shakes her head. "Oh, no. I don't think so. That woman loves you. She's still in love with you."

"Part of the stipulation to getting the role was that I stop dating her."

Crinkling up her nose, my mother turns her attention back to picking out a tea packet. "They made you date and then they made you break up?"

"Not our agents," I say. "Her father."

With the tea packet in her hand, my mother lifts her eyes back to me. "Why would he do that?"

"Because he's a control freak, and so is her mother." I set my feet on the ground and lean my forearms on the table. "It's like they keep Christina to themselves. I mean, her dad doesn't give two shits about her. He doesn't respect her career. He doesn't even acknowledge her when she's around. And her mother," I begin, and my voice rises.

I look behind me to see that I was loud enough Loki's ears perked up, and I probably woke my dad. But I don't hear him stirring.

"Her mother uses her for free publicity for her spas."

"That's shameful," my mother says.

"But after all of these lies, and us actually loving each other, and even getting engaged, it wasn't enough. He wrote it in the fucking contract," I say, and she swats my hand.

"Mouth."

"I can't help it. I couldn't have the role if I was with her."

"But you were engaged. And you got the role."

I've confused her further. "Yeah, well, then he produced the Mondragon movie and gave her the same ultimatum."

"Bastard."

Now I know I woke my father when I laughed hard at that.

"I hadn't signed the contract. I would have given it all up for her."

My mother's gaze softens, and she rests her hand on mine. "But she didn't do the same?"

Pressing my fingers to my eyes, I shake my head. "She signed her contract, gave back the ring, and broke it off with me."

"She wanted the movie more?"

I study my mother. "I think she did it so I got my movie," I say, admitting the truth that I've always felt inside and confirmed by what Milo told me. "I thought she loved me. But tonight—"

"She knows the deal with your movie? Has she talked to her father? I mean, what harm is there in the two of you being together if the movie is a bust anyway?"

The smile on my mouth is instant. She gets it. What in the hell would it ever matter if we'd been together or not?

"What do I do? I want her. I want her for life—and her dog."

"You do know your dog is in love with her dog, right?" she says, and we both look at Loki who is now napping on her kitchen floor.

"I thought that might be the case."

"If you date, or even get married, they fire you?"

I shrug. "I'd breach the contract."

"How important is it to you now?"

I consider that for a moment and then look her in the eye. "It's not."

Her mouth turns up in a supportive smile. "But her movie..."

"Right." I think about that. "I'll wait it out. And then I'll go to her father and tell him how I feel. I'll ask for her hand if that's what was missing. I'll take it without his blessing—that is, if she'll have me."

My mother lifts from her chair and pulls me to her. "Don't let her go. You don't need her father or your agents to make it in this town anymore. You both have solid footing. I don't see why you shouldn't be together."

And that's why I came here. I needed to hear that from the only other woman I love.

CHAPTER FIFTY-FIVE

CHRISTINA

And the entertainment reporter says, "Olivia Chase was released from the Italian hospital weeks after suffering a cardiac arrest on the set of the action film *Malibu Money*. Production continues to be shut down."

Dolly has taken up lying by the door. We haven't been to the park in two weeks. I'm afraid that Graham will show up again, and I'm not strong enough for that. But I know this is her subtle way of telling me that she misses her friend.

I finish packing up our bag for the next day. The crew has been awesome about having Dolly on set. She's super spoiled, and I think Penny spoils her the most. We have two days of filming, and then there is a break for Thanksgiving. After that, we will head to Michigan to get those outdoor shots in the snow.

Dolly lifts her head to watch me, then whines as she walks to her bed, circles it, and then lays down.

"You'll be fine," I say. "You'll see him again," I promise her, but I don't know that for sure.

When my phone rings with my father's ringtone, I stare at it as it lays on my counter. I haven't spoken to my father since he gave me the ultimatum to sign the contract and break it off with Graham. Well, let's be honest, my father hasn't spoken to me since then either. It takes two people to make any kind of relationship, right?

With an unsteady hand, I pick up my phone and swipe my finger across the screen to answer the call.

"Hello?"

"I need you in my office first thing in the morning," he barks out the order.

"Daddy, I'm filming in the morning. My call time is eight."

"Then I suggest you be in my office by six-thirty," he says.

"Can't you just tell me what this is about now?"

"Six-thirty, Christina. I'll see you then." And he disconnects the call.

I stand at my counter, my phone in my hand, and I shake my head. Dolly stands and walks to me, brushing her body up against my legs as if I need her grounding. And maybe I do.

My phone chimes again, in my hand, and when I look down, it's Graham's name that comes up.

I hold my breath. Why would he be texting me? He hasn't talked to me since he left the dog park.

Hi, his text says.

I wait a moment for more, but nothing else is said. So, I type in, *Hi*, and send the text.

A picture comes back of Loki laying on the couch next to Milo, whose head is back, and he too is asleep.

In return, I snap a picture of Dolly looking up at me and send it.

I think they miss each other, he says, and it squeezes at my heart.

I know they miss each other, and I miss him.

Have you talked to your dad?

I stare down at the message. What does he know that I don't?

No, I say. I'm not going to mention my meeting with him tomorrow. Maybe Graham will tell me what he knows.

Can I call you?

My palms go damp. I'm a glutton for punishment, so I type, *Yes*, and send it.

It isn't but a moment later that my phone rings, and I stare down at it as if I'm surprised to see that he's calling. Dolly lifts her head and looks back at me as she walks toward her bed.

Finally, I slide my finger over the screen and lift the phone to my ear.

"Hello," I say softly.

"Hey," he says, and my insides instantly turn to mush.

I lean against the counter and let myself sink into hearing his voice.

"I hope I'm not bothering you," he says, and I realize that my knees are soft, and if I don't sit down, there's a huge chance I'll fall.

He's said six words to me, and I can't even function. How did I hate this man for so long?

Sliding down the cabinets to the floor, I sit with the phone still pressed to my ear. Dolly must know I need her, because she prances around the island and comes to a stop next to me before she lays down against my leg.

"You're not bothering me." I choke out the words. "I was just packing up for tomorrow."

"You're on set tomorrow?"

"Call is at eight," I say, as if it matters.

"Can I come over?"

The question has me holding my breath. Why would he want to come over? I was curt and hurtful the last time I saw him. I've been nothing but a bitch to him since everything fell apart—hell, I'm not sure why he fell in love with me to begin with. I didn't make any of it easy on him.

"Christina?" he says, and I realize I'm only conversing with myself in my head.

"Graham, I don't know if it's a good—"

"It's a good idea," he finishes my thought. "Not only does Loki want to see his girlfriend," he says, and I grin down at my dog, "but I have something I need to talk to you about."

Dolly lifts her head and looks at me, as if she knows that Loki just might show up at her door.

"I suppose it would be okay."

"Great. I'll see you in twenty," he says. "Bye," he adds before the line goes dead.

I lower my phone and look at it. He's coming over.

"What is he up to?" I ask Dolly, who stands and walks back to her bed.

I push up off the floor and walk toward my bedroom. I have no idea what I look like at this point, and even though there is nothing between Graham and me, it would make me feel better if I knew I looked presentable.

As I study myself in the mirror, I pull my hair back into a ponytail and then add a bit of mascara and some gloss to my lips. I don't want to appear desperate, but a part of me is.

I'm still fussing with my hair and makeup when Graham texts me. *I'm here.*

Why he didn't use the code to get through the gate, I don't know—except that he's a stand-up kind of guy that wouldn't use a code that leads to a house he can't just walk into anymore.

Again, it makes my stomach do a little flip.

Dolly has to sense Loki is nearby. She hurries into my room, makes a circle, barks, and then runs for the front door.

It'll be worth having Graham here just so Dolly gets a few moments with her boyfriend.

Who am I kidding? It'll be nice to have Graham here so I can have a few moments with the man that still consumes me.

CHAPTER FIFTY-SIX

GRAHAM

And the Instagram post of Graham and Loki standing outside of Christina's gate says, "He's meeting her!!! Seriously OMG! Are they still together? Are they back together? #couplegoals #ilovegrahamcrowley"

Loki is pacing at my feet. The moment Christina's door opens, he barks, and she laughs. Then, I can hear Dolly barking too.

Christina buzzes us through the gate. I take off Loki's leash, and he takes off for her. I watch as Christina crouches down to love on him, but he then pushes past her to sniff Dolly. When the two are satisfied with their greeting, they take off into the condo.

Christina is still grinning after the dogs when I get to the door. She stands and then turns her soft eyes to me, and everything inside of me melts.

"Thanks for letting us come over," I say as I slide the leash into the messenger bag on my shoulder.

"She's been pretty miserable," she says, and then we just gaze at one another.

I refuse to think she doesn't want me. Even when she forces herself out of my life, she looks at me as she is now. This is love. No publicity stunt could ever make two people look at one another as we look at each other.

"Come in," she says. "I have some Cokes in the fridge if you'd like one."

I laugh. "You don't drink soda," I say, following her toward the kitchen.

"Well, you never know when company will want something other than water."

When she walks into the kitchen, she pulls open the refrigerator and waits for me to tell her what I want.

"I'm okay for now," I say, and she closes the refrigerator, then crosses her arms and watches me.

I set down my bag on the island and lean up against it. I could stand here all night and just look at her.

Her hair is pulled back, leaving her delicate neck exposed. How many nights have I dreamed of kissing her neck in the past six months? More than I can count.

There's a slight shine to her full lips, and her eyes are dark and needy. Maybe I'm needy. Just being in her presence makes me that way.

"You look beautiful," I say.

Pink fills her cheeks, and she looks down at the floor before she looks back up at me. "Thank you."

I realize the dogs have disappeared. I wonder if they're hiding so I won't take off in a huff with Loki, or if they're in a corner doing the things I want to do to Christina. The thought has the corner of my mouth turning up into a smile.

"What did you want to talk to me about?" she asks, and I let out a long breath.

"They shut down my film," I say. "For good."

Her face goes soft. "I'm sorry. I hadn't heard that."

I shrug. "Wasn't meant to be, I guess."

I take a step toward her, glad when she doesn't take a step back.

Turning back to my messenger bag, I pull out the book I have inside. I hand it to her, and her eyes go wide as she studies it.

"You got your book published?" A smile forms on her mouth and lifts into her eyes.

"It releases in August. This is your early copy," I say, and she presses it to her chest, wrapping her arms around it. "It's a super early copy. Its edits aren't even complete yet." I point to the cover where it says that it's an unedited copy.

She studies the bland cover and then lifts her eyes back to me.

"I'm so proud of you," she says with love in her voice, nearly the same kind of love my mother had when I'd shown it to her.

"Thank you." I lick my lips and keep my eyes on Christina. "Next week I'll have the script for it too."

Her eyes go wide. "You already sold movie rights?"

I run my hand over my hair. "King of Mischief Productions picked it up."

A line forms between her brows. "I have never heard of that company bef—" she stops as if it has all starts to make sense. "Loki is the god of mischief."

I nod.

"Are you the king of mischief, then?"

I nod again, only this time my smile widens.

Christina looks down at the book and back up at me. "You're producing the movie?"

"New adventure. Well, for me and my investors."

Her smile returns. "You're going to do great things."

"I hope so," I say as I close the gap between us. "I want to offer you a job."

Her lips part. "Me?"

"You see, I took a long time to write that book and to get it just right. It was written in my trailer after I'd do scenes with you. It was written in my office after I'd filmed with you. It just so happens that as I've been editing it with my editor, I realized I'd been writing you into it the entire time."

"Graham..."

I lift my finger to her lips and let it linger a moment before I drop my hand. "I want you to be the love interest in the movie."

"I don't—"

"Don't make your decision standing in your kitchen. Read the script first—read the book first," I amend. "It'll be another year or more before we can start production. But it was always your role." I lift my hand to her cheek. "It was written for you."

The dogs both walk into the kitchen and look up at us.

Christina shifts a look at them, and then back up to me.

"I can't wait to read it."

I smile down at her, wanting to kiss her so badly my hand is shaking as I withdraw it. But I step back.

I did what I came to do, and it opened the door for something else.

"I guess we'll get going," I say, picking up my messenger bag and hiking it up over my shoulder. "I'll be in touch."

She watches me walk toward the front door, and Loki slowly makes his way through the condo toward me, obviously not ready to leave Dolly behind.

As I clip on Loki's leash, Christina kneels next to Dolly and slings an arm over her.

"If you're not filming, your schedule is open?" she hesitantly asks.

"There's some word that Love Is in the Air has a role for me, even though my contract was bought out."

Her smile widens. "Interesting. I start filming at the beginning of the year on my next one. Well, as soon as I'm done with my current movie."

"You know, we're still their golden children."

She stands. "I was just thinking, maybe we could get the dogs together."

I'll take whatever she's willing to offer. "I'm very sure that Loki would love that."

"So would Dolly."

"I'll talk to you soon, then. Just let me know where and when you want to meet."

"I'll do that," she says.

I lift my hand in a wave, and Loki and I head home. I'm hopeful that I'll get my girl back, and Loki will, too.

CHAPTER FIFTY-SEVEN

CHRISTINA

And the talk show host poses the question to her Love Is in the Air guest, "What about the relationship between Graham Crowley and Christina Malloy? Did that surprise everyone? Rumors were that they didn't get along on set and would often get into fights."

"I guess it proves you can never judge a book by its cover," the guest says.

I'm exhausted.

I stayed up and read Graham's book—all of it. I couldn't help myself, even though I knew I needed to get to my father's office so early.

As the elevator comes to a stop on the floor that houses his office, I draw in a deep, calming breath, and look down at my dog.

Where I go, my dog goes.

Dolly walks so close to me as we walk through the door, she nearly knocks me over. I'm sure she's feeling my hesitation in going to my father's office.

My skin is hot. My heart is racing. My palms are damp, and I'm pissed off.

One of the things that changed the night that Graham and I walked that red carpet was me learning to lead my own narrative. Sure, we were tossed into something that we didn't have much control over, and then we agreed to it, but that night, my eyes were opened.

When Graham pointed out that my parents hadn't even checked up on me, or noticed that I'd left the awards ceremony, that was eye opening. Then, when I realized just how badly they treated those around them, it led me to realize how I treated Penny. Penny, of all people, who devotes herself to the success of my career—she deserved better. I hope over the past few months I've shown her how important she is to me.

And then there's Graham. I never would have thought it possible that I would fall in love with him like I did—but I did. I chose to love him. I chose to set him free. I choose to amend that.

I shouldn't be surprised that at six thirty, there are people moving about. Their day has already started.

My father's assistant isn't at his desk, and though I'm afraid of what's on the other side of the door, I push it open and walk into his office.

The door to his private quarters is closed, and I'm relieved. I'm not sure what I would do if I saw someone else in there. But no doubt, there is probably someone in there.

My father is sitting behind his desk, and when I walk in, he lifts his head.

It's six thirty in the morning, right on time. I'm there exactly when he asked me to be, and yet he looks toward the door as if he's a bit surprised to see me. Oh, not that I can see his eyes. They're shielded with sunglasses.

"The dog? In my office?" he says in lieu of good morning, or it's nice to see you.

"She goes with me," I say. "And since you demanded this is where I should be this early, she's here."

He presses his palm to his forehead before pointing to the chair in front of his desk—not asking me to sit, but rather suggesting I take the seat.

"I'm fine," I say, choking up on Dolly's leash to keep her tight to my side. "What did you want to see me about?"

My father picks up a piece of paper and pushes it in my direction. I take the step to pick it up.

I have to control my mouth to keep from smiling as I look down at a picture of Graham and me standing at the dog park in what appears to be a beautiful embrace.

Pushing the picture back toward my father, I pat Dolly's side.

My father leans in on his forearms. "You're forbidden to see him."

A pain zips through my jaw I clench it so hard. "Forbidden," I repeat the word. "I thought I was only contracted to not date him."

My father chews on his bottom lip. "Christina—"

"Did you have someone poised behind a tree to get that photo? I mean, I publicly broke up with the man, and I haven't spoken to him in over five months. But the one time I happen to run into him at the dog park—and when I say run into him, that's exactly what happened—and you have a photo of that. Isn't that convenient?"

My father fists his hands on the top of his desk. "You're not dating him?"

"My guess is that you've been having me followed in some way for this long. You know that I'm not dating him. Not only that, that picture is two weeks old. Your spies aren't very good."

"Christina," he says again in a growl, as if that's going to stop me from speaking.

"And why exactly is this such a big deal? Why couldn't I be

involved with a man that I love? A man that asked me to marry him?"

"You have a reputation to uphold, and it doesn't include you running off with some two-bit actor."

My heart is racing now as I inch closer to his desk. Dolly keeps herself pressed up against me as if to keep me not only protected but grounded.

"Two-bit actor? You're the one that hired him to be your next big thing."

"That's business," he says.

"Do you hear yourself? He's not good enough for me, but you'll spend millions on him?" Then I reconsider that. "Or am I not good enough for your new star?"

My father comes out of his chair, but I don't step back. I'm not going to let him ever make me cower again.

"Your mother and I have worked very hard to get where we are. The least you can do is obey our wishes."

I have Dolly's leash wrapped around my hand so tightly I'm losing feeling in my fingers.

"I think the expiration date on me obeying your wishes ran out twelve years ago."

"You signed a contract," he says, his voice rising.

I nod. "I sure did." Instead of resigning to the fact that I did indeed sign a contract that basically forbade me to be with the man I love, I begin to laugh.

"Christina," he says my name again, as if this is how he controls me.

I hold up my free hand. "I quit," I say, and my father's eyes go wide.

"You can't quit."

"I sure can. I can breach the contract. I can walk away. I can be fined and sued, but I can quit."

His lips flatten tightly, and he takes off his sunglasses. "I've never had you talk to me like this."

"You're right. For the past thirty years, I've been nothing but someone you parade around in front of the media to make it appear as if you have a good family." I snort out another laugh. "I've walked the line my whole life. I'm not going to walk it anymore," I say, my eyes focused on him.

"Contracts are what run this town," he counters, because obviously he's still stuck in the thought that he has control of me.

Easing my grip on Dolly's leash, only slightly, I move from my position in front of his desk and walk toward the door that connects his personal space.

"Christina, what are you doing?" He takes a hurried step as I reach for the doorknob.

"How important are contracts, Daddy?" I ask, raising a brow, my hand gripping the knob. "If I open this door, I won't find out how little long-term contracts matter, will I? Contracts that hold together marriages and families. I won't find someone in here *just cleaning?*" I ask using air quotes with my free hand. "How important are those contracts?"

"Christina." His voice lowers, but not in anger, I realize. There is a defeated grumble in him saying my name now.

"I love Graham, Daddy. I love him enough to walk away from everything. I love him enough to have signed your stupid contract so he could have the role he always wanted, and then I walked away for five months and resigned to never see him again. I love him enough to stand here and quit a movie I love and that I'm passionate about because, well, I still love him. And he'll wait for me to finish this movie if I ask him to. But I really don't want anything to do with a movie that you're part of."

"That's enough." His voice rises—and the knob on the door turns in my hand.

I step back as the door opens and Olivia Chase blinks tired eyes at me.

I turn my attention back to my father, whose eyes have gone

wide. In this moment I know that extra amendment to my contract is null and void.

"Goodbye, Daddy."

CHAPTER FIFTY-EIGHT

GRAHAM

And the meteorologist on the morning news says, "Don't get too comfortable with the weather. It'll change on a dime. But change is good."

I hear the doorbell, then I hear Loki. My room is still dark, the blinds drawn. A moment later I hear another dog barking, and that causes Loki to bark more. Then, there are voices. Milo is still home.

I sit up in my bed and run my hands over my face. The clock on my nightstand says it's just past seven o'clock.

My head is fuzzy as if I drank all night. Truth is, I stayed up until early this morning working on a new book. It was as if the words wouldn't pour out of me fast enough after I left Christina's house. Talk about a muse.

The knob on my bedroom door turns and the door opens. A moment later Loki prances in, followed by Dolly.

But it's the woman that follows them that has my body temperature rising.

The light behind her shadows her face, but I can see her weary smile.

"Hi," I say, gathering the sheet up around me.

"Hey," she croaks out the word. "I'm sorry to bust in on you, but..."

"No. I'm glad to see you," I say, dropping my legs off the side of the bed and rubbing my eyes. "Is everything okay?"

Her breath shudders, and she moves to me. Instinct has me reaching for her, no longer concerned with my state of nakedness.

Christina moves to me, wraps her arms around my neck, and pulls me to her. My cheek rests against her chest, and I can feel her body shake.

"Honey, tell me what happened," I say, looking up at her.

She's crying—sobbing—but smiling.

"I quit," she says on a breath.

"You quit?"

Christina nods. "I quit. I won't do a movie that my father has money invested in. I won't be part of something that keeps me away from you. I'll give it all up if it means I get to be with you."

"Christina," my voice comes out accusingly. "You can't do this."

"But I can. I did." She kneels in front of me, taking my face in her hands. "I love you. I don't know if you still feel the same, but—"

I take her hands in mine. "I've never stopped loving you," I say, and she sighs.

"I don't know what will happen. I mean, I might get sued over all of this. But a man who doesn't even cherish the vows he shares with his wife doesn't have a right to keep me from the man I love."

I have to take a moment to absorb everything she's told me, and it goes much deeper than some stupid clause in a contract.

"You need a lawyer," I say, reaching for my phone.

Christina eases back on her heels as I scroll through my contacts.

"I haven't even checked my phone yet. Surely, they're looking for me. I didn't go to the set."

"Let's go." I stand, the sheet still wrapped around me. "We're going to do this together."

"Do what?" she asks as she stands.

"You're not going to get fired or sued. You're going to get your happily ever after," I promise as a smile lifts the corners of her mouth.

∼

Amelia Post, the director, comes at us as we walk on set. Her eyes are angry and her hands are fisted to her side. It's been two days that Christina has missed, and Amelia is understandably angry.

As she raises a finger in anticipation to cut Christina and I off with her words, I reach for her gently.

"We need a word," I say calmly and softly hoping to keep any reaction from her from stirring those working on the set. "We have some legalities to go over."

Amelia's eyes go wide, and she shifts a glance in Christina's direction and then at the man in the suit standing behind us.

Christina squeezes my hand as Amelia gives us a nod and motions toward Christina's trailer.

Christina opens the door to her trailer and turns on the light. We each pile in and sit in the cramped space.

"There's a lot to unpack right here," Amelia says looking around the room. "You two are together?"

"We are," I say.

Amelia worries her lip. "Christina, your contract—"

"Is something we need to discuss. Kirk McDonald, counsel for Ms. Malloy," my lawyer says as he sets down the contract amendments he drew up for us. "As of this morning, Charles Malloy Productions has pulled out of production."

"I'm sorry, what?" Amelia asks, gathering up the paperwork.

Christina rests her hand atop Amelia's, directing her attention up to her.

"I've cut ties with my father," she says.

"Christina, I don't want to be part of some family drama."

"My family drama will not affect production. My family drama will stay within my family."

Amelia looks up at me and then to Kirk. "If my producer has backed out, I'm screwed."

"We have a producer in place to take over," Kirk says as he sets a packet of papers on the small table. "Though production might be extended as we get everything in place, the movie is in safe hands."

Amelia studies the papers in front of her. "King of Mischief Productions? I've never heard of it."

I smile down at Christina. "It's my production company," I say, looking back at Amelia. "I'm ready to step in and make sure everything keeps going smoothly."

She eyes me carefully. "And exactly how many movies have you produced?"

"Well, this will be the first, but I assure you, I have a qualified team of associates and investors."

Amelia puckers her lips. "Is this all so you two can be together? I saw the contract. That clause that was added about you two was asinine."

Christina looks up at me, grinning. "It's a bonus, that's for sure," she says. "And my father has a lot going on in his life. This movie and crew are not so important right now."

Amelia studies Christina for a moment and then nods as if she might know what Christina is talking about.

"Well, let's get a meeting scheduled with the new production company, lawyers, and crew. It appears this production just took a turn for the better, and I'm anxious to be part of it," Amelia says, and Christina leans against me as if she can finally relax.

Not only will she still get her Penelope Mondragon film, but we also get to be together. This is going to change my plans going forward—well, only slightly, but it's so worth it. We're in charge of our destiny, and our destiny is to be together.

CHAPTER FIFTY-NINE

CHRISTINA

Three Years Later

And the Instagram post from the gossip site says, "Graham Crowley is fit! The action hero / producer / writer status looks good on him. But we have noticed that Christina Malloy hasn't been seen in the past few months."

My stomach threatens to betray me. I'm sewn into this dress, and I can't breathe.

The last time I was this uncomfortable, a rumor had been started about me and Graham Crowley dating.

I can't help but smile at the thought now, twisting the diamond on my finger even as my insides fight for space. I owe everything to the first person who passed on the rumor nearly three years ago, and to our agents who wanted to capitalize on it.

Dolly brushes up next to my chair and I rest my hand on her back. She's been keeping an eye on me—my protector.

"I'm okay, sweetheart," I say, running my hand down her back. "It's going to be a long night."

"And I promise not to leave your side," Graham says from behind me, and I turn to take him in.

He's dressed in a custom-made tuxedo that accents his wide chest and shoulders. Action heroes don't fit into tuxedos easily—we've found humor in this knowledge for the past few weeks leading up to the premiere.

Graham reaches a hand out to me, and I take it, easing from my seat.

"You look radiant," he says as he runs a finger over my jaw, down my throat, and into my cleavage, grinning like a teenager being allowed his first touch. "I can't wait to get you out of this dress."

That has me lifting his hand away and lacing our fingers together. "Mr. Crowley, you know that this dress isn't coming off without a trained seamstress in attendance."

The corner of his mouth lifts. "I'd pay extra just to tear it off of you."

I lean into him, careful not to get my makeup on his jacket, and his arms come around me. "Tempting. Oh, so tempting," I tease, taking a step back and blowing out a breath before I suck in another.

Concern contorts his face, and his eyes grow darker. "Are you okay?"

"Don't judge me, but I'm sure before the night is out, I'm going to be sick."

"We don't have to do this," he says, and I shake my head.

"We most certainly do have to do this. We have a lot invested in tonight," I remind him as I brush a piece of lint off his jacket. "I've never wanted to attend a movie premiere more than I do this one. *Whisked Away*"—I use my hand to envision the marquee—"written by Graham Crowley and based on the bestselling book by Graham Crowley. Produced by Graham Crowley.

Starring Graham Crowley," I say with a laugh. "I'm so proud of you."

He pulls me to him. "If only I hadn't had an affair with my leading lady." He winks at me.

"Yeah, well, that affair is what makes me so uncomfortable in this dress," I remind him.

Graham runs his hand over the swell of my stomach. "Oh, so worth it."

Loki joins us, and Graham pats him on his side. And, just as Dolly had, Loki brushes up against me to let me know he's here for me too.

"Your mom said she's ready," he says, and I nod.

"And your parents?"

"Their car is waiting for them downstairs too. Mom has changed her dress three times."

I laugh at that. I think she might be more nervous than I am.

~

My mother checks her lipstick in the mirror of her compact. She radiates a glow of a happy and successful woman.

I know she'd say it was the new technology she's invested in for her chain of spas that makes her look so young and beautiful, but I think that divorcing my father and moving into my condo when I moved in with Graham is what did that for her.

In the past few years, she's moved on from therapy, opened six more spa locations, and though she's tried to hide it, I've heard a rumor that she's seeing a plastic surgeon—romantically that is.

Before she closes the compact, she adjusts her earrings, which were custom made from the rings that my father had bought her over the years. Once they were divorced, and my mother had taken her share of my father's wealth, he admitted to multiple affairs, and those rings were tokens of guilt.

As of yet, I haven't mended my relationship with my father. I'm not sure when I'll be ready for that—or if I'll be ready for that.

Penny hands me my clutch as the car pulls up in front of the theater.

"Thank you," I say, patting her hand before she pulls it back.

She smiles wide in her custom-made dress, her own clutch on her lap.

King of Mischief Productions has become a lifeline for all of us. Graham swooped in when my father pulled out of my Penelope Mondragon movie, and not only did it save the movie, but I'm contracted for two more Penelope Mondragon movies. The first was box office gold, and they're banking on the others to have the same kind of success. And the memes that circulate social media comparing me to Meg Ryan are epic, in my opinion.

Of course, I also got to be with the man I love, and no contract or rumor could keep me from him.

I became Graham's business partner only a week after we got married in a private ceremony with my mother, his family, Penny as my maid of honor, and Milo as Graham's best man in the backyard of Graham's house—our house. I can guarantee that Loki and Dolly were excited to have their parents get married.

Once I was a partner in King of Mischief Productions, we hired Penny to run the office, and Milo became an investor. He's no longer the safe friend who isn't involved in the industry.

Graham has written two more books, and he says the words flow since I'm his muse and he wakes up next to me every morning.

Graham takes my hand and gives it a squeeze. "Are you doing okay?"

I nod with a smile, trying to reassure both of us. "I'll be fine. But I hope you have an escape plan if we need it."

Graham leans in and brushes a kiss over my lips. "In a few

minutes, the whole world will understand our need to sneak out if we need to."

I bite down on my bottom lip. This dress is so tight, there will be no speculation about why I look sick. But we've planned our entrance, and this will be our announcement without saying a word.

As the car comes to a stop, the door is opened, and my mother takes the hand offered to her.

There is a roar of applause for her, and for the first time, I can't help but enjoy her moment with her. She deserves appreciation from the masses.

Milo exits the car next and offers his hand to Penny.

"This is our dream come true, right?" Graham says. "We have it all now?"

I run my hand over my belly and smile back at him. "We have it all."

"Wait until they see our next publicity stunt," he says, resting his hand over mine.

"It'll be epic."

He eases in and presses a kiss to my lips. "Let's go stir things up."

Graham moves to the door and climbs from the car. The noise from those outside escalates as my gorgeous, action hero husband is seen by the crowd. He gives them a wave before reaching for my hand.

As I step out of the car, his arm comes around me, and his hand goes directly to my belly. We share a smile and then wave at those who have amassed to celebrate the man who brought this moment to life.

It's also that moment that our baby kicks for the very first time.

Graham's eyes go wide, and I cover his hand with mine.

"Did you feel that?" he asks.

I laugh and lean into him. "Of course I felt it." I let a sigh move through me. "You know what this means? This baby is already addicted to this kind of attention."

Graham's brows draw inward. "I'm now understanding your father's need to keep us apart."

I rest my hand on his chest. "Yeah, well, that didn't work out, did it?"

"Thank God."

Another wave of sickness moves through me. "Do you have an escape plan?" I whisper on a breath, willing away the nausea.

"I can have one in place in a hot minute."

I nod. "If we sneak out, the rumors will fly."

He leans in and kisses me. The cheers surrounding us are muted by the sound of my heartbeat resonating through me just by having him near.

"I say we go with the rumors. I'm guessing they're going to notice that I knocked you up."

"You think?" I say with a laugh.

"Let's go make our appearance and then get home to our dogs."

"I like your plan, Mr. Crowley," I say as Graham takes my hand and we begin our walk into the theater, waving at the fans who have gathered to see their favorite TV movie couple in real life—in love, happily married, successful, and expecting a baby.

∼

And the interview in the magazine that showcases Graham Crowley, Christina Malloy, and their daughter on the cover says, "Could anyone have predicted that what started as a publicity stunt would turn into a happily ever after?"

RATE AND REVIEW

We hope you enjoyed *Publicity Stunt* by Bernadette Marie. If you did, we would ask that you please rate and review this title. Every review helps our authors.

Rate and Review: Publicity Stunt

MEET THE AUTHOR

Known for her bestselling contemporary romances, Bernadette Marie is a fervent advocate of Happily Ever Afters. As a devoted wife and mother of five, she cherishes the notions of love at first sight, whirlwind romances, and the power of second chances. Beyond her literary pursuits, Bernadette is a dedicated martial artist with a 3rd-degree black belt in Tang Soo Do and holds certification as an instructor. Her passions extend to the tranquility of Tai Chi, exploring Disney parks, and indulging in lunch outings with friends. When she's not crafting compelling narratives or overseeing her own publishing house, 5 Prince Publishing, Bernadette can often be found immersed in a beloved Rom-Com, effortlessly reciting cherished one-liners.

OTHER TITLES FROM 5 PRINCE PUBLISHING

www.5princebooks.com

Spring Showers *Sarah Dressler*
Secret Admirer Pact *Bernadette Marie*
The Publicity Stunt *Bernadette Marie*
A Trace of Romance *Ann Swann*
Descendants of Atlantis *Courtney Davis*
Holiday Rebound *Emily Bybee*
Rewriting Christmas *S.E. Reichert & Kerrie Flanagan*
Butterfly Kisses *Courtney Davis*
Leaving Cloverton *Emi Hilton*
Beach Rose Path *Barbara Matteson*
Aristotle's Wolves *Courtney Davis*
Christmas Cove *Sarah Dressler*
A Twist of Hate *T.E. Lorenzo*
Composing Laney *S.E. Reichert*
Firewall *Jessica Mehring*
Vampires of Atlantis *Courtney Davis*
A Rocky Mountain Romance *Jessica Mehring*

Milton Keynes UK
Ingram Content Group UK Ltd.
UKHW012309060524
442290UK00005B/247

9 781631 123771